Shattering Obscurity

EVERGREEN SERIES IV

Joann Herley

ACKNOWLEDGEMENTS

Cover Photo by: © Alanpoulson | Dreamstime.com

Cover Photo by: © 1enchik | Dreamstime.com

Cover Design: Joann Herley

Edited by: EBH and P. Maier

Ebook formatting by: P. Maier

Dedication

Pam Maier

For making the entire journey with me!

Your friendship and encouragement have been unwavering!

Thank You!

Special Thanks

To my husband for his never ending love and support.

To my friends and family that have encouraged me to keep writing.

To my readers for taking a chance with a new author and making the complete journey through the Evergreen Series

History of the Island of Alltree

Long ago, strong ships carrying brave explorers discovered its lush forests, fertile earth and crystal clear rivers. Hearing of the beauty of the land, Lord Evergreen boarded a ship and sailed to Alltree to see the land for himself. Captured by its beauty, he returned home to tell everyone of the faraway island and his plans to build Evergreen Castle. Returning to Alltree with skilled craftsmen, he proceeded to build a castle on the west side of the island that overlooked the sea. After a decade, his castle was finally complete, and he brought his family to the island.

One by one, Lords Cumberland, Fallon, Draglaw, and Heinrich made their journey to Alltree and began building castles of their own. They were all peace loving men, and the five lords pledged to refrain from war and live in peace.

It wasn't long before immortals heard of the island and began to sneak aboard ships to make their way to Alltree. Once they arrived, they changed everything.

Prologue

Astra ran from her cave to wait for the final item that would break the curse and allow her to leave the mountain. She no longer donned the cape to hide her once translucent face or the gloves that prevented death from a single touch. Her body was completely whole again, and her magical powers had been restored. They were weak, but with a little more practice, she would regain all that she had lost.

Reaching the abandoned camp site, Astra stood eagerly watching the sky for the appearance of the white hawk. She couldn't believe that she would finally be able to leave the mountain. If it hadn't been for Thomas and Tate searching the mountain for Lady Lara, she never would have been able to end the curse. Climbing up on a large boulder in hopes of seeing over the tops of the trees, she scanned the sky for any sign of Gavenia's white hawk.

It wasn't long before she saw a small white speck in the sky. She stared while clasping her hands under her chin as the speck grew larger and moved closer to her. Astra could feel the pounding of her heart as the hawk circled above her and then swooped down to drop a small leather pouch into the palms of her hands. Clutching it to her chest, she watched the white hawk circle once more and then fly back toward Evergreen Castle. Astra hung the strands of the soft leather ties around her neck and felt the pouch rest safely against her body.

"Baxter," Astra yelled, without thinking. "Baxter, do you hear me?"

"Yes, Astra," Baxter replied, as he held the sides of his head. "Loudly, I might add."

"Forgive . . . me, please," she stuttered. "Gavenia was here. I have the pouch, and she is on her way back to you. I owe you my life for this kindness. I don't know how I will ever repay you."

"I am so happy for you," Baxter said. "Hopefully, we will see you soon."

"If all goes well, I will return to my cottage in Primrose Pond. For now, I am heading to the place where the shield blocks my departure from the mountain. There I will attempt to cross through to my freedom," she exclaimed. "You will hear my tears of joy when I have escaped this dreadful place."

"I look forward to hearing them," he whispered. Hearing nothing more than her rapid breathing, Baxter shouted, "Run Astra, don't wait any longer."

Astra jumped from the boulder and ran toward the shield and her freedom. It wasn't long before she saw the shimmer of the shield that had imprisoned her to the mountain. Standing before it, she reached out her hand and gently touched it with her finger. Small circles rippled away from her touch, but the shield did not break.

"I have the last item," she shouted, showing her frustration. "You must let me pass."

Astra waited and watched, but the shield stood firm and ignored her request. Taking the pouch from around her neck, she carefully opened it and withdrew the small vial. Holding it between her thumb and forefinger, she watched a tiny flashing light dart within a rose colored vapor.

Now, what do I do? Do I drink it? Do I release it? What if I make a mistake?

Gathering up all her courage, she opened the vial and watched the rose vapor swirl up into the air carrying the tiny light with it. For fear that she had made a mistake, Astra held out her hand hoping it would return to her.

"Tell me what to do," she begged, hoping someone would speak to her. "Please, tell me what to do."

The tiny light slowly drifted toward her and gently rested upon her open palm. Feeling a gentle tickle, she laughed as she looked up to see the once clear shimmering shield had turned a soft rose. Confused, she looked at the shield and then at the twinkling light within her palm.

"You are a little kiss," she softly said. "A beautiful little kiss. What do I do with you? What does someone do with a kiss upon their palm?"

Suddenly, she understood what she needed to do. Bringing her palm toward her mouth, she inhaled slightly and then blew the kiss toward the shield. As the kiss made contact with the rose colored shield, it shattered into a million tiny pieces. Watching the pieces of the shield fall to the ground, she started to cry as she realized what it meant.

"I'm finally free," Astra cried, through her tears as she ran from the mountain without looking back. "I'm free."

Chapter 1

Thomas could hear the sound of Lara's bare feet against the stone floor, and see the candlelight reflecting in her hair as she walked toward him with outstretched arms. A gentle breeze blew in from the open window and caused the sheer fabric of her sleeping gown to flutter around her legs. Without speaking, he wrapped his arms around her and felt her body rest gently against his own. He could feel her hands brush against his skin causing a momentary feeling of peace to fill his mind. Pulling away to look upon her face, Thomas bent down and touched his lips to hers. Closing his eyes, he let the softness of her mouth consume him. When he opened his eyes to look at her again, she had vanished.

Startled, Thomas gasped as he woke to the familiar weight of Lara's body, and the feel of her soft silken curls splayed over his chest. Relief set in when he realized he was awake and no longer dreaming. The scent of lemon and mint lingered in the air, and it brought back vivid memories of the first night she had lain within his arms. A thousand times he had dreamt of that night with her body next to his own, and a thousand times he had awakened alone to feel a crushing pain within his chest. Night after night, he had begged for the dreams that would momentarily soothe his mind, but he soon realized that when he woke to find her gone, it had done nothing more than torture him.

Will the fear of losing her ever go away?

Closing his eyes, he forced the pain from his mind and ran his fingers over her bare arm. She was back in his arms, and they had eternity to love one another. Comforted by the feel of her, it wasn't long before he drifted back to sleep and began to dream.

Lara stood in the middle of the meadow thick with wildflowers. The air was warm, and the rays of the sun brought out the red highlights within her hair. As he moved toward her, he could see that she was heavy with child. Standing before her, he brushed the wisps of hair from her face and kissed her forehead. Wrapping his arms around her shoulders, he drew her against his body. Her hands reached around him, and he suddenly felt sharp pain pierce his back. Pulling away, he looked down to see Magna's flame red hair tangled around his arms. Her laughter bombarded his senses causing his nostrils to flare while moving his hands to her throat. Her shrill cries for help filled the air around him until they were silenced by her broken neck. Letting her body fall to the ground, he savored the relief that surged through his body. Lowering his eyes to take one last look at her, he froze. There among the wildflowers was Lara. He had killed her. He had killed Lara.

Lara could feel the tense quiver of his body and his sudden gasp as he woke from another nightmare. She knew it had been hard on Thomas without her by his side for all those years. She had felt the same pain as she woke alone every morning.

So much had happened before she had run from the castle. He had just regained his sight, her sister had died a final death, and she, herself, had recovered from a near fatal wound. The surprising news of a child and a possible threat to her life had terrified her. She had willingly left him alone to take care of everyone's recovery after the attack by Jario's army, knowing she would never be able to return. Fortunately, their lives were joined back together by the loophole of a simple loving embrace. One, she would be grateful for the rest of their days.

"Another nightmare?" asked Lara, as she gently kissed his chest and sat up letting the bed linens fall from her body.

"My dreams were once my only connection to you," whispered Thomas, as he raised up to lean his shoulders against a pillow. "It was waking to find you gone that brought me pain, not the dreams."

The look of sadness in his eyes made her determined to make him smile. She wanted to see the light in his silver-grey eyes again.

"Then, I shall make it my personal endeavor to take the pain away," she smiled, as she brushed his hair from his eyes and leaned forward offering him a kiss. "My love, I shall give you things to think upon that will make you eager to wake each day."

Seeing a mischievous grin replace his once pursed mouth, she knew her plan was working.

"I am more than willing to partake in this new personal endeavor of yours," he said, as he licked his upper lip.

Straddling him, Lara laughed as she teasingly drew a heart on his bare chest with the tip of her finger. His hands were quick to encircle her waist, and he slowly brought her forward to claim her mouth with his own. Heat raced through his body and ignited his desires. His mouth trailed kisses over her neck and across her shoulder.

"I find that I am already looking forward to tomorrow," he whispered.

"Tomorrow? Oh, my love, I think I should start my endeavor today. Why should we wait until tomorrow?" asked Lara, as she crawled from their bed.

"Where are you going?" asked Thomas, as he playfully reached for her trying to pull her back to him.

"The stars must be very bright this evening," she said, while slipping on her robe and tying its sash around her waist. "You know how much I love to look up at the stars. Come with me, my love. Let's gaze up at the stars together."

"Could this celestial adventure of yours wait for another time?" he asked, as he reached for her again, with his mind on nothing but covering her body with kisses. "I was perfectly content with my arms wrapped around you. Why must you leave me?"

"I think not, my love. I wish for you to make love to me under the stars. Will you join me in the courtyard?" she asked, pleased that his expression immediately changed.

Without hesitation, Thomas leapt from the bed. Grabbing his tunic, he pulled it over his head and swept Lara up into his arms.

"My love, you have somehow made the stars much more appealing," he laughed, as he headed for the courtyard.

Chapter 2

Sitting on a stool while Caprice brushed and braided her hair, Laralynn closed her eyes and replayed the night she was formally introduced to the people of Evergreen Castle. It had been overwhelming to see everyone, including her parents, kneel before her, and it had literally taken her breath away. Baxter had felt her sway from the surprise, and thankfully, he had kept her from falling. She had danced with her father for the very first time, and when he didn't think she was looking, she had seen him wipe a tear from the corner of his eye. It was a wonderful evening. One, she would never forget.

"Laralynn, Laralynn," her mother repeated, as she lightly touched her shoulder trying to gain her attention. "What are you thinking about?"

"I'm sorry mother," she replied. "I was thinking about the celebration. Wasn't it the most glorious evening?"

"It was," she said, as she took hold of her daughter's hands. "Caprice, let's get her dressed. I want her to walk the grounds with me. She needs to learn about the people of Evergreen."

Caprice lifted the pale green gown from the door of the armoire and draped it over her arm as she approached Laralynn. With her arms over her head, Caprice and her mother lifted the gown and placed it gently over her head. She could feel the soft fabric against her arms as it slid down her body. While her mother began the process of tightening the laces, Caprice retrieved her slippers.

"Mother, do you dress like this, every day?" asked Laralynn, as she felt the strings of the corset tighten and struggled to take a breath. "This dress is so heavy and awfully tight. It is much too special to wear outside. I am sure I will get it dirty. I will never be able to run to the stable or roam about the forest."

Laralynn saw Caprice press her lips together tightly to keep from laughing and then the furrowed brow of her mother.

"What? Did I say something wrong?" she asked. "I can't possibly wear this type of garment every day. I saw several of the women wearing breeches or a woolen skirt. Doesn't that seem more suitable for spending time in the stable? You know how dirty my woolen skirt got in Primrose. Just going outside got the hem of my skirt muddy."

"They may be suitable for another day, but I don't think it is appropriate for today," her mother replied. "We will be making personal visits today. This requires you to look your best."

Laralynn sighed knowing her mother was trying to teach her about her new responsibilities. She knew she had a great deal to learn, but she just wanted to be comfortable while doing it.

Slipping her toes into her new slippers, she turned to have her mother give her final approval. Seeing the smile upon her mother's face made her happy, and she quickly forgot about the stable. Following her mother to the door, she wondered who she would meet today. More than anything, she wondered if she would see Baxter.

The hallways were cool, and the darkness was only brightened by occasional lanterns that hung upon large metal hooks. The path seemed to twist and turn several times before they reached a narrow set of steep stone steps. Following her mother, Laralynn lifted her skirt and carefully took the worn steps that spiraled to a large wooden door. She noticed the door open before her mother could lift her hand to rap upon its surface and announce their arrival.

Entering the candlelit room behind her mother, Laralynn observed a woman sitting in a chair sipping tea with a book floating above her lap. She tried not to stare, but she was surprised to see her long curls floating above her head. Looking at her mother for some explanation, her mother smiled and patted her hand.

Sending her book to a small table and her teacup to rest beside it, Meadow waved her hands to usher Laralynn to sit down before her.

"Come see me, child," Meadow requested. "Come take my hands."

Feeling her mother gently nudge her toward Meadow, Laralynn took hold of her hands and sat down on the floor in front of her chair. Meadow closed her eyes and drew Laralynn's young spirit into her mind. As she did, she opened her own mind to allow Lady Lara to see the same. Meadow carefully examined the pictures of Laralynn's past and her future. Pulling her hands back into her lap, Meadow took a deep breath.

"I am sorry that you had to endure the sadness of your mother's death. I did all that I could to protect her," she softly said to Laralynn.

"It was not your fault," Laralynn replied. "My mother explained everything to me, but I thank you for your kind words."

"You are welcome," she replied, cupping Laralynn's chin with her hand. "Would you like to know what I have learned about your spirit?"

Confused but eager, Laralynn nodded her head.

"You have a strong connection to animals like your mother, as well as a loving heart." Meadow looked up to see a smile upon Lady Lara's face and then continued. "Your spirit is as wild as the wind. It will lead you on a journey much different from your mother's path. You are curious and adventurous by nature. You will test the spoken word that other's offer you. It will not be out of distrust, but an inner knowledge of wanting to know the truth. You have been blessed with a powerful element of nature. You hold the power over water. You must remember it can be as gentle as a whisper and as dangerous as a storm."

Lara looked at Meadow and gently shook her head for their conversation to end. Adhering to her wishes, Meadow left her remaining thoughts unsaid.

"Be cautious, my child," Meadow whispered, as she gently stroked the side of Laralynn's face and then folded her hands back into her lap. "That is all for today. I must return to my reading, but I thank you for the visit."

Laralynn slowly stood and watched as the book gradually moved back over Meadow's lap, and the teacup met her hand. Laralynn felt her mother take her arm and gently lead her toward the open door.

"It was nice to meet you," Laralynn said, as she looked over her shoulder at Meadow. "I hope to see you again."

Meadow nodded and gave her a smile before she took a sip of her tea.

As they left her chamber and started down the stone steps, Laralynn heard the door close and the sound of the latch click into place. Eager to get to the bottom of the stairs, she impatiently followed her mother's slow and steady pace. Finally reaching the bottom, she started to speak, but her mother shook her head.

"We will speak of this later," she whispered, with a stern tone. "This is not a conversation to have in the hallway for others to hear. We have many more people to visit before we return to your chamber. We must pay a visit to Charlotte. I have congratulations to offer her, and I hear that she has a young son named Patrick. Besides, I am sure you will be curious about many more things before our visits are through."

"But," Laralynn said, before her mother tilted her head and placed a finger over her lips.

Holding her breath and pursing her lips, Laralynn placed her hands behind her back and made tight fists.

"Laralynn, I have learned that our world is full of hidden enemies. A single word repeated could bring danger to all of us.

You must learn that secrets are best kept secret for a reason," her mother cautioned.

She knew her mother was right; it was clear her questions would have to wait.

* * *

Charlotte looked up from the table to find Lady Lara and Lady Laralynn entering her kitchen. With her hands covered in flour, she pulled up the corner of her apron and tried to remove what she could.

"My Lady, Lady Laralynn," she said, bowing her head and bending into a quick curtsey. "I was not expecting you. The kitchen is too untidy for visitors."

"It is not the kitchen that I have come to see. It is you, Charlotte," Lara replied. "It has been much too long."

"I fear time has changed me," she shyly replied, as she brought her hand to her face and left a bit of flour upon her cheek. "While you were away, I married and have become a mother. All in all, it has aged me and Woodward, but it has brought great joy to our lives."

"I was pleased to hear of your marriage to Woodward and to find you have a son," she said. "I am sorry that I was not here to celebrate with you."

"Thank you, My Lady," she replied.

"In addition to offering my congratulations, I have come here to thank you," Lara said, as she stepped toward Charlotte and took hold of her flour covered hands. "I know that you watched over Lord Thomas while I was away. I am truly grateful for your kindness."

"It was my honor, My Lady," Charlotte replied.

Interrupted by the sound of sloshing water, they all turned toward the open door. A young lad of twelve stood facing them. He was fair skinned like his mother, but his father's eyes, smile, and hair made him a spitting image of his father.

"Mother, I have the water," a young boy's voice filled the

kitchen.

Seeing visitors in the kitchen, he stood perfectly still and looked at his mother for guidance.

"This must be Patrick," said Lara, as she smiled at the young boy holding two full pails of water.

"Patrick, this is Lady Lara and her daughter, Lady Laralynn," Charlotte said, as she moved toward her son.

He gently placed the pails upon the floor and bowed slightly, "My Lady, Lady Laralynn."

"He is quite a handsome lad," Lara said. "He looks very much like his father."

"He is his father's son," she laughed. "I find it hard to keep him from roaming the forest with his bow. He hopes to be the Forest Warden, someday."

"May I go with you?" Laralynn boldly asked. "The next time you . . . roam the forest with your father. I would like to go with you and learn to use the bow."

Patrick started to laugh and quickly pursed his lips when he saw his mother's stern expression.

"Mother, I would like to learn everything," Laralynn pleaded, before her mother took hold of her hand. Looking up at her mother and over at Patrick, she felt her face flush with frustration.

"We will speak to your father about your request," she replied. "However, your father made many trips into the forest with Woodward and learned a great deal from him. If your father approves and Woodward is agreeable to teaching you, I will approve of your request."

Feeling her frustration fade, a smile soon appeared on Laralynn's face, and she felt satisfied with her mother's response.

"We have many more people to visit," Lara announced. "Charlotte, it was good to see that you are well."

"My Lady, we are all pleased that you and Lady Laralynn were able to return to us," Charlotte offered. "You were truly missed."

Lara nodded and turned to leave the kitchen. Laralynn followed her mother but stopped for a moment to look over her shoulder at Patrick.

"We will become good friends, Patrick," she said. Seeing him grin made her happy. "I see you like that. I like it too."

Thrilled to have made a new friend, Laralynn turned and hurried from the kitchen. She eagerly followed her mother hoping to meet someone else her own age, and she greeted everyone that passed her in the hallways. After peeking in every open doorway, she was disappointed to find no one even close to her age.

Stopping in front of a large door, her mother rapped three times. The door slowly opened to reveal stone steps that plunged into darkness. The hallways in the castle were cool, but as they descended the stone steps to the lowest level of the castle, the cool air was replaced with an unusual thick warmth. Confused, Laralynn swept her hand through the air as if she could touch it.

"It is spelled to keep the prisoners secure," she smiled, impressed that her daughter had recognized the difference in the air. "To know everything about Evergreen, you must see the evil that we and others face. It is our duty to protect our people from those that would do us harm." Lara saw her daughter hesitate to move forward. "You will be safe, my dear. They cannot harm you."

Laralynn stood outside the chamber that held the locked cells of those that had been arrested by the Evergreen Army. The pungent air smelled of sweat and blood. Even though her mother had told her she had nothing to fear, chills ran down her spine. Her mother unlocked the door and pulled it open. A sudden clamoring of voices yelling obscenities filled the chamber. Men reached from their cells trying to grab her mother with their dirty hands.

"Laralynn, these men have been imprisoned for horrible crimes," she explained. "They have raped, murdered, stolen, and committed treason against Evergreen. It falls upon me to judge their crimes and determine their punishment."

"Will they die?" she asked.

"Some will die or be given their final death," replied her mother. "It will be done quickly and with as little pain as possible. For those men who are truly remorseful, they will be given their freedom."

The men continued to yell hoping to gain Lady Lara's attention. A few made obscene gestures and fondled their manhood to draw the turn of young Laralynn's head.

"Mother, may we go?" she asked, as she reached for her mother's hand. "I have seen and heard enough."

Her mother nodded and turned toward the door. Before she could grasp the handle, a leather boot hit the wall beside the door. Instantly, her mother stood before the cell door with her hand gripping a man's throat. He stared into her eyes and began to laugh. It wasn't long before he calmly rested his arms at his side and closed his eyes. Pulling her hand free from the man's neck, she told the man to step back against the wall. He followed her request without hesitation and stood quietly against the wall.

Looking back at her daughter, she said, "Now, we can leave."

After seeing the men in the dungeon, Laralynn wanted to go back to her bedchamber, but her mother insisted they make one more visit to see Flora.

The quiet of the Healing Room calmed her nerves as they waited for Flora to finish tending to a man that had burns covering one arm. It was a dreadful sight, and Flora's gentle touch did little to quiet his moaning. After washing her hands and drying them on a clean cloth, Flora greeted them with a smile.

"My Lady, Lady Laralynn," she said, making a quick curtsey.

Lara reached for Flora and lovingly wrapped her arms around her.

"It has been far too long my dear Flora," she quietly whispered. "I have missed you."

"It is good to have you back at Evergreen," she replied, as

she released Lara and took a step back. "Your daughter is lovely."

"Laralynn, this is Flora. She is Evergreen's healer and my dearest friend," her mother's smile beamed. "Flora, this is my daughter, Laralynn."

"It is an honor to meet you, Lady Laralynn," she offered.

"Thank you," she shyly responded, as she glanced at the man that Flora had been tending. "Do you find it difficult to look upon such a dreadful sight?"

"No child," Flora smiled. "It gives me great satisfaction to help those that are ill or wounded. I once helped your mother recover from a tragic attack."

"Mother, you were attacked?" she gasped.

"That is a story for another time," her mother gently caressed the side of her face. "Flora, where is Niobe?"

"She has gone back to Wintergreen Mountain," replied Flora. "She wanted to return to her village. Niobe had learned a great deal under my watchful instruction, and she felt she had much to offer them. Will escorted her back to her village, and Lord Thomas sent enough coin for her to secure a cottage to do her work."

"I am sorry I was not here to see her go," Lara sighed. "I will not keep you from your work. Flora, promise me that you will come have tea with me and tell me all about the things I have missed."

"I would enjoy your company," Flora replied. "Lady Laralynn, you are welcome to visit the Healing Room, anytime. I am sure those that fill these cots would enjoy your visit. A smile or a kind word does much for those that suffer."

"I am willing to learn all that you are willing to teach me," declared Laralynn. "I will gladly be of help in any way that I am able."

Lara listened to her daughter offer to help Flora, and she knew that her daughter would make her proud.

Chapter 3

Magna sat by Velsa's hearth hoping to warm her body, but she couldn't feel the heat of the flames. She hadn't been able to feel the heat or the cold since the white wolf's brutal attack. Somehow, her spirit had managed to separate from her body that had been concealed by her sister's appearance. She had watched as the imposter clung to her sister as they fell to the stone floor of the dungeon. Everyone had rushed to Lady Lara's aide leaving her own headless body sprawled on the floor. Following Elda as she carried the remains of her body outside, she had seen the sun ignite its flesh and witnessed the ashes swirl up into the wind before they vanished.

After seeing Magna at her door, Velsa had helped her into her cottage and sat her in her favorite rocking chair. Seeing the dazed look upon her face, she carefully entered Magna's mind. She gasped as she saw the graphic visions Magna offered from her memories. Velsa had seen the moment her spirit had separated from its host and hovered above the turmoil as her head was removed from her body. She could see the blood drip from the white wolf's mouth, and Gautier kneeling to run his fingers through her fur. Shaking her head to try and remove the images from her mind, she stepped closer to Magna.

"Magna, where have you been all this time?" asked Velsa.

"Black Thistle Castle," she grumbled. "I have been walking the hallways looking for a way to escape. Something was keeping me there, and I was unable to leave the castle walls. It even prohibited me from standing in the moonlight within the stone wall that surrounds the castle."

"Could no one see your image?" she asked. "Could no one hear you speak?"

"Not my image or hear my cries for help," she sighed. "Not until recently."

"What happened?" Velsa asked, as she leaned closer to Magna and stroked her glove covered hand.

"I received a surprise visit from Jario," she said. "He was covered by his haze, but I knew that he was there. A faint image of his body was visible to me. I don't understand how, but I was able to touch him. I could feel his sadness over my death and his desire for me. I couldn't help myself; I pierced his skin with my fangs and drew his blood. I believe that is what allowed me to leave the castle."

"Then you know of Jario's demise," she said.

"I do," Magna replied. Closing her eyes for a moment, she then looked down at her hands. They were clutching the edge of her cape tightly against her body. "He is held within a dagger that has been spelled to an emblem that hangs within the Great Hall of the castle. I tried to remove it. I wanted to bring it to you so that you could free him, but it was bound securely in place. Nothing I did would allow the dagger to break free."

"I would not have been able to free him from Gautier's curse," Velsa replied. "He can only be released if the loophole is found, or Gautier decides to free him. Until that time, he will be securely held in place."

Magna suddenly stood and her image began to fade. Velsa felt her pass through her body as she headed toward the door.

"Wait, where are you going?" asked Velsa.

"Back to the castle," she said. "You can't help Jario, and I have nowhere else to go."

"Magna, stay here with me. I may be able to help you," she said. "I cannot promise you that I will be able to bring your body back, but I will try."

"For what price? I have nothing to give you," Magna replied.

"I never thought I would say this, but I will do it . . . because . . . well, because," she stuttered. "I may want to ask a favor of you in the future. Would a future favor be agreeable to you?"

Magna looked around the tiny cottage and shook her head.

"There is not enough room for the two of us in this tiny cottage. Everywhere I look there are herbs, sacks, bundles, disgusting jars of salves, and it smells of smoke," she whined. "It smells bad. I am used to fine linens, a soft bed, and pillows stuffed with goose down. Velsa, you live in a pigsty."

"You are starting to sound like your old nasty self," Velsa flinched, as she clenched her fingers into fists and threw handfuls of sparks around the cluttered cottage. "You sassy little vampire, is this more to your liking? I wouldn't want you to do without your luxuries."

Magna looked about the grand sitting room and nodded. Seeing the open door to a bedchamber, she drifted toward it. A bed piled high with cream linens came into view. Looking over her shoulder, she saw Velsa standing with her hands on her hips.

"You have outdone yourself," Magna said. "This is much more to my liking."

"Go rest your pretty little head," Velsa ordered. "If I am going to bring your body back, I had better get busy. I don't intend for you to be a permanent resident around here."

"Nor do I want to be," Magna grinned. "I am not sure where I will go. Do you know of a safe place that I might use for shelter from my sister and the Evergreen Army?"

"I hear the Lord of Crimson Claw is unable to return to his castle," Velsa smirked. "You might find the new commander to your liking. I hear he is a giant of a vampire, and he once sailed the mighty sea. Rumors on the wind tell me he once was in love with a mermaid."

"Very interesting," Magna replied. "A giant of a vampire, you say. I will have to pay him a visit."

"Be cautioned, there is a witch that lives at the castle. We aren't the best of friends," Velsa laughed. "I caused the death of her sister, and she is here on Alltree Island to avenge her death. I am not aware of a romantic involvement between the vampire and the witch, but I would tread lightly."

"This sounds fun," Magna giggled. "A new castle, a new vampire, and a new witch to entertain my fantasies. Thank you for the warning. I will be cautious and see which way the witch's temper blows."

"Get some rest," Velsa ordered. "I need some quiet."

Magna huffed and headed toward the new bedchamber. As she reached the door, a candle beside the bed came to flame and the coverlet pulled back. Entering the chamber, Magna blew Velsa a kiss and closed the door.

Does she really think that I am going to help her, thought Velsa? That vampire has never shown me a single kindness. Oh, the fun I will have with her.

Chapter 4

A new stone pedestal had been erected outside the main entrance to the castle, and the stone statue of Killian's wolf had been securely positioned upon it. As he had guarded and protected Lady Kayleigh, it would now stand guard at the entrance to Black Thistle Castle. A grand ceremony had marked the occasion with colorful banners and fine words delivered by Lord Gautier. For his courage and sacrifice, Killian had been awarded the honor of "The Great Guardian". Alicia had proudly climbed the wooden ladder during the ceremony to place the elaborate medal around the stone neck of Killian's wolf. The bravery Killian had shown that day would never be forgotten.

Alicia felt the loss of Killian more than anyone. Her heart and her wolf constantly ached for him. She felt lost without him. The sweet dreams she had of Killian had turned into repeated nightmares of the moment he had been turned to stone. To try and ease her aching heart, she often walked along the edge of the forest thinking about their sprints through the trees, splashing their paws in the small streams, and resting in the cool shade after a long run. Those memories brought moments of happiness that quickly faded to sadness. They couldn't heal the pain caused by his absence.

For some unknown reason, she found herself in the Great Hall instead of standing at the edge of the forest. It was one place she had deliberately avoided. A fire roared in the hearth, but the flames did nothing to warm her or give her comfort. She looked up at the elaborate emblem that hung far above the mantle. It held a boar's head surrounded by thistles with two crossed swords. It had been removed by the craftsmen to permanently affix the spelled dagger that held Jario. It then was remounted securely to the wall, well beyond anyone's reach. She hated the sight of it, and even more, she hated what Jario had done to Killian.

Her wolf mourned the loss of her beloved black wolf, and Alicia had been unable to bring her forth since Jario's attack. She had tried numerous times, but her wolf had withdrawn and refused to acknowledge her pleadings or those offered by Lady Kayleigh. Her wolf had hidden away, leaving Alicia completely alone.

"I promise you, Killian. I will find the loophole that will set you free," she screamed. "I will bring you back to me."

Startled by the sound of her echoing voice, Alicia ran from the Great Hall as tears began to fill her eyes. Unable to breathe, she burst through a set of wooden doors and found herself outside of the main entrance to the castle. There, she collapsed on the stone steps gasping for air. Losing Killian had been too much for her to endure. She longed to see his smile and hear his voice again. Through her tear-filled sobs, Alicia heard a soft and soothing voice. Wiping her eyes with the back of her hand, she looked around for the person that had invaded her privacy. She found no one but heard the soothing voice again.

"Alicia, it is me, Killian," he softly repeated, trying not to frighten her.

Confused, she looked up at the wolf statue and studied its stone features.

"How can this be?" she said, as she continued to stare up at the solid stone face of the wolf through tear filled eyes. "I have surely fallen ill and must find my mother for a cure. She will know how to help me."

"Alicia, you are not ill," he replied. "Even though we have been turned to stone, I find that our spirits are still alive. I heard your tears and your beautiful promise to me. In return, I promise you that one day I will return to you. I do not know when, or how, but I will return to you. I ask that you be strong for me. We will figure this out. There must be a way to undo what has happened to me."

Alicia could feel her wolf begin to awaken to the knowledge that Killian had spoken to them. She could feel her agitated wolf pushing to be released. Sensing that she was trying to communicate with his wolf, Alicia stood on her toes and placed her hands upon the back paws of the statue. Closing her eyes, she let her wolf reach out to his wolf. She could feel her joy and her sudden rage.

"Take care of your wolf," Killian begged. "She is filled with anger."

"I promise to take care of her," she whispered. "We will find a way, Killian. We will find a way to bring you both back to us."

Turning toward the open wooden doors, Alicia felt hope lighten the heavy sorrow her heart had been carrying. It wasn't much, but she finally had hope, and the sound of Killian's voice to keep her strong.

Walking quickly through the hallways, Alicia was desperately looking for Lady Kayleigh. As she turned the corner to head for the library, she found herself floating above the stone floor.

"You are in quite a hurry," Desirae teased. "We would have both been sprawled upon the stone floor had I not heard your frantic footsteps and stopped you midair."

"I'm sorry, but he spoke to me," she told Desirae. "I need to tell Lady Kayleigh."

"Who spoke to you, child?" she asked, as she gently set Alicia down upon her feet.

"Killian spoke to me. Well, his spirit spoke to me," she quickly replied, as excitement filled her eyes. "I was outside, and he just spoke to me. I could hear him in my mind."

The rustle of fabric and hurried footsteps preceded her before Lady Kayleigh appeared behind Alicia.

Turning Alicia to face her, Kayleigh asked, "What happened? I heard Killian speak. My wolf recognized him."

"Lady Kayleigh, he spoke to me," she replied. "He isn't gone." Alicia lowered her head and began to cry. Looking back up at Lady Kayleigh, she wrapped her arms around her waist. "Lady Kayleigh, please help me find a way to bring Killian back. I could feel how lonely he has been."

"We will try," Kayleigh replied, as she looked up at Desirae feeling helpless. "Alicia, I promise you, we will try."

Chapter 5

Upon arriving in Primrose Pond, Astra had found a field of sweet grass where her little cottage once stood. Prepared to find nothing, she felt no sadness upon finding it was gone. Too many years had passed for it to have remained. A partial stone wall that had bordered the path to the village was all that was left. She faced a clean slate.

Ready to start her new life away from the view of the mountain, she set about conjuring herself a new cottage. It was small, but it had several windows that allowed the light to brighten the space. Dark clouds and dark caves had hindered her life for too long, and she wanted to see the sunlight. Hoping she would not find trouble at her door, she made certain that her cottage had two doors. If trouble should enter through the front, she could easily escape through the back. Astra knew it was silly, but it gave her mind great comfort.

The usual items were conjured and put into place. The stone hearth was large enough to heat the cottage on a cool evening and the cooking pot for her meals. A table sat in the middle of the room flanked by two benches. She hoped her new friends would come for a visit and join her at the table for food and long conversations. Wanting to watch the sunsets, a wooden chair was placed by the window to allow her to take in the beauty of the vivid colors. It was a simple thing, but she knew that none of those things interested her more than her bedchamber. It was a cozy space with a wooden bed that was completely covered by a large pillow stuffed with the softest goose down feathers. It was the most delightful thing she had ever felt. Gone were the nights of sleeping on the hard ground and using rags for bed linens. She would sleep in a real bed that would allow her to dream sweet dreams every night.

It would take her a long time to forget the misery of the mountain. She would have to replace those bad memories with new memories of the friends she had made upon that mountain. They would always hold a special place in her heart, and she longed to see them again.

Settling into her chair to wait for the sky's colorful display, she felt a familiar pushing on her mind. She gladly accepted the intrusion as she waited to hear his voice.

"Astra, are you there?" Baxter asked.

"Yes, I am here," she replied. "I am sitting in my cottage waiting for the setting sun to show me its wonderful colors. Would you come for a visit? Our time on the mountain was very short. I would like to properly meet you. I owe you my thanks for everyone's kindness."

"I would like that very much. Can you describe how I might find you?" he asked.

"My cottage is at the end of the dirt road that leads south away from the village of Primrose Pond. It is easy to see. I have chosen a spot beyond the shelter of the trees. I can see the sunrise, sunset, and hear the sounds of the sea. It is a perfect location."

"I will be there shortly," he replied, as he broke their connection.

Astra anxiously waited for Baxter outside her cottage door. Catching a glimpse of him coming through the trees, she lifted the edge of her skirt and ran to meet him. Throwing her arms around his waist, Astra placed her head against his chest.

"Thank you, thank you," she whispered. "How will I ever

repay you for your kindness?"

Taking hold of Astra's arms, he gently pushed her away from him and looked directly into her eyes as he spoke, "It is you that deserves our thanks. If not for your help, we would have never been able to return Lord Thomas and Tate to Evergreen. They would have been lost to us. Because of your bravery, I have been sent to invite you to Evergreen Castle. Lady Lara and Lord Thomas wish to offer their thanks in person."

"I would be honored to meet them," she shyly responded. "May I also meet Gavenia? I have only seen her beautiful white hawk. I would love to meet her. She risked her own life helping me."

"I am sure it can be arranged," Baxter grinned. "I shall return for you tomorrow and take you to Evergreen. Are you brave enough to flash with me to Evergreen?"

"After my stay on the mountain, I believe that I am brave enough for almost anything," she laughed. Sensing that he was about to leave, she took hold of his hand. "Baxter, would you sit with me and watch the sunset before you return to Evergreen?"

"It would be my pleasure," Baxter replied, as he allowed Astra to lead him to her cottage.

* * *

The sun was just starting to rise, and Astra woke to the sound of birds chirping outside her window. Remembering that Baxter was coming for her, she quickly sat up and slipped her body out from under her coverlet. With both feet securely on the floor, she suddenly felt a bit dizzy from the rapid beat of her heart and leaned back against her bed. Lifting her hand to her forehead, Astra tried to focus her thoughts on the gentle sway of the sweet grass that surrounded her cottage to calm her nerves. She had never been to Evergreen Castle, and it had been a long time since she had been around others.

Taking a deep breath, she set to work preparing for Baxter's arrival. Pouring water from her pewter pitcher into a wooden bowl, she could see her reflection staring back at her. Smiling back at herself, she dabbed the water with the tip of her finger as she returned the pitcher to the table. Amused at how the rippling water made her image blur and then disappear, she splashed the cool water on her face to wash the sleep from her eyes.

After brushing and braiding her hair, she methodically twisted it into a perfect crown upon her head. Securing it with long pins that held red poppies, Astra began to struggle with what to wear to meet Lord and Lady Evergreen. She opened the tall narrow armoire and studied her choices. Touching several of the colorful fabrics, she pulled out her prettiest gown of cream lace over black satin. Delighted with her choice, she laid it across the foot of her bed and retrieved her leather slippers.

Adjusting the thin satin straps over her shoulders, she pulled the laces to tighten the bodice of her gown and tied them in a bow at her waist. Waving her hand, Astra created a reflection of herself and turned in a circle to view her beautiful gown. Lifting her hand to her bare neck, she quickly conjured one necklace after another. Deciding on a pendant that held a deep red stone, she hung it from a simple black ribbon and tied it loosely around her neck. Pleased with her appearance, she felt ready to visit Evergreen Castle.

A soft rap at the door drew her attention and caused her reflection to disappear. Knowing it was Baxter, she hurried to the door to greet him.

"Good morning, are you ready to go to Evergreen?" asked Baxter.

"I am ready but very nervous," she replied.

"Astra, you will be among friends. There is no need to be nervous," Baxter said, trying to reassure her. "I thought I would show you about Evergreen. It will give you a chance to meet Gavenia and Tate."

"Yes, I would like that very much," Astra replied.

Taking Astra's hand, Baxter gave her a smile as he asked,

"Ready?"

Seeing her nod, they vanished from her tiny cottage.

* * *

Baxter and Astra suddenly appeared in the Command Center to the fierce sound of clashing blades and heavy grunting. Noticing Baxter holding the hand of a young woman, the men lowered their blades and turned to face them. Looking about at the shirtless men, Astra's cheeks flushed, and she quickly lowered her eyes to the floor.

"Have I come at the wrong time?" she whispered to Baxter. "I seem to have intruded upon their quest for power."

"No, no," Baxter replied, gripping her hand a little tighter. "They are simply brandishing their blades to better their skills and to stay strong in body and spirit. Evergreen relies on these men to protect Lady Lara and Evergreen."

As the men came closer, Baxter felt Astra's hand begin to tremble.

"Who might this be?" asked Oliver, as he balanced the tip of his sword on the toe of his boot.

"My good friends, this is Astra," Baxter announced. "She helped me retrieve Lord Thomas and Tate from the mountain. She saved them from their final death."

It took but a few seconds for the men to realize the importance of the young woman that stood before them. One by one, the men knelt placing with their fists upon their bare chests.

"Astra, we thank you for your bravery and are honored by your presence," bellowed Oliver. "I, for one, willingly pledge my service for your protection."

The echoing sound of men's voices affirming Oliver's pledge filled the Command Center. Completely surprised by the men's tribute, Astra stepped forward breaking her contact with Baxter. Raising her hands in a silent plea to have them stand, she watched the men stand before her.

"It is I that is honored to be standing before you," Astra boldly said, as she addressed the men before her. "You see; I was cursed to live upon the mountain. It had been such a long time, and I had given up hope of ever leaving that dreadful place. The chance meeting of your Lord Thomas and his brother, Tate, allowed me to receive the items I needed to escape that curse. I will forever be indebted to all of Evergreen for those gifted items. I thank you, fine men of the Evergreen Army, for your generous pledge."

One by one, the men came forward and introduced themselves to Astra. Feeling a bit overwhelmed by trying to remember all of their names, it wasn't until Oliver introduced himself that she felt a sense of calm take over her body.

"Astra, I am Oliver," he said, as he looked upon her gentle face and offered his hand.

"He is my best friend," Baxter declared, as he slapped Oliver on the shoulder. "I owe him my life."

Astra smiled, and in return, she offered her hand to Oliver.

"I thank you for saving my new friend's life," she replied, as she felt his large callused hand grasp her own and a strange surge of power pass between them.

Releasing her hand, Oliver raised a brow and looked down at the palm of his hand. Shaking his hand and then rubbing his palm against his breeches, he looked up at Baxter for an explanation.

"You have a powerful touch, little lady," Oliver teased. "Next time, a kind warning would be helpful. I was not expecting such a strong hand."

"Oliver, she is a witch," explained Baxter.

"I am sorry, Oliver," she whispered. "My powers were taken from me. I have just recently regained them, and it appears they are still a bit unruly. Please forgive me."

"Never you mind, little lady," he replied. "It was a surprise, nothing more. I harbor no ill will."

The sound of laughing drew Astra from Oliver's apology. Seeing Tate enter the Command Center holding the hand of a beautiful woman with a long red braid hanging over her shoulder, she immediately determined her to be Gavenia. Excusing herself from Baxter and Oliver, she made her way toward Tate.

"Astra," shouted Tate. "It is so good to see you."

Astra quickened her step and threw her arms around his waist. She could feel his kind spirit and lingered for a moment to enjoy his comfort. Pulling herself back, she looked up at Tate's broad smile.

"I must say that you look much better than the last time I saw you," said Astra. "You were an awful sight."

"Indeed," Tate replied. "I believe that we all have improved since leaving that dreadful mountain."

Astra nodded her head and glanced at the woman standing next to Tate.

"Astra, this is my little white hawk, Gavenia," he said, as he heard her soft sigh.

Feeling overcome with emotion, tears began to well in Astra's eyes.

"It is so good to finally meet you," she said, as her chin began to quiver.

Immediately, she felt Gavenia's embrace and the comfort of her hawk.

"I am sorry that you had to stay all alone upon the mountain," whispered Gavenia. "It broke my heart that you could not leave with Baxter."

"If not for you, I would have been lost upon the mountain," Astra replied, as she pushed back to look up into Gavenia's eyes. "I will never forget your act of kindness."

"Nor will I forget your bravery," she replied. "You allowed Tate to return to me."

Baxter approached Astra and gently placed his hand against her lower back.

"We have much to see before your meeting with Lord Thomas and Lady Lara," said Baxter. "I thought you might like to visit Meadow. She has been expecting you and is eager to spend time with you."

"Meadow?" asked Astra.

"She is also a witch," Baxter replied. "Come, let me show you the way."

"We hope to see you again," Gavenia said, as she gave Astra one last hug.

"Enjoy your visit with Meadow," Tate chuckled. "You will find her most interesting."

Oliver turned and watched Astra and Baxter leave the Command Center. Looking down at his hand, he saw a strange red mark that looked like a star burst on the palm of his hand. Annoyed, he tried to rub it off onto his breeches. Taking another look and seeing it was still there, he felt worry invade his mind.

"She has marked me," Oliver muttered under his breath. "The little lady has marked me."

* * *

Baxter opened the door to the courtyard for Astra to enter. With her by his side, they walked toward Lord Thomas, Lady Lara, and Lady Laralynn that were seated by the fountain. Nervously, she took hold of Baxter's hand.

"My Lady," Baxter said, as he looked at Lady Lara. "I am pleased to introduce Astra."

"Lady Lara, it is an honor to meet you," Astra replied, as she bent into a deep curtsy."

"We are honored to have you visit Evergreen," Lara replied. "Please sit with us."

Baxter waited to seat Astra until Lord Thomas had seated Lady Lara and his daughter. As he helped Astra with her chair, he noticed the concerned look upon Laralynn's face and gave her a smile hoping to ease what might be bothering her.

"I must thank you for helping me break the curse that kept me prisoner on the mountain," Astra sincerely stated, looking at Lady Lara. "Lady Laralynn, I thank you for the item that finally set me free. Without your help, I would still be upon that horrible mountain."

"I am glad that I could help," she replied, as she studied the way Baxter looked at Astra. "Now that you are free, where will you call home?"

"I have a cottage in Primrose Pond," replied Astra. "The tall trees block the view of the mountain, which is much to my liking."

"Primrose Pond was my home until my father came for me," she said, as she lovingly looked at her father. "I find there are times when I miss it and my friends."

"You are welcome to visit me anytime," offered Astra. "It was my home too, before the curse. I am glad that I was able to return."

"Is there anything that we can do for you?" asked Thomas.

"No, My Lord," she replied. "You have done so much for me already. It is I that owes you for your kindness."

"I understand that you met with Meadow," Lara said. "Was it a good meeting?"

"It was; however, I did find her a bit unusual," Astra smiled and saw Laralynn attempt to cover a smile. "She finds that my powers have returned, but they are still weak. She has offered me help if I feel I need it. I know I must spend time practicing to improve my skills. She has also offered the use of her small library to me. I may spend some time going through her resources. Her magic has recorded much of the history of the island. Because of the curse, I have missed so much."

"Do you have family here on the island?" Laralynn asked, as she looked from Astra to Baxter and back again.

"I do," she replied. "I have a sister."

"A sister?" Thomas repeated. "There are very few witches upon this island. Are you related to Desirae?"

"No, My Lord," Astra replied. "My sister's name is Velsa."

Astra was not surprised to see the look of shock upon his face.

"Yes, she is my sister," she confessed. "Sadly, she is the one that cursed me to the mountain."

"Why?" Thomas asked, just before Laralynn interrupted him.

"Your own sister did that to you? She cursed you to the mountain? Did she curse the creature too?" Laralynn asked, as she impatiently waited for her to speak.

Astra was not surprised by the questions, but she didn't want to repeat the story she had tried for so long to forget.

"It is nothing I wish to remember. Might we speak of something else?" she politely requested.

A sudden silence filled the courtyard as she began to rub circles in her palm with her thumb and tried to think of something else to talk about.

"I'm sorry if I upset you," Laralynn said. "It was not my intention. Will you forgive me?"

"Of course," Astra replied and reached for Laralynn's hands to reassure her.

In doing so, Laralynn noticed what looked like a raised mark or red rash upon Astra's hand.

"Astra, are you hurt?" Laralynn gasped. "Is there blood upon your palm?"

Astra pulled her hand away and looked at the bright red mark upon her palm.

"No, this can't be," she muttered. "No . . . No . . . No."

She looked up to see Lady Lara standing before her and quickly hid her hands behind her back.

"Let me see," urged Lara. "I will have our healer, Flora, help you."

"No one can help me," she replied. "No one can help me."

"What do you mean? Flora has healing powers. I'm sure that she can help you," Lara replied, as she tried to reach for Astra's hand.

"Not with this she can't," she declared. "What's done is done."

"What is done?" asked Thomas. "Baxter, please take Astra to the Healing Room."

"You don't understand," Astra tried to explain. "This can't

be healed. It is the mark of my intended mate. It can't be undone."

With a furrowed brow, Thomas asked, "Who is it, Astra?"

"I don't know," Astra replied, as tears ran down her face. "I am a Seer, and I don't know. I have not been able to see the future since I escaped the mountain."

Laralynn watched Baxter take a few steps toward Astra. She felt a sudden ache in her chest as Astra turned and pressed her face tightly against Baxter's chest seeking his comfort. He wrapped his arms around her shoulders trying to quiet her trembling body. When his eyes met Laralynn's, he could see her concern. He lifted his hands and looked at his palms. Turning them over, he let Laralynn view his unmarked palms. Seeing her shoulders relax and hearing her sigh of relief, Baxter returned his focus back to Astra.

"There is no need to cry, Astra," Baxter said, trying to reassure her.

"Baxter take me home," Astra whispered. "Please . . .I want to go home."

"Yes, of course," Thomas said. "Shall I have Tolin ready your horses?"

"My Lord, I flashed Astra here. I will take her home the same way," Baxter replied.

"Off with you then," offered Lara. "It was a pleasure meeting you, Astra. Please know that you are always welcome at Evergreen."

"Thank . . . you," she stuttered through her tears. "It was an honor to meet you."

Laralynn stepped forward and wrapped her arms around Astra. She quietly whispered something in her ear for no one else to hear. Astra nodded her head and gave her a forced smile. With a nod to Baxter, he took hold of her hand, and they vanished.

"It saddens me that she is not happy," Thomas said, as he reached for Lara's hand.

"She has been through so much. It doesn't surprise me.

When she is ready, she will open her mind and her heart to her intended mate," Lara replied.

"She has to find him first," laughed Laralynn.

"I have a feeling that he will have to find her," offered Thomas.

Chapter 6

After multiple attempts to return her body back to its previous state, Magna sat cross-legged on the floor of Velsa's cottage with blue hair and ears the size of her feet.

"Your talents are lacking," Magna cursed, as she stood and stormed over to the cot and sat down. "It appears you have lost your magic touch."

"I wasn't the one that jumped from my body," Velsa fussed, trying to keep from laughing. "Don't blame me for your predicament."

"If I hadn't jumped, I wouldn't be here," she growled, smacking the lumpy cot with her gloved covered hand out of frustration. "Give me some of that power you brag about. You can't expect me to stay this way." Flapping her ears with her fingers, she saw Velsa start to laugh. "It isn't funny. I am in a worse state than I was before I came here."

Velsa turned her back on Magna and tried to regain her composure. She had given her colorful liquids to drink, thrown purple sparks at her, and made her body shake uncontrollably. None of it was the answer to her problem, and she knew it. It had all been a wonderful game, and she had enjoyed every delightful moment. Knowing she had reached Magna's limit for understanding, she turned and stepped toward the floppy eared vampire.

"Let me try one last thing?" she asked.

"Just put me back the way you found me," Magna begged. "It doesn't appear that a spell can help me regain my full appearance."

Nodding in agreement, Velsa placed her hand upon Magna's head and started to chant.

Return, return to where we started!
Go back, go back before it parted!
Turn time, turn time to when she came!
Make right, make right, her troubles tamed!

Magna's ears began to warm, and her head felt like it was being stung by bees. As Velsa's chanting ended, Magna's ears slowly returned to normal. Scratching her head, Magna lifted the ends of her long tresses to see that fiery red color she loved had returned. Relieved, she flopped back on the cot and covered her face with her hands.

"Thank the stars," she whispered. "I have had enough of your spells."

"We could try," Velsa started to speak but was cut off by Magna.

"No! I have had enough," she shouted. "It is extremely clear that you can't help me. I think it is time for me to leave."

"So soon?" asked Velsa with her hand covering a smile.

"It is time," she replied. "I appreciate the lovely bed and all your efforts to help me, but it is clear that I must obtain help from someone a little more powerful."

Those words bristled against Velsa's spine. She hadn't helped the vampire because she had nothing to gain from it. Magna had always been selfish, and it was clear that she hadn't changed.

"Shall I take you to Crimson Claw Castle?" Velsa asked. "It is a long walk."

"No, I still have my gift of flashing," she replied.

Magna made her way to her bedchamber and returned wearing her cape. Pulling the hood up over her head, she headed for the door. Standing before its rough surface, she turned and nodded to Velsa before she vanished leaving a very faint wisp of red smoke.

* * *

Appearing in the cool shade, Magna could see the thistles that surrounded Black Thistle Castle from the edge of the forest. To her, they were lovely little creatures that had once kept her company. As a child, she had played among them and had felt the pricks of their thorns upon her hands, arms and legs. She never understood why Velsa had taken her hatred out on them. They appeared to be dead and sometimes dangerous to others, but Magna knew how to make them come alive. She could make them dance in the sunlight and sway in the evening breeze. Her blood had been the secret, and they had always loved her for it.

Making the last few steps toward the thistles that lined the stone walls, she noticed how the moonlight highlighted their sharp thorns. The desire to play once more among the brittle flowers and feel them touch her was overwhelming. Standing before them, she dropped her cape and removed her gloves. As she took her first step between their rows, the thistles began to quiver. One by one, they began to sense her arrival and eagerly turned toward her. Lifting her hands to caress their thorns, she felt the sweet sting of their affection. Their cries for her attention entered her mind, and she moved about trying to greet each and every one of them.

Feeling dizzy from the sound of their songs of devotion and the stings of their venom, Magna laid down to rest. Slowly the thistles moved toward her and nestled themselves around her body. After completely covering her, they began to gently pierce her skin. Her muffled whimpers continued until they were all united with her body. Closing her eyes, Magna drifted into a deep comforting sleep.

Startled by the sound of clashing swords, Magna sat up and rubbed the sleep from her eyes. A hint of the morning sun was just beginning to rise, and she could feel a gentle warmth from its rays upon her skin. Remembering where she was, Magna quickly stood and brushed the dirt from her skirt and ran to retrieve her cape. Draping it over her shoulders and covering her head with the hood, she reached for her gloves. She noticed her hands were covered in blood. Smiling, she tugged her gloves over her swollen fingers.

"I must leave you," Magna whispered. "I promise; I will return to play with you again."

Hearing their soft sad cries, she knew they had heard her, and she quickly vanished leaving a wisp of vivid red smoke behind.

Arriving at the Dragon's Tear River that bordered Crimson Claw Castle, Magna removed her gloves to wash her hands within its rippling water. Dipping her hands into the cool water, she splashed her hands within the gentle current and watched the blood that covered her hands slowly wash away. Feeling refreshed, she stood and dried her hands on her heavy skirt. Looking across the river, she could see the red stone castle before her. As she started to shield her eyes from the bright sun, she gasped at what she saw. Ripping her cape from her shoulders, she stepped into the dappled sunlight. Lifting her arms, she couldn't believe her eyes.

"I am whole again," she sang, as she danced in circles looking at her hands. "I have found the loophole. My precious thistles were the cure." Plunking down upon the soft grass, she examined each finger and the palms of her hands. "How lovely to see my fingers."

Feeling emboldened, she looked again at the red stones that graced the castle walls. She had been told of the vampire and of the witch that resided there. Could she persuade them to allow her to stay at the castle? Would her friendship with Velsa harm her chances? There was only one way to find out.

"It is time to meet the big bad vampire," she said, just before she vanished into a swirling wisp of red smoke.

Chapter 7

Laralynn woke to sunlight streaming through her open window. She had deliberately left it open hoping the morning light would wake her. Pushing back her coverlet, she quietly slipped from her bed and tiptoed across the stone floor. Trying not to make a sound, she carefully opened the heavy armoire door. Nothing but fine satin, delicate lace, and rich brocade hung before her. Taking a deep breath, she moved the delicate fabric from side to side searching for something that would be appropriate to wear outside. Almost giving up, she noticed something on the bottom shelf next to her numerous pairs of slippers. Running her fingers over it, she immediately recognized the woolen fabric. It was the skirt she had worn most days working around the cottage. Folded beneath it were her under-slip, stockings, and woolen vest with the flowers she had embroidered herself. Snatching them from the armoire, she hurried back to her bed.

Removing her sleeping gown and tossing it on the foot of her bed, she quickly began to dress. Looking down at her stocking feet, she tried to remember where she had seen Caprice put the soft leather boots she had worn when she arrived at Evergreen. There was no place to store them since no other cupboards or trunks were in her room. Heading for her bathing chamber to look in the tall cabinet, she suddenly remembered seeing Caprice placing something under her bed. Hurrying back to the bed, she squatted down and lifted the ornate fabric that skirted her bed to find her boots along with her leather satchel. Grabbing her boots, she made her way to her door. Pulling the heavy door open just enough to peer out into the hallway, she saw that no one lingered about, and she timidly stepped into the hallway and quietly closed the door. With a boot in each hand, she ran through the hallway.

Feeling happy about escaping the torture of being pampered and dressed by Caprice, she carelessly ran around a corner and halted immediately. Coming toward her was her uncle. With no place to go, she hid her boots behind her back and walked toward him with a smile.

"Good morning, uncle," she said.

"Good morning, niece," he replied, as he gazed down at her stocking feet. "Where are you off to this morning?"

"I am going to the kitchen to ask Charlotte for some carrots and then to the stable," she truthfully declared.

"Your boots might serve you better if they were upon your feet," he laughed.

"I did not want to wake anyone with my noisy boots," she said, as she drew her teeth over her bottom lip hoping he would believe her.

"You mean you didn't want to get caught. Sneaking about the castle might find you in a bit of trouble with your mother," Tate sternly replied, as he saw her lower lip begin to quiver and quickly regretted his harsh words. "Your mother is a kind woman, Laralynn. She also loves the horses in the stable. I am sure she would love to join you."

"I was afraid that I would have to dress in satin again today. I have done nothing but visit those about the castle since I have arrived here. Everyone is very nice, but I have not had a moment to explore. Life at the castle is much different from the cottage where I grew up," Laralynn said, as she lowered her eyes to the floor. "I miss my friends, the shade of the forest, and I am lonely without my friends around me."

"I will speak to your father about teaching you to ride if you promise to speak to your mother about what you have told me," he said. "She won't know how you feel unless you tell her."

Laralynn nodded her head and started to turn around to head back to her bedchamber.

"Since you are already dressed for the stable, would you like to take a short ride with me?" he asked. "I am sure Twiggs would enjoy a carrot from the kitchen."

"Yes, yes," she grinned.

"Go ask your mother. I will wait here for you," he ordered. Seeing her frown, he pointed down the hallway toward her chamber. "I don't want your mother to find you missing. She would send me to the dungeon if she knew me to be the cause of her worry."

He was relieved to see her smile as she turned and headed off to seek permission to ride with him. Leaning against the stone wall, he began to laugh as he thought about his brother giving Laralynn fatherly advice. Thomas was going to have his hands full learning to deal with his daughter.

* * *

As Tate pulled back the heavy stable door, Laralynn was greeted with the strong scent of fresh straw. She could see several horses leaning their heads over their stall gates and anxiously stepped forward to find one for herself. Leading her to the first stall on the right, Tate was greeted by a solid black stallion. Rubbing his fingers between his ears, he beckoned Laralynn forward.

"This is your father's stallion, Midnight," he said. "Do not worry. He won't bite."

She timidly raised her hand and stroked his black mane.

"He looked so fierce when my father road him. Is he gentle?" she asked.

"He is a handful for most, but your father has good control over him," he replied.

Midnight lowered his head toward Laralynn's pocket and tried to nibble on her woolen skirt. Stepping back and covering her pocket with her hand, she pointed her finger at Midnight.

"You found the carrots, smart boy," she laughed, as she reached into her pocket and retrieved a small piece of carrot. Holding it in her palm, she watched as Midnight eagerly took the morsel from her hand.

"I believe that you have made a friend," Tate smiled. "I hope you have enough carrots in your pocket for the others."

Laralynn greeted each of the horses with a carrot or a handful of green beans. She found that Arrow liked to nibble the end of her braid if he wasn't rewarded with more than one carrot. She was familiar with Twiggs since she had ridden behind her uncle to the castle, but he still stomped about his stall when she refused to offer him more than one treat.

"These horses are greedy," she snapped, as she pushed Mona's nose away from her pocket.

"Your mother frequently brought them treats," he said. "She devoted as much time as she could to her horses."

"I hope to do the same," she replied. "They are such beautiful animals."

Laralynn had hoped to find a horse for herself. It was disappointing to find they all belonged to someone else, and she would have to ask their permission to ride them. Seeing one empty stall next to Tolin's room, she looked up at her uncle.

"Where is the horse that belongs in this stall?" she asked.

"It has remained empty for some time. My Gavenia has used this stall to transition into her hawk on occasion. Now that we have taken a bedchamber with a balcony, she has no need of the stall. It sits empty awaiting a new horse," he replied. "I will tell you a secret if you promise not to tell anyone that I told you."

"Oh please, I promise," she replied, as she clasped her hands together under her chin. "Tell me, please."

"This empty stall is for your new horse," he said.

"Mine?" she asked. "A horse just for me?"

"Yes, it should be here soon," he said. As he watched her jump up and down on her toes with excitement, he heard the stable door open.

Laralynn turned to see Baxter enter the stable and greeted him with a wave.

"Remember our secret," Tate whispered. Seeing her give him a smile, he turned to retrieve Twiggs from his stall.

"Baxter, we are going for a ride. Would you like to join us?" she asked, hoping he would say yes.

Hearing her invitation, he looked over at Tate and grumbled under his breath before he gave Laralynn his answer, "I would My Lady. Which horse have you chosen?"

"I will be riding with my uncle on Twiggs," she replied.

Disappointed in her reply, Baxter lifted the latch to the stall of his horse and readied him for the ride. Leading him from the stall, Laralynn greeted Copper with a gentle stroke of his mane. As she did, he lowered his head searching for her pocket.

"I see that you have spoiled my horse for me," Baxter smiled, as he saw Laralynn's eyes brighten with his comment.

"I have, and I intend on doing it often," she replied.

"Come Laralynn," Tate shouted, from the far end of the stable. "It will be a short ride this morning. Since you haven't had your morning meal, your mother will be angry with me if I keep you out too long."

Laralynn headed toward her uncle with Baxter close behind her. As she looked over her shoulder, she saw a scowl upon Baxter's face. Turning toward him and walking backward, she stuck out her tongue at him. Seeing him smile, she turned and ran toward her uncle.

"It will be fun, Baxter," she shouted. "If it isn't, I will polish your boots."

Baxter laughed and mounted Copper.

"I like my boots polished until they shine, My Lady," he replied. "I hope you are up to the task."

Chapter 8

Magna closed her eyes as she ran her fingers over the red stones of the wall that surrounded Crimson Claw Castle. Its rough texture reminded her of the stones within Black Thistle's dungeon, and it pained her to think of them. She loved the feel of those cold stone walls. Quickly setting those troubling emotions aside, Magna continued along the wall until she stood facing the entrance to what she hoped would be her new home. The ornate arched gate that greeted her stood tall and wide. The heavy ironwork held two fierce dragons facing each other with wings spread and talons ready to attack. Iron flames flared from their mouth's creating an elaborate swirl of decorative and intimidating spikes.

Hoping to draw someone's attention, she pressed her fingertip to one of the spikes letting it pierce her skin. Watching the blood run down her finger brought a sudden wave of hunger and a frantic need to quench her thirst. Grasping the talons of the dragon, she tried to steady herself. If no one came to her aid soon, she would be forced to return to the forest to find some unsuspecting animal.

"Who stands before the gate of Crimson Claw Castle?" the guard shouted.

As he made his way to the gate, Magna could see he had

drawn his blade. It would have given him little protection if she had remembered to feed, but he had found her lacking the power to attack or defend herself.

"My name is Magna. I am an old friend of Lord Jario's," she offered, hoping he would open the gate to her.

"This castle no longer belongs to the wayward vampire, Lord Jario. Lord Seth rules this castle," he shouted his response.

"Then, I will see Lord Seth. I was told by the witch, Velsa, that I might find shelter here," explained Magna. Holding tightly to the iron gate, she tried to control the red vail that appeared before her eyes. "I am in great need of assistance."

"Fitz, I will deal with the hungry vampire. See that a cell is readied for her imprisonment," Desirae ordered, as she walked toward the gate.

"Yes, Mistress," he replied, as he sheathed his blade and hurried off.

She kept her eyes on Magna as she listened to the guard run to obey her order.

"Mistress? Are you Lord Seth's whore," Magna asked, as she clutched her throat and tried to focus on the woman before her.

"Why? Is that why you have come to the castle? Are you seeking that position?" Desirae sarcastically asked.

"I am here for shelter. I can no longer live among the walls of Black Thistle Castle. The warlock and his wolf have made it unbearable to do so," barked Magna.

"Whether you stay or you are turned away will be up to Lord Seth. I will take you to the dungeon and make sure that Claudia sees to your needs. If you are in agreement, place your hands behind your back and turn around," ordered Desirae, as she moved closer to the gate.

Feeling dizzy, Magna did as she was asked. She felt her hands grow cold just before she felt her back against cool stone and cuffs around her wrists. All attempts to stand were denied by a new feeling of paralysis. Even though she could not seem to focus her eyes, she heard the cell door open and light footsteps coming toward her. The scent of blood flooded her senses as a goblet was raised to her lips. A warm hand held the back of her head as the goblet was tipped up allowing her to consume the luscious liquid. Licking her lips to gain all that the goblet had offered, Magna leaned her head back against the cool stone wall and closed her eyes. Her hunger had been sated, for now.

* * *

Desirae found Lord Seth bent over several old unfurled parchments in a large chamber he had named the Hunter's Glory. It was filled with heads of beasts he and his new army had hunted, killed, and mounted upon the walls. Several old banners of red dragons striding against black backgrounds hung from the high ceiling. Their wings seemed to move in the flickering light of the torches that stood burning along the walls.

A shield bearing a crowned dragon with crossed swords hung over the hearth that was six men wide and that again high. It was a masculine room and was fitting for the new lord.

"I beg your pardon, My Lord. May I interrupt?" asked Desirae.

"You may," he sighed. "I find my eyes weary of studying these faded maps."

"Do you wish my help?" she asked, with concern in her voice.

"No, I need only rest," he replied. "A remedy that is completely within this old vampire's control."

Smiling at his unusual gentle response, Desirae silently sent a soothing spell that would help him fall asleep the moment his head touched his pillow.

"I distracted you. What brings you to the Chamber of Heads?" he smirked. "Yes, I know of your distaste for the trophies that are mounted around me. I have heard others repeat your new name for my favorite chamber."

Trying her best to ignore his words and hide a smile, she straightened her back and prepared to advise him of the new visitor in his dungeon.

"Lord Seth, we had a visitor today," she said. "A vicious vampire that I have imprisoned in the dungeon. She is safely restrained by my paralysis spell."

"Is this the vampire you discovered that had returned from a final death?" he asked.

"The same," she replied. "I do not trust her. The wind has shown me many disturbing images of her wickedness." Hesitating for a moment, she sighed before she continued. "She also knew Jario . . . intimately."

Hearing her last statement caused him to laugh uncontrollably, and she brought her hand up to conceal her own broad smile.

"Well, let's visit the little vampire that Jario fancied," he laughed, as he threw the stone he was holding onto the table before him.

* * *

His boots echoed through the dungeon as he descended the stone steps. Standing before her cell expecting to see a snarling vampire, he was surprised to see a beautiful woman with tears streaming down her face.

"My Lord, please release me," Magna begged. "I have been unfairly treated by your mistress. I come only requesting shelter."

"I doubt that this is the only reason, but I will grant you shelter," he responded.

Magna lifted her arms to present her cuffed wrists to Seth. He only shook his head and turned to speak to Desirae.

"Can you control the vampire if I grant her release from the cell?" he asked, as he continued to look at Magna.

"I do not believe that is wise," she replied. "She is dangerous."

In an instant, he pressed Desirae against the wall with his face inches from hers.

"I did not ask for your opinion," he shouted, raising his hand ready to strike her.

"I am sorry, My Lord," she quickly apologized. "Yes, I can block her gifted powers. It will only be temporary, but I can do it."

"Very well, release her from her restraints and block her powers," he angrily responded. "I will have Claudia prepare a bedchamber for her. In the future, I expect you to answer a question that is asked of you."

"Yes, My Lord," Desirae replied, as she lowered her eyes to the floor and hearing a faint snicker coming from Magna.

Seth took one last look at Magna huddled on the floor of the cell and stormed from the dungeon.

Looking over at Magna, Desirae saw the nasty smirk upon her face. Raising her hands and gathering a bright ball of light, Desirae whispered a few words and threw the ball of light directly at Magna. The impact caused Magna's body to shake uncontrollably. Desirae stood watching Magna until she finally gave into the darkness. Gripping the heavy lock in her hand, she applied a bit of pressure and felt it release.

"This is the last kindness I will show you, Magna," she whispered.

Opening the cell door and waving her hand in a circle, she watched the cuffs fall from Magna's wrists. Taking hold of her arm, Desirae closed her eyes as she searched for Claudia. Finding her placing a decanter of sweet wine on a table in a bedchamber, Desirae vanished with her charge. Appearing at the foot of the bed, she let Magna slump to the floor.

"Claudia, she is released to your care," Desirae declared. "I have removed her powers. Beware, it is only temporary. If you desire a spell of protection, I will gladly offer one for you."

Seeing Claudia shake her head in denial, Desirae nodded her understanding and quickly left the bedchamber.

I am afraid that my days at Crimson Claw have come to an end.

* * *

Magna sat alone in her bedchamber sipping sweet wine and gazing up at the moon. It had been a difficult day, but the day had finally come to an enjoyable end. She found her new accommodations more than grand and hoped to offer her gratitude to Lord Seth in person.

A sturdy rap at the door was all the announcement Lord Seth offered before he barged into her bedchamber and slammed the door behind him. Startled, she stared at the huge vampire that stood before her. He had removed his tunic and wore only a leather vest that displayed the large tattoos that covered both his arms and his neck. She could see the red that rimmed his steely eyes. Magna sat her goblet of sweet wine down on the small table that stood beside her chair. Unsure if she should fear him, she stood slowly and stepped away from the chair.

As she tried to put distance between them, he watched her movements like the predator he was. With one swift movement, he took hold of her arms and pressed her body tightly against his own.

"We meet again, my beautiful Magna. It has been far too long," he proclaimed before he forcefully claimed her mouth.

Chapter 9

It was clear that Seth and Magna had a history, and Magna delighted in flaunting her new-found status at Crimson Claw. When Lord Seth was busy instructing his army of vampires, she spent most of her time ordering Claudia to bring her wine, help her bathe, or brush her hair. When not pestering Claudia, she managed to find Desirae and talk endlessly about her tales of being trapped as a bodiless spirit at Black Thistle Castle. Desirae was at her wits end and eager to leave the castle.

Desirae's bedchamber and the library seemed to be the only places she could avoid the annoying vampire. Closing the door to the library, she leaned back against its elaborately carved surface and sighed with relief. She was finally alone and had the quiet she longed for. A few more days was all that was needed to finish her research. She had almost completely finished documenting Velsa's history when news came of Jario's demise. With him gone, Seth had become the new Lord of Crimson Claw Castle and needed help to secure all within its walls, including his army. She had been helpful, and he had been appreciative. Their relationship had been nothing more and nothing less, until Magna arrived.

Determined to keep her mind off of the vampires and focus on her research, she made her way to the large table and sat down on the cushioned stool. Desirae took a book from the five remaining books she had left neatly stacked at the end of yesterday's research. Placing it on the table in front of her, she carefully opened the fragile cover, removed the ribbon that had marked her place, and began to read.

Desirae was looking for any weaknesses she could use against the troublesome witch. If she could cast a strong enough spell against her, she could possibly end her life or remove her magic. Since only the curses or spells that were cast out of anger or hatred could be reversed with her death, many of her spells would stand even though she was gone. Her focus was to document every single spell cast from hatred to bind it in the spell that she would throw at the old hag. Derora, her sister, was long past saving, but there were others that would benefit from her revenge against Velsa and her magic.

Several hours had passed since Desirae entered the library. Her eyes grew weary, but she forced herself to continue reading. Her dedication to her goal had allowed her to return two books back to the wooden shelves. At this rate, she would be ready to leave by tomorrow evening.

Hearing light footsteps coming down the hallway, Desirae immediately replaced the ribbon to mark the page and closed the book. Waving her hand, the book in front of her and the two to her left were rendered invisible. With the snap of a finger, a book of Alltree Island flowers was now open in front of her. Looking down at the lovely drawings, she waited for the troublesome vampire to invade per privacy. Magna opened the door without knocking and barged into the library.

"So, this is where you have been hiding," she barked. "I have been roaming the halls for hours looking for you."

"Is there a problem? Does Lord Seth need me?" asked Desirae.

"No, Lord Seth does not need you," snapped Magna. "What could he possibly need you to do for him?"

"If Lord Seth doesn't need me, you must be in need of my help," Desirae said, as she bit the inside of her cheek and tried to remain calm.

"I was curious where you had been spending your time," she smirked, as she pulled a slender book from the shelf and opened it. Running her finger down the page, she looked over at Desirae and back at the book. "I simply do not understand what people see in books." Closing the book with a snap, dust billowed in the air. "They are dusty and dirty things." Throwing the book onto the table in front of Desirae, she proceeded to walk around the table to look at the pages that had drawn Desirae's attention. "You are looking at a book of flowers. Do they have drawings of thistles? I love thistles."

Desirae flipped through the pages until she found several colorful drawings of thistles. The bright purple flowers looked strange to Magna. She had only seen the black withered thistles that had encircled the wall of Black Thistle Castle. Picking up the book, Magna studied each of the beautiful drawings.

"These purple flowers do not look like the thistles at Black Thistle," she sighed. "How odd they look."

"The thistles at Black Thistle are cursed. They were cursed by Velsa during the War of the Witches," explained Desirae. "Her curse turned them black."

"Well, I like the black thistles much better. They are my dearest friends. I would change them all to black if I could," she barked, as she closed the book and handed it back to Desirae. Magna made her way to the door. Hesitating for a moment, she began to speak to Desirae without turning around. "You are requested to join us for dinner. Don't be late." Before Desirae could respond, Magna had vanished and left an irritating swirl of red smoke behind.

Dinner? Only one more night, Desirae thought. Only one more night.

* * *

Claudia escorted Desirae to the courtyard. There, a table was draped in red linen and tall glowing candles. Three pewter plates and goblets were set ready for the meal to be served. As Desirae approached the table, she noticed Lord Seth and Magna walking arm in arm under the wisteria covered arch on the far side of the courtyard. She was a tiny thing compared to the large vampire that stood at her side, but to be sure, the evil in Magna far outweighed that of the large vampire. Desirae had read little of the written history of Magna; however, the few pages she had read were appalling.

"Desirae, it is nice to have you at our table," Seth announced, as he seated Magna at the table next to his chair. Pulling the chair out for Desirae, he assisted her and then made his way to his own chair. "I thought a meal under the stars would be a welcome change for you. I understand that you have been taking your meals in your chamber."

"With Magna's arrival, I felt I would be intruding," she replied.

"Guests in my castle should never feel that they are intruding," he responded. "You are always welcome to dine with me."

"Thank you, My Lord," Desirae replied. "It is a lovely evening, and I appreciate the thoughtful invitation."

"I told Lord Seth about the books that you have been reading," Magna said. "He has given me permission to have a small garden of black thistles. I would hope that you would be able to provide this for me."

"I can create black thistles for you," Desirae replied. "If you are in need of thistles like those that surround Black Thistle Castle, the curse would need to be applied by Velsa."

"Why can't you do it?" whined Magna.

"I don't know the exact curse she used," explained Desirae. "Each witch has her own chants and curses. It would be a simple request of Velsa."

Magna pounded her fist upon the table and looked at Lord Seth for help.

"Now, Magna," he softly said, as he placed his hand upon her arm. "We will invite the witch to the castle and ask her to provide your precious thistles. Now, let's enjoy the evening and our meal."

Magna glared at Desirae as she nodded her acceptance of his recommendation.

Relieved that the conversation surrounding the thistles had ceased, Desirae knew she needed to leave Crimson Claw before Velsa made her grand appearance. If Magna had her way, Velsa would be appearing tomorrow. Determined to leave before she arrived, Desirae decided to collect the remaining three books from the library and take them to her bedchamber. Once there, she would pack them among her few belongings and leave before the sun brightened the morning sky. She only had one remaining problem. She had nowhere to go but Black Thistle Castle.

Surely, Lord Gautier would offer me sanctuary, she thought.

Chapter 10

Velsa stood staring at her tattered old book of spells. It had been nothing but an empty journal when her mother had given it to her. Along with the journal, she had received rigorous daily instruction from her mother. She had insisted on perfection, and Velsa understood why when she had accidentally turned her own ears into the wings of a seagull. Living with flapping ears for several days had been embarrassing, and she had been left on her own to undo it.

"You must face the consequences of your actions," her mother repeated, over and over at every lesson. "You must be prepared to resolve the wrong you have created. The harm you cause may not only impact others, but it could impact you, as well. Your deeds will be noticed by others. Do your best to shatter the darkness."

Her mother had practiced white magic and taught her the same. Velsa had eagerly watched as each spell she perfected magically imprinted itself within the crisp parchment pages of her journal. The celebration of each of her accomplishments was short lived, as her mother gave her a hug and immediately began instruction for the next spell.

It was not until Gautier's betrayal that everything changed. She let anger and jealousy rule her thoughts. The spells she had loved as a young girl slowly began to fade from her journal and were replaced with dark spells that were often written in heavy black ink or blood. With each dark spell, her magic grew darker and more deadly.

Remembering her mother's words always left a bitter taste in her mouth. Rubbing her tongue against the roof of her mouth, she quickly turned and spit into the flames of the hearth causing purple sparks to race back at her. Smelling smoke, she looked down to see that they had singed the intricate lace cuffs of her new gown. Furious, she tore the cuffs from her sleeves and threw them into the flames.

"I remember mother. I remember every word you said to me. Even now, you manage to punish me," she screamed, as she looked at her tattered sleeves. "It is not my fault. It is Gautier's fault, his and the little white wolf that betrayed me. It is their fault that I have changed."

Furious, she raised her hands over her head and began to mumble as she wildly waved her arms in the air. Her eyes rolled back and her body began to shake. Outside the sky began to fill with dark clouds and a strong wind swirled among the trees. Thunder and lightning filled the sky, and rain began to pound the ground. Pleased with her effort, she sank into her rocking chair and propped her feet up on her new milking stool listening to the raging storm. She was just beginning to relax when the door shook from the force of someone's incessant knocking. Knowing who stood at her door, Velsa waved her arm, and the door flew open to reveal a familiar tall vampire.

"Is this your doing?" asked Balgair, as he squeezed the water from his long silver hair onto the floor.

"I was thinking about my mother," she replied. "I let my thoughts get out of control."

"Are you still out of control?" he asked, as he took a step back away from the witch. "For if you are, I will come back later."

"No, I am quite composed," Velsa replied, as she stood waving her open hand in the air and then closing it into a tight fist making the storm suddenly stop.

"I had to leave the wagon filled with your supplies at a farm outside of Echo Bluff. It will take days for all of it to dry," complained Balgair. "It took hours to get it hauled off the ship and onto the wagon. I'm not sure all of it will survive the rain. What do you plan on doing with all of it?"

"Never you mind," she snapped. "Balgair, never you mind."

He could see a purple glow creeping from her hands up to her elbow. Taking a step back, Balgair considered flashing to a safer place on the island. He watched as the purple glow grew brighter and slowly lifted his hand to point at her arm.

"I am sorry, Balgair. I'm just not myself," she muttered. "The day has not been a good one. You mustn't worry. I will see to the wagon of supplies. Your task is complete."

Hearing his sigh of relief, she made her way to her cluttered table and opened the lid of a small wooden chest. The twist of one crooked finger and she retrieved a vial that contained a silver liquid. As Balgair approached and extended his open hand to her, Velsa placed the vial upon his palm and closed his fingers around it.

"Do not open this until you are ready to use it," she warned. "It is only good for a few moments. Once used, it is gone."

"I understand," he replied. "Again, I thank you."

With a quick bow, Balgair vanished from Velsa's cottage.

Relieved that she was alone, Velsa looked over at her book of spells. With a smirk, she closed her eyes and mentally searched for her wagon of supplies. Finding it hidden in a farmer's barn, she quickly vanished.

* * *

Balgair appeared outside the gate of Crimson Claw Castle. He had already attempted to penetrate the boundary but found it held a protection spell. Since hearing of Magna's return from her final death, he wanted to speak with the vampire. He was interested in finding out how she had managed to escape. If it was a gift, he intended on taking it for himself. Such a gift would be a prized item. Withdrawing the vial from his pouch, Balgair removed the lid and brought the edge of the vial to his lips. Tipping the bottom up, he let the silver liquid wash over his tongue and down his throat. With one long stride, he was inside the protected walls of the castle. Pulling his haze, he headed for the closest entrance into the castle to search for Magna.

As Desirae gathered her things to leave the castle, she suddenly felt the protected barrier around the castle sway and then crack. Someone had been able to penetrate the protection spell. Knowing nothing good could come from this breach, she quickly grabbed the books she had taken from the library and stowed them in her bag. She knew another witch would be the only one that could slip through the spell. Fearing it was Velsa, she searched for the intruder. She could feel something much different and was surprised to find it had been a vampire that had entered the castle walls.

A vampire would need the assistance of a witch, she thought. There is only one witch that would offer a spell to revoke another witch's spell, Velsa!

With that thought, Desirae picked up her heavy bags and immediately vanished from her bedchamber.

* * *

Magna sat alone in her bedchamber sipping blood from a pewter goblet and dipping small pieces of warm bread into honey before letting them melt upon her tongue. Since leaving the dungeon, she had not had the desire to return to its dreary cells. The comforts of her bedchamber had far outweighed the rank smell and darkness of Seth's dungeon. Even though there were new vampires chained to its walls, the need for their blood had been replaced with her uncontrollable desire for Seth. He had afforded her anything her cold heart desired, as well as joining her in her favorite games of torture. She was treated as the Lady of Crimson Claw, and she had come to enjoy it.

Magna had felt the coolness of the shimmering silver mist a moment before she saw it and the man that appeared before her. Jumping from her chair, she cautiously waited for his attack. Preparing to flash, she was stopped by a slight wave of the intruder's hand.

"I am not here to harm you," he proclaimed. "I have come to speak with you. Let me introduce myself. I am Balgair. You have probably heard others refer to me as the Silver Fox or the Power Collector." Seeing a hint of acknowledgement in her eyes, he continued. "I will release you if you will sit quietly and answer my questions. If not, I can force you to speak. It is up to you."

Her body began to tremble and panic filled her mind. She had heard of the Power Collector and knew him to be the vampire that had turned her sister. She knew he could steal a vampire's gifted powers. Jario had told her of the night this vampire had taken his smoke. It was done with great pain, and she wanted no part of it.

"I will sit quietly," replied Magna. "Please . . . do not harm me."

Balgair simply nodded his head and released her from her paralyzed stance. Taking one of the empty chairs by the hearth, he watched her slowly take the other.

"I have heard rumors that you escaped your final death," he began, as he glared into her eyes. "Is this rumor true? Do not lie to me, Magna. I will know if you lie. I have the gift."

"Did you take it from someone?" taunted Magna, before she could stop her sassy outburst.

"I did," he replied with an evil grin. "Now, let's get on with the matter at hand."

"To be honest," she smiled. "I do not know how it happened. I had taken the appearance of my sister trying to protect myself. Gautier's white wolf attacked me. As my head was torn from my shoulders, I felt myself drift or escape the body that fell to the floor of the dungeon. Until recently, I was trapped as an invisible voiceless spirit. I was a prisoner for well over a decade in Black Thistle Castle. I was not seen as I walked the castle hallways. Sadly, I was not heard when I screamed for help. I was a lonely bodiless spirit that wandered the castle, alone."

"What allowed you to leave the castle?" he asked.

"Jario came to the dungeon," she replied. "Somehow, I was able to take his blood. I believe that was what allowed me to leave."

"You are clearly not an invisible image anymore. How did this happen?" Balgair sat completely baffled as he listened to the story he was being offered.

"I can only tell you that I woke within the thistles outside of the castle. My hands and arms were covered in my own blood. When I flashed to the Dragon's Tear River, I washed the blood away with its water. That is when I realized that my form had truly returned, and I was no longer an invisible spirit," she explained, hoping he would ask no more questions.

Balgair stood and walked toward Magna. He could see the fear in her eyes as he lifted her wrist to his mouth. Letting his fangs descend, he sank them deep into her cold flesh and drew her blood into his mouth. As the truth of her story filled his senses, he released her wrist.

"I find all that you say is truthful," he said, as he backed away from her. "I have learned all that I can from you."

Drawing her eyes to his, he compelled her as he spoke, "You will not remember my visit or the words you have spoken to me."

With a deep bow, he vanished leaving a silver mist that slowly disappeared from her bedchamber.

Chapter 11

Since Alicia had discovered she could mentally converse with Killian, her wolf was eager to come forth and run. Hearing Killian's voice had given her wolf hope. She knew that Alicia would try to find a loophole to return her beloved black wolf, and she longed for that day. For now, they would both stay strong. They would protect each other and Lady Kayleigh. If staying strong meant joining her on a run, they were both ready and eager to enjoy the exhilarating feeling of a moonlit run.

As Kayleigh ran through the castle gate toward the forest, she could hear the warnings being shouted by Gautier. As the sound of his words filled her ears, she could sense his love for her.

Without hesitation, she gently sent her loving words back to him, "You are my one and only love. We will stay safe."

Seeing Alicia's wolf ahead of her, she increased her speed and followed her toward the narrow stream. It was the thrill of the chase that drew their wolves to its water, and the animals that stopped to quench their thirst. If they were lucky, their wolves would be gifted with the thrill of a challenging chase.

Gautier stood and watched the wolves until they were gone from sight. Leaving his mind open to Kayleigh in case she needed him, he turned to make his way back to his courtyard to wait for her. A sudden shimmer in the night air caught his attention. He pulled his dagger from its sheath and prepared for danger. As Desirae suddenly appeared, two heavy bags landed noisily beside her feet.

"My dear Desirae, are you leaving us?" asked Gautier, as he pointed his dagger toward her bags while waiting for a response.

"No, I have fled the Crimson Claw Castle," she gasped, as she held her hand to her throat. "Seth has received a visitor that I could no longer tolerate, and I have come hoping that you will grant me your hospitality. If not, I will be forced to look elsewhere."

"You are always welcome here at our home," Gautier reassured her. He placed his dagger back into its sheath and studied Desirae for a moment. "But, I am curious. What visitor could make you leave Crimson Claw?"

Gautier heard a deep sigh before he heard her blurt out a long forgotten name.

"Magna!" snarled Desirae. "She is crazy. Why won't that vampire stay dead?"

"What?" he choked, looking confused. "I saw her head torn from her shoulders, and her blood spread across the floor of my dungeon. It was Elda that took her remains outside for the sunlight to turn her body to ash."

"I know," she muttered, as she shook her head. "I heard the whole story, numerous times. Magna insisted on telling and retelling her dreadful tale."

"How did this happen?" he groaned. "Was it some spell that brought her back?" Before she could respond, Gautier gasped. "Velsa! Did she have a hand in this?"

"Magna could not explain it. She said her spirit jumped from her body when the wolf tore her head from her shoulders. Magna saw her sister's body drop to the floor and Elda take it from the castle," she explained. "She was invisible to all and trapped in Black Thistle for over a decade. Sadly, it wasn't long enough."

"Something or someone must have allowed her to leave. Who was it?" he demanded, as he began to pace back and forth in front of Desirae. "Who could have done this? I will make certain they shall feel my wrath."

"It appears to have been Jario," she replied. "Unknowingly, he must have made a visit to the dungeon before he attempted to kill Lady Kayleigh. She was able to take his blood, and she believes that single act allowed her to leave her confinement."

"Well, at least, we have Jario secured," Gautier barked. "He will not be bothering us, but Magna will be trouble. She is deadly. She cares not for humans or anyone else but herself. I fear the new Lord of Crimson Claw Castle will soon tire of her. When he does, she will be drawn to this castle. She has a fascination with those deadly thistles that surround the castle walls. I have done my best to try and remove them, but they still stand."

For a moment, Gautier stood quiet as if listening to someone speaking. He began to smile and silently nodded his head.

"Excuse me," he politely offered. "Kayleigh was informing me that she and Alicia are on their way back to the castle. There are hunter's roaming the forest. Let's go to my courtyard and wait. Kayleigh will join us when she has returned. We can continue our discussion there. I will see that your bags are taken to your old bedchamber."

* * *

Gautier stood to greet Kayleigh with a kiss as she entered the courtyard. Seeing Desirae, she stepped forward and reached for her hand.

"This is a surprise," Kayleigh said. "What brings you to our home?"

"My dear, let's sit. Desirae has been telling me about Magna's return," he smirked and waited for her shocked reaction.

"Her what?" Kayleigh asked, as she slowly took her seat. "How? I tore her head from her shoulders. If that didn't kill her, my bite should have ended her pathetic life."

Desirae looked at Gautier hoping that she would not have to repeat the tale. Seeing him shake his head, she was relieved to hear him speak.

"Magna believes that her spirit leapt from her body after your attack," he tried to explain, as he held her hand to calm her. "She roamed our castle for over a decade in an invisible state. Apparently, Jario entered the dungeon before he succumbed to my binding spell in the library. She was able to draw his blood and believes that allowed her to leave the castle."

"Is she still invisible?" Kayleigh nervously asked. "Can she come back to our home?"

"Desirae has seen her. Her body and her powers have returned," he replied. "I am sure if we ask Desirae she will offer a protection spell against the unruly vampire."

Kayleigh looked from Gautier to Desirae to see her nodding her head. Closing her eyes, Kayleigh took a deep breath and let it out slowly trying to calm the rage that was stirring inside her.

"Magna believes the thistles provided the magic she needed to reclaim her body," he continued. "She played among them as a child."

"Let's destroy them," cried Kayleigh. "If they help her, we need to destroy them."

"They hold magic from Velsa. I am unable to destroy them. I have tried to no avail," Gautier replied, trying to explain their continued existence. "After all this time, they have not harmed us. In some ways, they have protected us. Kayleigh, anyone that tried to attack us would have to come through those deadly weeds. They would find themselves attacked, keeping us safe."

"I find this all very disturbing," Kayleigh muttered, shaking her head. "Does Lady Lara know of her sister's return?"

"I will send word to Lord Thomas. Magna has been a proven threat to them both," he stated. "The more eyes we have to watch for the troublesome vampire the better."

Kayleigh nodded her agreement with Gautier's statement and

grasped both his and Desirae's hands. Angry at herself for feeling weak and afraid, she felt her wolf offering her the comforting strength she needed at that moment. She was willing to come forth to attack the vampire and feel her neck within her jaws once again. Kayleigh felt deep in her heart that Velsa had somehow helped Magna. If not directly, she had provided her help through the spell on the thistles. She feared Magna would be indebted to her. Velsa always demanded payments for her bargains, and she worried they would help each other in the future. If Velsa was plotting to take Gautier from her, she would kill the witch. After what she had done to Gautier and herself, she owed her a painful death from the fangs of her wolf. Seeing the worried look upon Gautier's face, she was determined not to give Velsa another thought, she lifted her chin and smiled.

"Let's not speak of Magna anymore this evening. It is a beautiful evening. The moon is almost full, the sky is full of stars, and we are joined by our dear friend, Desirae," Kayleigh declared. "Let's enjoy the rest of the evening."

Velsa, watch your step, she thought. Gautier is not yours for the taking. He belongs to me, and I will kill you and your little friend to prove it.

Chapter 12

The day was covered in heavy dark clouds, and the sun had not shown a single ray of sunlight. A small excited crowd of young and old lined the road leading to the main entrance of Evergreen Castle. News had quickly spread of the coming visit from Lord Cumberland and his son Hamish. He had been rumored to be quite handsome and a good match for Lady Laralynn. However, this did not deter the young ladies that stood next to their fathers just wanting to get a glimpse of the young lord.

Banners of emerald green bearing shields of gold hung on either side of the castle's open gate. Seeing them flap in the gentle breeze, Laralynn thought about the story her mother had told her about her great grandfather's journey to Alltree. The banners bore his colors, and the standing lion holding a dagger had been chosen by him to signify the strength of a defender. She was proud of her great grandfather and felt the weight of her new found responsibility to defend the meek as her ancestors had done.

The sound of cheering filled the air, and Laralynn looked up to see three riders followed by guards proudly displaying Cumberland's crest as they entered through the open gate. The castle guards, dressed in their finest, quickly came to attention, and she flinched at the sound of their polished boots snapping together. As her parents made their way down the steps, the three men dismounted their horses. Tolin gathered their reins and led all but one horse away. The young lord held tightly to the reins of the silver-grey mare and stepped forward to hand them to the commander before taking his place beside his father.

"Lord Cumberland," Thomas said, as he greeted him with an outstretched hand. "We are honored with your visit to Evergreen Castle."

"Lord Evergreen, I must apologize," he replied. "Our visit is long overdue."

"Apologies are not needed among friends," Lara softly added, as she offered him her hand. "We were pleased to hear of your desire to visit us. What of the Lady Cumberland?"

"Agnes is heavy with child, and I feared the journey would have been most uncomfortable," he replied. "She was pleased to hear of your return to Evergreen, and of your daughter."

"I understand," she replied. "It was sometimes difficult to stand when my time was near." She felt Thomas take her hand in his and felt his distress. She gently squeezed his hand to comfort him. "Flora has the gift of healing. If you find need of her gift, please send word."

"As always Lady Evergreen, your kindness is appreciated," he declared. Gently taking her hand in his, Lord Cumberland bent to place a kiss upon the back of her hand. Stepping back, he caught sight of the warm smile she offered his son.

"And who is this young man that stands by your side?" asked Lara.

"This is my eldest son, Hamish," he replied.

Hamish stepped forward and made a slight bow before he nervously spoke, "I am honored to meet you, Lord and Lady Evergreen. I would like to present you with a gift for the Lady Laralynn."

Hamish reached for the reins the commander offered him and brought the mare forward. As he attempted to hand the reins to Lady Lara, she placed her hand over his to still his attempt.

"Hamish, might you prefer to present this gift to our daughter instead of me?" asked Lara. Seeing him nod, she turned to her daughter. "Laralynn, please come meet Lord Cumberland and Hamish. He has brought a gift for you."

Laralynn felt her uncle take her elbow before assisting her down the steps to stand beside her mother. Gracefully, she bowed her head and made a deep curtsy before her guests.

"Lord Cumberland, it is an honor to meet you," she softly said. Seeing him nod, she smiled and looked at Hamish. "It is an honor to meet you, Lord Hamish." Seeing his face flush, she stood quietly waiting for him to speak.

"Lady Laralynn, it is my honor to present you with this gift from Cumberland Castle," Hamish said, as he handed her the soft leather reins.

Laralynn reached up and rubbed the bridge of the mare's nose. Seeing the mare make several nods with her head and try to nuzzle her hand made Laralynn laugh. Hamish stepped back with a look of great relief on his face.

"It is a wonderful gift, Lord Hamish. The color of her coat reminds me of the stars in the night's sky. I shall name her Starlight," she announced, to everyone's delight.

Hearing nothing but the nervous heartbeats of his daughter and Hamish, Thomas grasped Lord Cumberland's arm.

"Enough of all this formality," Thomas barked. "Let's go inside. I am sure you are hungry and thirsty after your long journey. We can relax and call each other by our given names as we partake of some food and drink. What do you say, Hammond?"

He grinned and eagerly slapped Thomas on the shoulder.

"Thomas, I find your invitation very appealing," he replied. "My throat is parched and in need of a good strong drink. Show me the way, my friend."

"Tolin, please take Starlight to her new quarters," he stated. "Give her fresh water. She has come a great distance and needs a bit of pampering." He looked at his daughter and saw her sweet smile of approval. "Now, let's go in. I hear that Charlotte has made her bread pudding. You have not lived until you have tasted it."

After Tolin retrieved the mare, Thomas escorted Lord Cumberland toward the castle. Tate took Lady Lara's arm, and they noticed the polite offering of Hamish's arm to Laralynn. She shyly accepted, and they quietly followed behind her uncle's lead.

Evergreen's Grand Hall was filled with the dancing light from candles. As they took their seats at the long table, beams of bright colored light began to filter through the stained glass windows. It was as if the clouds had known of Lady Lara's plan to greet Lord Cumberland and covered the sun to protect her.

Large platters of food and pitchers of ale were carried and placed upon the table, each more tantalizing than the next. The talk was energetic, and the laughter was infectious. All seemed to be enjoying the food and conversation but one. Baxter sat at the far end of the table to the left of Lady Lara. Unfortunately, Laralynn sat at the other end of the table. She sat between her father and Hamish. Since they were both on the same side of the table, it made it difficult for Baxter to see her. He could hear her laughter, and as unsettling as it was, he tried to ignore it.

"Baxter, are you troubled?" asked Lady Lara. "You have barely eaten anything."

Quick to hide his worry, he responded, "No My Lady, I have decided to wait for Charlotte's bread pudding. It has a special meaning for me."

"It does for me as well," she replied. "I woke from a near fatal wound to the aroma of the decadent delight. I believe that it cures all that ails us."

"I hope it does, My Lady. I hope it does," Baxter muttered.

Lara leaned toward Baxter and whispered for only him to hear, "Be patient, she is young. Her heart is warming. Give it a chance to blaze. You will both be happier for it."

"I seem to have little control over the fire that burns within me," he confessed. "It rages when another is near her. I fear a match will be made before I am able to profess my love for her."

"It is true that Hammond has requested a match between Laralynn and his son, Hamish, but a match will not be made without Laralynn's consent," she declared. "If I know my daughter, as well as I think I do, the spark between you has already been ignited. You must coax the flame before it goes out; however, be very careful. Her father would see to your end if she is harmed, and my wrath would be worse than his."

Baxter was suddenly speechless. He nodded his head in understanding and prayed that the bread pudding would soon be presented to allow a distraction from any further conversation regarding his affection for Laralynn.

For a moment, Lara's thoughts drifted back to the time she was introduced to Hamish's ancestor, Lord Charles Cumberland. They had both been very young, not unlike Laralynn and Hamish. It had been an arranged marriage that ended almost before it began. Even though he was kind, it had been difficult for both of them. Even though he tried to be a loving husband, her heart felt nothing for the young lord. When he died, she blamed herself for letting him die without love in his heart. As a result, she would make sure that her daughter's marriage would not be arranged by anyone.

* * *

The next morning, Baxter and Elda stood watching the Cumberland guards prepare their horses for the return to Cumberland Castle. Baxter clenched his teeth as he watched Hamish kiss the back of Laralynn's hand and say good-bye. Again, she offered her thanks for their gift of the mare and their visit. Standing with her parents and Tate, she watched Lord Cumberland and Hamish escorted by their guards leave through Evergreen's gate. Once they were out of sight, she followed her parents and her uncle back into the castle.

"What did you think of Hamish?" her father asked.

"He is very handsome and very shy. He doesn't talk very much," she offered. "I found myself trying to think of things to say to get him to talk."

"That might have been because his father did most of the talking," he laughed.

"I know, but father, he didn't like to dance. He didn't like Charlotte's bread pudding, either," she added. "I think he was a little boring. He was nice but boring."

Following close behind, Baxter could hear everything Laralynn had to say about Hamish. Feeling his shoulders relax, he tried his best to hide a smile.

* * *

It was well past midnight, and all of their official duties were complete. As Thomas closed their bedchamber door, he took a moment to watch Lara walk toward their bed and remove her slippers. He leaned back against the door completely mesmerized by the way she pulled her long braid over her shoulder revealing her delicate neck. Keeping his eyes on her, he removed one boot and then the other. As her fingers began to untie the ribbon that was intricately woven into her braid, Thomas was no longer able to keep from touching her.

Placing his hands upon her bare shoulders, he whispered in her ear, "Let me help you."

Pulling her braid back over her shoulder, he began to gently unravel the silky ribbon from her strawberry blonde strands. With her hair finally free, he gathered it up into the palms of his hands and inhaled its sweet fragrance before moving it back over her shoulder. He ran his index finger from her neck down over the laces of her gown and tried to untie the bow at her back. He shook his head at his fumbling fingers.

"It has been much too long since I have loosened your gown's laces," he sighed with a bit of frustration. "It is taking all my will power to keep from ripping this lovely gown from your body."

Lara turned and cupped his face within the palms of her hands. She saw flecks of red that had started to conceal the silver-grey of his eyes.

"When was the last time you fed?" she asked. "Your eyes tell me that it has been much too long."

"I have been reluctant to drink blood in front of our daughter. I fear she will think badly of me," he replied.

"Oh Thomas, our daughter knows what we are. I have explained everything to her, and she understands our need for blood. She loves you. You must not put others or yourself at risk by letting the madness take hold of you," she cautioned. "I could not bear to lose you."

"You will never lose me," he blurted, as he brushed her hands aside and bent down pulling his dagger from his boot.

"Turn around," he ordered. "I will sever your laces and remove this abundance of satin that keeps me from touching your body."

Lara felt his heavy hand upon her shoulder and the back of his dagger at her waist as he slipped the blade beneath the laces of her gown. The sound of each taut lace as it snapped made her gasp. He was on the edge of losing control, and she could sense his madness. With the last lace released, Thomas quickly pulled her gown down over her body. Before she could step from the puddle of satin, he picked her up in his arms and dropped her among the soft linens of their bed.

"I do not need lectures from my mate. You are all I need to quench my thirst and the heat of my desire," he snarled, as he pulled his tunic over his head and dropped it on the floor. "I feel them both raging inside of me, and I can feel them begging to consume you." Untying the leather laces of his breeches, he pushed them down over his thighs and kicked them aside. As his eyes devoured her body, he placed both hands against the edge of their bed and stared into her eyes. "I can make you a promise, my sweet Lara. My need for blood will be completely satisfied, and we will both be sated by morning's light."

Taking hold of her outstretched hand, he heard her whisper his name before darkness took him.

Chapter 13

The breeches and tunic given to her by Elda felt foreign to her, and those that stared at her must have thought the same thing. Everyone had stopped what they were doing the moment she entered the Command Center. Some immediately knelt, others lifted their hands over their hearts, and some stood with an open jaw before they realized their error.

"My Lady, are you ready for your first lesson with the bow?" asked Baxter.

Turning away from the curious stares, Laralynn tried to focus on Baxter's question. She could feel the flush on her cheeks and thought she had made a foolish mistake. Feeling embarrassed, she lowered her eyes to avoid looking at him or anyone else.

Noticing the men consumed with watching Lady Laralynn instead of attending to their practice, he decided that removing the distraction from the Command Center was the best option, for her and for himself.

"Let's go outside. I think you will be more comfortable if we study the bow without so many prying eyes," he said. "Besides, a few stray arrows would be better suited for the trees than the men in the Command Center."

Laralynn nervously laughed as she watched Baxter pick up the bow, quiver full of arrows, and two odd shaped pieces of leather. Eager to be away from those that continued to stare, she followed Baxter out the door to a small clump of trees next to the stable.

Leaning the bow and quiver against the tree, he held up the two leather pieces for Laralynn to examine.

"These are for your protection," he explained. "This small strip of leather is an arm guard. It goes over your arm above your wrist to protect your arm from the slap of the string." He was pleased to see that she was watching and listening. "This is your vest. You will wear both every time you pick up the bow to practice or to hunt."

Baxter laid the vest on the ground and held the arm guard out toward Laralynn.

"With which hand do you hold a spoon or write with a quill?" he asked. Seeing her lift her right hand, he nodded toward her left hand. "The guard will go on your left."

Laralynn slipped her hand through the narrow opening and watched Baxter slide it up over her arm. She detected a sudden warmth as his fingers brushed against her hand. Noticing his reaction, he must have felt it too. As he pulled on the laces, she could feel the pressure on her wrist. With one last tug of the laces, she gasped.

Concerned that he had made the guard too tight, he quickly asked, "My Lady, have I harmed you."

"No! No! It is very comfortable," she reassured him. "The pressure of the laces surprised me."

Picking up the vest, he stepped toward her and let her touch the firm leather.

"The vest goes over your head," he explained, as he lifted the vest and carefully brought it down to rest upon her shoulders. "My Lady, you must lift your arms. I need to tighten the laces."

She followed his command and stood perfectly still holding her breath as she felt his fingers lightly brush against her body as he tightened the laces under her arm. Warmth spread quickly through her chest, and she tensed as he moved to her other side. Again, he tightened the laces, and she held her breath waiting for him to finish.

"Breathe," he laughed. "This isn't a torture devise. I have seen your mother wear a leather vest many times."

Laralynn pursed her lips trying not to laugh. She couldn't picture her mother wearing a leather vest or carrying a bow. Especially since she had worn nothing but satin and brocade since returning to Evergreen.

"How does it feel? Is it too tight?" he asked, while picking up the bow.

"It isn't too tight. It just feels . . . strange . . . it's stiff," she replied, as she twisted her body from side to side.

"You'll get used to it," he laughed. "We all felt the same way the first time we wore the vest."

He held out the bow, forcing her to take it with her left hand. She awkwardly held onto the bow and waited for his instruction.

"Now, turn your body to allow your left shoulder to face the trees and spread your feet apart. A little further, My Lady," he tapped her boot with his own.

He grinned when she pushed the toe of her boot back against his own. Ignoring her playful attempt to draw his attention, he pulled an arrow from the quiver and turned to face Laralynn.

"Point the bow at the ground," he said, as he handed her the arrow. "Place the shaft of your arrow here." He pointed to the ridge close to where she gripped her bow. "Hold the arrow with three fingers, one above and two below." He helped her place her fingers properly around the arrow. "See the notch," he nodded toward the feathers. "Insert the string into the notch."

Laralynn listened carefully and tried to follow his instructions. As she lifted the bow, she pointed it at Baxter.

"Like this?" she asked.

"My Lady, lower your bow," he sternly ordered. "Keep your bow pointed at the ground unless you are ready to release the arrow at a target. I have had one arrow through my chest, and I do not desire another one."

His gruff voice startled her, and she quickly lowered her bow after hearing his command. She raked her teeth across her lower lip trying to quiet her nerves and stop her hands from shaking. Taking a deep breath, she looked at Baxter.

"I am sorry, Baxter. Like this?" she softly asked again.

"Yes, very good," he replied. "Are you ready to try and hit a target?"

"I'll try," she nervously said. "A target as large as the stable will do nicely."

"Don't be discouraged if it doesn't go well your first day. It is much harder than it looks, and I am the only one that will see," he grinned.

Stepping back away from Laralynn, he pointed at the tree and waited for her to lift her bow. He could hear her nervous sighs and pursed his lips to keep from laughing.

"Raise your bow, aim the arrow at the base of the tree, and draw back the string," he said, as he waited for her to respond. "My Lady, whenever you are ready."

Laralynn dropped her arm and looked at Baxter, "Can you show me, please?"

Baxter took the bow and arrow from her outstretched hands.

"Come stand beside me," he coaxed. "It will allow you to see where I place my hand and fingers."

Laralynn moved to stand beside Baxter and watched as he skillfully raised the bow. She leaned in to see his fingers and the way he drew back the string with the arrow sliding through his fingers.

"Now, you try it," he said, as he lowered the bow and handed it back to Laralynn.

She took her stance and tried to mimic the way he had placed his feet. Seeing his nod of approval, she notched the arrow in the bow. Raising the bow, she aimed at the base of the tree. Pulling back the string and arrow, she heard Baxter say release. She closed her eyes and released the arrow.

"My Lady, open your eyes," he laughed. "You missed the tree, but your arrow went quite far for a first attempt. Try again."

Laralynn pulled another arrow from the quiver and took her stance. This time she felt more comfortable. Raising her bow, she exhaled and quieted her shoulders. Pulling back the arrow, she took aim at the base of the tree and silently wished for it to hit its mark as the arrow flew through the air. Seeing it go well beyond the tree, she pounded her thigh with her fist in frustration. Not waiting for Baxter to speak, she quickly drew another arrow from the quiver, but it offered her the same result.

"I will never be able to do this," she grumbled.

"My Lady, it is your first day of practice. It will come in time," he tried to reassure her. "Now, go retrieve your arrows. We'll try again."

Still frustrated, she closed her eyes and stomped her foot. Opening her eyes, she looked for her arrows. She could see the feathers peeking out from the tall grass. Bending down, she picked them up and held them over her head to show Baxter she had found all of them, but he was running toward her.

"How did you do that?" he gasped. "How did you flash?"

* * *

With the quiver of arrows against his back and the bow over his shoulder, he clutched Laralynn's hand as they ran towards the Command Center.

"Where was your mother this morning?" Baxter asked, as they ran.

"I saw her at breakfast in her bedchamber," she replied. "Why? Have I done something wrong?"

"No, you did nothing wrong," he replied, as he held the door open for her to enter the Command Center.

Baxter noticed Tate speaking with Preston. They were both reading a parchment and seemed to be worried over something it contained. As he continued to hold Laralynn's hand and lead her toward the hallway, he saw Tate look over his shoulder at them. Baxter silently motioned for him to follow.

"What's happened?" asked Tate, as he looked back and forth between Baxter and Laralynn.

"We need to speak in private," demanded Baxter. "Let's go to the Council Chamber."

"Baxter, why all the secrecy?" he sternly urged a response.

"I will tell you once we are behind closed doors," he whispered.

Confused by Baxter's actions, Tate followed them, but he started to worry when he noticed the anxious look upon Laralynn's face. After entering the chamber and closing the door, Tate stood waiting for Baxter to speak.

"I will just come right out with it," declared Baxter. "Lady Laralynn flashed."

"She what?" blurted Tate.

"She flashed," repeated Baxter. "She was learning to use the bow. She released her arrows. I must say it went a good distance." He looked at Laralynn and smiled.

"Baxter!" growled Tate.

"Sorry, she had her eyes closed. I told her to retrieve her arrows, and the next thing I knew she vanished and reappeared next to her arrows," added Baxter.

"I didn't do it on purpose. I'm so sorry," Laralynn sniffled, trying not to cry. "I didn't even know that I had . . . what you called it . . . flashed."

Tate saw the tears begin to run from Laralynn's eyes, and he quickly embraced her.

"You did nothing wrong. You need not worry. You did nothing wrong," he softly whispered, trying to reassure her.

"Go find Lady Lara," Tate ordered. "I will stay here with Laralynn until you return."

The chamber fell deathly quiet after Baxter left. The only thing she could hear was her own breathing and an occasional sniffle. After she had calmed herself, Tate gently sat her down and took the chair next to her.

"Did you have a visit with Meadow?" he asked. Seeing her

nod, he continued. "Did she tell you that you could flash?" He saw her look down at her lap and shake her head. "Did she tell you that you had any special powers?"

"She told me I have the power of water," she replied. "What does that mean, uncle?"

"I do not know for certain. It could mean many things. Have you spoken to your mother or father about your visit with Meadow?" he asked.

"She was with me when I visited Meadow. She heard everything Meadow told me, but she has been busy seeing after everyone here at the castle. I have not bothered her with questions. I am not sure my father is happy to be around me. He no longer eats with me," she said. "Is something wrong with me?"

"Never doubt that your father loves you," he said, as he grasped her hands in his. "Laralynn, nothing is wrong with you. We are all different in our own way. Gavenia can turn into a hawk. I can bring flames to my hands. Your father can walk in the sunlight, and you have the power of water. You have learned today that you can flash. These are gifts, Laralynn. They are meant to help us or allow us to help others."

Laralynn embraced her uncle. Through the sniffles, she said, "I was so afraid that something was wrong with me. Thank you."

As the door opened, Laralynn looked up to see her mother enter the chamber. She quickly ran to her mother and wrapped her arms around her waist.

"I will leave you two to talk alone," offered Tate.

He stepped through the open doorway and closed the door behind him. He saw Baxter leaning against the wall.

"I have some bad news," Baxter said. "Your brother is in the Holding Room."

"What?" he choked, in surprise.

"I was as surprised as you are. Lady Lara took him there herself. Seems he has not been feeding properly. The madness has started to take hold of him. He is afraid of what his daughter will think of him," he explained.

"Stand ready if Lady Lara should need you. I am going to visit my brother," he stated. "As long as we are sharing bad news, I have some of my own to offer you. Lady Lara's sister has survived her final death. She has taken refuge at the Crimson Claw Castle."

"When did this happen?" asked Baxter.

"We just got word from Gautier. It seems the witch, Desirae, brought word of her survival to Gautier. After leaving Crimson Claw, she has asked for his hospitality. She could not deal with the red-haired vampire," smirked Tate. "She is back and so are her powers. We must do all we can to protect Evergreen and all within it. Maybe this bit of news will bring my brother to his senses."

Baxter took his position outside the door as Tate left to confront his bother.

* * *

Tate opened the door to the Holding Room and found his brother in cuffs and chains sitting on the floor with his elbows on his knees and his head in his hands.

"My Lord and brother, I see you have trespassed beyond your boundary. Was being restrained in chains the first time not enough for you? I seem to recall the bitterness of those chains, and I want no part of them" Tate sternly stated, as he looked for some reaction from his brother. "Have you given no thought to others within this castle? Have you given no consideration to your mate and your daughter?"

Thomas flinched at Tate's words. He knew that he had let the madness take him. It had not been on purpose. It had slowly crept upon him like the darkness takes the daylight, but he had let it happen.

"Have you seen Lara?" he timidly asked, without looking up. "She has not come to see me."

"She is with your daughter," he snapped. "Laralynn is

troubled, and she has gone to comfort her."

Thomas quickly lifted his head and struggled to stand from the weight of his restraints.

"What troubles Laralynn? Tell me," he demanded.

"While learning the bow with Baxter, she discovered the gift of flashing. She thought she had done something wrong," he shouted, as he glared at Thomas. "Neither you or her mother have taken the time to explain what she heard when she visited Meadow. Also, she thinks you don't want to be around her. Is this true? Have you been avoiding her?"

"She is human, Tate," he chocked, trying to get the words out. "I am afraid I will hurt her. I am a vampire. What will she think of me?"

Tate was furious with his brother's pathetic excuses. He reached for the chair that stood before him and threw it across the room. Watching it shatter against the wall and fall to the floor did little to calm his anger.

"Thomas, she is your child. She loves you. Have you not seen the light in her eyes when she looks at you?" he groaned with frustration. "She has accepted you into her heart. Thomas, she has accepted everyone for what they mean to her, not for what they are."

"I love Laralynn," he whispered. "I truly love my daughter."

"Then, tell her," shouted Tate. "She won't know unless you tell her."

Thomas turned his back to Tate. He knew he deserved every harsh word his brother had spoken. It was all true. He had failed Laralynn and Lara. Turning back around, he saw Tate at the door.

"Help me," he begged. "Tate, help me. I need them more than my own life."

"Shall I send Laralynn to see you?" he asked.

"No!" he shouted, as he raised his hands and heard the sound of the chains drag against the floor. "Not like this!"

"Do you think she will be afraid of you?" he asked. "She might surprise you. That child has so much love in her heart, she will not even see the chains. You need to trust her. You need to tell her how you feel."

Thomas ran his hands over his face and through his hair as he paced back and forth.

Tate could see the internal struggle he was going through. He didn't want to make things worse, but he had to tell him about Magna. The news would either draw him back or push him away forever.

"There is one more thing I must tell you," Tate tried to remain calm.

"There is more?" Thomas gasped. "How could there be more?"

"I am afraid there is . . . Gautier has sent word that Magna has survived her final death, and she is living in Crimson Claw Castle."

Thomas stood shocked for a moment before a ferocious growl filled the air.

"Let me out of here," he demanded. "I need to be with Lara and my daughter."

"I understand; however, I have no power to remove your chains. Your freedom rests solely with Lara," he explained. "Let go of the madness completely. It is your only chance to leave this dreadful place. Fight it, Thomas. You did it once. You can do it again."

Tate opened the door and looked back at him. He could see how tormented his brother had become. If the news he had brought him did nothing to help him fight, nothing would help.

The sound of soft footsteps drew his eyes down the hallway. He could see Laralynn carrying a pitcher and coming toward him.

"What is this?" he asked.

"I have come to see my father. He needs my help," she softly replied.

"Are you sure?" he questioned her safety more than her desire.

"He is my father, uncle. He won't hurt me," she assured him.

He nodded and held the door open for Laralynn to enter the Holding Room. He watched her slowly walk toward the table and place the pitcher of blood down upon its surface.

Without turning around, she calmly said, "Uncle, you may close the door. He won't hurt me. After all, I am his daughter."

Tate looked beyond Laralynn at Thomas. He stood quietly looking at his daughter.

"Do as she asked, Tate," he said. "I would like to speak with my daughter."

Tate closed the door, but stood leaning against its hard surface.

Take this opportunity she has given you, my brother. Make things right.

Chapter 14

With news of Magna's survival, the Evergreen Army was assigned additional patrols. Meadow was called upon to cast a protection spell for the castle and for Laralynn. With the confinement of Lord Thomas, Tate had assigned Baxter and Will to guard Lady Laralynn and Frances to guard Lady Lara. It was well known that Magna could change her appearance, and warnings had been sent out to the surrounding villages asking them to be vigilant.

Elda and Oliver had continued patrolling the Echo Bluff Harbor and the tavern in the village. These were both frequented by Magna before her attack on her sister, and they all assumed she would not be able to stay away. For Oliver, he was glad to have gotten the order to patrol the tavern. There was a special lass that he had not seen for some time and looked forward to another playful visit.

On their most recent patrol, several wagons waited in line eager to transport goods from the harbor for a fair wage. Elda recognized most of them and surveyed the crowd of newcomers. It appeared to be the usual crew members, a young family greeted by an older gentleman, and several men carrying bedrolls.

"I find no immortals among them," Elda whispered. "Those

men are probably looking for work."

"I don't see anyone here that concerns me," Oliver replied. "Let's head on over to the tavern. Those men will no doubt head that way, as well. It will be a good way to see how they interact with others."

"You mean, it will be a good way for me to see how they will interact with others," Elda jabbed Oliver in the ribs. "You will be scampering up the stairs with your little lass."

Oliver shrugged his shoulders and gave her a big grin.

"Scampering is not what I had in mind," he playfully swatted her backside.

As they walked toward the tavern, Elda felt a strange presence and slowly put her hand on the dagger she wore at her hip.

"Do you . . . feel that?" she stuttered with apprehension. "It's like the air around us has closed in on us.

Oliver quickly took his place behind Elda, and he walked with his back against hers, searching for the cause of her concern.

"I feel it, but I don't know what to make of it. I see nothing following us. I don't see a threat, but we should be ready for an attack," he cautioned.

After walking a few more paces and surveying the area, they both felt the strange feeling vanish. The air around them no longer felt thick.

"Whatever it was, it is gone," she sighed. "I didn't feel it earlier at the harbor. I sensed nothing unusual. If it was an immortal, it had power enough to hide its imprint."

"There was definitely something there, and I am glad it's gone," Oliver moaned. Taking his place next to Elda, they continued to walk toward the tavern with their hands at ready upon their weapons.

As they approached the tavern door, they could hear Lulu's voice echoing harsh words through the open windows. A recognizable twang was heard just before something heavy hit the floor. Opening the door, they could see Lulu standing over a man that was sprawled on the floor. Two other men stood and were backing away from her.

"Lulu, do you need any help?" shouted Elda, knowing full well the men had Lulu's full attention.

Hearing a familiar voice, she grinned and shook her head.

"I believe I got my point across," she snickered. "That is the last time he will be taking liberties with the curves on my backside."

Oliver bit the inside of his mouth trying to keep from laughing. He could see Zeb looking on from his place behind the bar. He held a mug dripping with foam in one hand and waved a shovel in the other.

"What do you plan on doing with that?" Oliver laughed.

"Nothing, I was prepared to toss it to Lulu if she needed it," he shouted.

"I see . . . you let the women do the dirty work around here," Oliver nodded approvingly.

Elda picked up the man from the floor and sat him back in his chair. She looked at his friends and directed them to take a seat. Lulu gave them a stern look and headed back to the bar.

"No more trouble from you tonight," Elda glared at the men. "I am much more trouble than Lulu, and I don't believe that you want to find out how much."

Elda turned and headed toward Oliver. He was leaning with one elbow on the bar with an outstretched hand offering her a mug of ale. As she made her way through the tables full of men, something in the far corner of the tavern caught her eye. The light from the hearth was reflecting against something silver. Two men blocked her view, and she took a step back to get a better look. A man with long silver hair looked up from his meal and made eye contact with her.

Noticing her frozen stance, Oliver looked over his shoulder to where Elda's eyes were focused and back at her troubled expression.

"Elda, Elda" he shouted. Drawing her attention away from the man, he lifted the mug again. "I'm not holding this to exercise my arm."

She blinked her eyes and looked over at Oliver. Confused, she returned her eyes back to the man with the silver hair, but he was gone.

What's got you looking like the eyes of death just looked at you?" asked Oliver.

She took the mug from his hand and raised it to her mouth, eagerly consuming its contents.

"I must be seeing things," she muttered. "I thought I saw Balgair. He was sitting in the corner, and he looked right at me."

"The vampire that kidnapped Lady Lara?" he asked.

"The same," she replied, banging the mug on the bar. "Zeb, I need another, please."

Obliging her request, Elda lifted the mug to her mouth and gulped it down.

"I'm sure it was him" she said. "I need to get back to Evergreen. The army needs to know that Balgair is here on the island. You coming with me?"

A sudden shriek filled their ears. Oliver immediately recognized the shrill sound and looked about the tavern to find the pretty lass. As he turned and took a step away from the bar, he felt the weight of her arms around his neck and her legs anchor securely around his waist.

"Oliver, my Oliver," she mumbled in between pressing her lips to his.

Wrapping his arms around her waist, he stumbled toward the stairs. The sound of men's cheering filled the tavern as he moved his hands down around the curves of her bottom trying to regain his balance. Blindly searching for the first step of the stairs with his boot, his hands began to shake. A fierce burning pain stopped him in his tracks. Jerking the lass from his body and placing her feet on the floor in front of him, he looked down at his hand. A pulsing red starburst filled his palm.

"What the hell?" he groaned.

He rubbed his palm against his breeches, and the pain slowly disappeared. Relieved by the sight of the fading mark, he picked up the lass and threw her over his shoulder. As he took a step towards the stairs, the pain caused him to drop her to the floor.

"Have you cursed me, lass?" he stared into her eyes waiting for an answer.

She reached for his hand and turned it over to look at his palm.

"I have seen this only once before," she began to cry. "Your intended mate has marked you. It will not allow you to touch me. Oliver, we can never be together."

Wiping the tears from her eyes, she reached for his face with both hands and kissed him one last time. He could feel her sadness and his own as she dropped her hands to her sides and backed away. Oliver lifted his hand to touch her cheek, but she turned and fled up the stairs.

Pounding his fist on the bar, he looked at Elda searching for an answer to the curse that had stricken him.

"Let me see?" Elda asked, taking Oliver's hand. "It looks like a burn. Who has marked you?"

"It can't be," he blurted. "Not the little witch. This must be undone. Do you hear me? I must find a way to remove this mark."

"Forget the mark. We need to get back to the Command Center to tell Preston about Balgair," Elda said, as she headed for the door.

As Oliver followed her, she began to laugh.

"What is so funny?" he roared.

"You, Oliver," she continued to laugh. "You have a mate. I pray the stars will protect her."

"She will surely need protection if she doesn't release me from this curse," he barked through gritted teeth. "She doesn't know the wrath I can offer."

"I think she has you well in hand," Elda joked.

Seeing him purse his lips and lower his brows, she knew she had gone beyond what Oliver would tolerate. Without hesitation, she started to run.

"You better run," he shouted. "You know what I will do if I

catch you."

She knew he was right on her heels, and she hoped he wouldn't catch her. If he did, he would bury her up to her neck and leave her until morning.

"You will have to catch me first," she shouted, as she ran for her life.

Chapter 15

Every morning since her unexpected talent of flashing was discovered, Laralynn met with Baxter to continue her training with the bow. It wasn't long before she could hit the center of a target at fifty paces, and Baxter felt she was finally ready to go on a hunt with Woodward.

Laralynn nervously walked by Baxter's side holding her bow, and her shoulder felt slightly stiff from the weight of the quiver of arrows against her back. It would be her first real adventure in the forest surrounding the castle, and she had dreamt of what it would be like. Standing next to the low stone wall that bordered the forest, she could see Woodward and Patrick waving. She immediately felt her neck and shoulders relax when she saw Patrick's smile, and she quickened her pace to join them.

"My Lady, are you ready for your first hunt?" asked Patrick.

Seeing the flush upon her face, Patrick stepped forward and took hold of her hand.

"My Lady, don't be afraid," he said. "We will all protect you."

"I am happy to have such fine men to care for my safety," she replied, and noticed Patrick puff up his chest after hearing her compliment.

"We have been tasked by the kitchen to bring back rabbits, but I will not expect you to make the kill," Woodward said. "It is not fitting for My Lady."

"You will not find me weak of heart," she replied. "I have readied many a rabbit and chicken for the cooking pot. The kill was not made by an arrow but from the twist of my hand upon their neck or the blade of an axe. I would prefer using the arrow. It would allow me to avoid the look of fear in their eyes."

Baxter coughed back a laugh at her blunt statement. She had lived a much different life in Primrose Pond, and he was just beginning to learn the strength she possessed.

"Well, let's be off," said Woodward, as he led the way into the thick of the trees.

Laralynn took notice of the forest and decided it wasn't much different from the one near Primrose Pond. She was surprised to see so many more eatable mushrooms and wild onions. The forest floor seemed to be covered with them.

After walking for quite a while, Woodward raised his hand and everyone immediately stopped. A moaning sound could be heard coming from off in the distance.

"It sounds like a hurt or wounded animal," he said.

They all stood perfectly still. Hearing the sound again, Baxter pointed off to their right. Unsure of what they would find, Baxter kept Laralynn safely behind him. Walking in the direction of the sound, it was quickly replaced with the rustling of branches. Entering a small clearing, they could see a large cluster of bushes jerk back and forth. Baxter pulled an arrow and raised his bow ready to kill the animal should it attack while Woodward and Patrick followed Baxter's lead. Laralynn's boot made contact with a dry twig, and the crack it made beneath her foot caused the animal to lurch from its shelter. A deer caught in a trap raised up for a moment and then stumbled to the ground.

As Baxter took aim, Laralynn screamed, "No! It's hurt."

Before Baxter or Woodward could stop her, Laralynn ran

toward the frightened animal. It laid on its side and tried to kick free from the trap. As she fearlessly knelt by its side, it seemed to calm and closed its eyes as she stroked its side.

"Please help her," Laralynn begged.

"Her leg is broken," Woodward said. "We need to end her pain,"

"Take the trap from her leg," she insisted. "We must try and help her."

"Laralynn, she will not survive with a broken leg," Baxter said, as he tried to reason with her. "She will be too weak to defend herself from other animals that will want to kill her. Her death could be much worse than a well-placed arrow."

"Give me your water skin," Laralynn demanded, ignoring his plea. "She needs water."

Baxter dropped his bow and took the skin from his waist. As he handed it to her, he knelt down and looked at the shattered bone. He knew there was nothing that they could do to help the poor creature. Seeing Laralynn's demanding glare, he took hold of the trap and pried it open. The deer flinched but didn't attempt to move. Laralynn poured water into the palm of her hand and held it to its mouth. The deer made no attempt to drink and her breathing appeared to slow. Not knowing what else to do, she poured the water from her hand over the bleeding wound.

Tears began to run down her face as she stroked the deer's neck.

"She is gone," whispered Laralynn, as she continued to gently stroke the deer's neck. "We were too late to save her."

Baxter took Laralynn's arm to help her stand. As they took a step back, Baxter reached down to pick up his bow.

"We weren't in time, but it did seem that you gave her some comfort," he replied.

"What shall we do with her?" she asked, looking at Baxter and then up at Woodward. "We can't leave her here."

"Take Laralynn back to Evergreen. Patrick and I will take care of the deer," Woodward said. "She has seen enough for today."

Not waiting for Laralynn to object, Baxter took hold of her hand and vanished.

Woodward leaned his bow against a tree and pulled his blade from its sheath. Before he could kneel next to the deer, she struggled for a moment and then stood on all fours before him. Hearing Patrick's gasp, the deer leapt toward the cover of the trees.

"Father," Patrick shouted.

"I cannot believe my eyes," he replied. "Her leg has healed, and she drew a breath after she had taken her last."

"How?" asked Patrick.

"I do not know, son," he replied. "Do not mention what you have seen to anyone. I will speak with Lady Lara. It appears Lady Laralynn has healed the deer."

Chapter 16

Velsa sat high in a tree clutching securely to a branch overlooking the stream where she had seen the white wolf stop for a cool drink on several occasions. She had patiently sat among the treetops hoping to discover the wolf's favorite and most frequented paths through the forest, and this seemed to be her favorite. The banks of the stream were covered in soft moss, and the gentle ripple of the water filled the forest with a soothing sound. She, herself, had found this to be the most relaxing spot in the forest.

With the full moon filtering through the tops of the trees, she was certain that tonight the white wolf would make an appearance. It wasn't long before she heard the sound of paws sprinting toward her; however, the sound she heard was much different. Listening carefully, she studied the echoing sound and determined there were two animals in a furious chase. Eager to see the white wolf chasing her prey, she hid herself from view. To her surprise, the white wolf followed by a grey wolf leaped into the clearing along the water's edge.

She watched as the wolves drank from the cool water and seemed oblivious to the fact that she was very close to them. She was so close that with a snap of her fingers she could have easily ripped the tail from the white wolf. Her fingers began to twitch and her hands began to shake. She had let the tempting thought linger in her mind for a moment longer than she should have. Realizing her dilemma, she held her breath desperately trying to control her wildest desires. It wasn't enough to rip her tail from her body, she wanted to see the wolf suffer. Simply taking her tail would not give her the enjoyment she needed. Looking away from the wolves, she tried to refocus her thoughts. She had to stay true to her plan, or she could face failure. Gazing up at the moon and back down at the wolves, she noticed how the moonlight made their fur glisten.

Maybe I shouldn't stop at her tail, she thought. Her soft white fur would make a lovely rug beneath my bare feet.

Going over her plan in her mind, she struggled with the idea that the white wolf may never be alone. Two wolves would make her task a bit more difficult. A simple spell could easily contain them, but the grey wolf would be a witness to her actions. She would inform Gautier, and he would be easily led right to her cottage door. It would be best if the white wolf was alone. After all, she had no grudge against the grey wolf and would not harm her unless she foolishly attacked her.

Velsa had been watching the wolves for some time and knew the path they frequented. If she was going to take the white wolf's tail, this would be the most obvious place to set the trap. It would have to be well hidden and appear to be the trap of a human hunter. If the grey wolf was near, she would surely run for help. This would allow the time needed to remove the white wolf's tail and leave before help arrived.

Bored with the napping wolves, Velsa vanished back to her cottage. Standing in front of her table, she began to rub her hands together. She was pleased to have found Kayleigh's most frequented path. Since her favorite time to run was in the evening and during a full moon, she decided that would be the best time to place her trap. The darkness would make it easier to hide, and the full moon would make the wolf more eager to run and less cautious.

She picked up her book of spells and ran her hand over its

cover. She could feel the smooth worn leather and its slight vibrations before her index finger felt a prick along with a burning sensation. Without lifting her hand, she began to hum a gentle melody and the burning stopped.

"I know you are anxious. I am anxious too. We shall have the white wolf's tail, and it will allow us to complete the spell to avenge the wrong done to me," she lovingly whispered. "With her tail, I will have everything I need to erase Gautier's memories of Kayleigh and the hidden chamber. Once again, I will have Gautier by my side, and he will love me, only me. It will be Kayleigh's turn to suffer."

Bringing the book to her lips, she gently kissed the worn leather and placed it back upon the table. Satisfied with her discovery in the forest, she sat down in her favorite chair and began to rock. As she sang the words to the tune she had been humming, the words swirled around her head making her dizzy.

The love you took from me, now burns bright in another's heart.
But once I have her tail, your love will fall apart.
Apart! Apart! Apart! Your love will fall apart.

Velsa sang the words over and over until her eyes slowly closed, and she slipped quietly into her dreams.

Chapter 17

The heavy door of the Holding Room opened, and the sound of rustling fabric drew Thomas' attention. As he looked up, he could see the candlelight reflecting in her eyes. They were the same beautiful blue, but they held a sadness that kept the sparkle from her eyes. A sadness he had caused. He wanted to run to her and take her in his arms. He wanted to kiss her bare shoulders and take her mouth with his own, but he sat perfectly still as he watched her walk toward him.

Stopping a few feet from him, Lara studied Thomas' eyes. She had been told they had cleared days ago, but she had waited to visit him. His neglect was serious, and she wanted him to be able to think about what he had done with a clear mind. She was treating him no different from any other vampire that had gotten too close to the madness.

"I find we have returned to where we first began," Lara said, followed by a deep sigh.

Hearing the pain in her sweet voice crushed him, but he didn't look away.

"Again, you have saved me," Thomas replied, remembering the moment he had realized that he was held against his will in the Holding Room.

"Again, you needed saving," she whispered.

"And I am grateful," he quickly replied, as he stood letting the chains fall to the floor.

Lara took a step back and began to wring her hands. The sight of the chains hanging from his wrists disturbed her. For a moment, she remembered the weight of wearing those chains as she fought the madness as a new vampire. Pushing those thoughts away, she focused her attention on his eyes.

"Do you recall what I told you when we met in the library after your release from this chamber?" she asked.

Seeing the tilt of his head as he tried to remember, she continued to search his face for recognition.

"I told you that the madness is never completely gone. It will always be there waiting to take hold of you again," she reminded him. "Letting yourself refrain from drinking animal blood invites the madness to return. You put yourself and others in danger. You could have been a danger to our daughter."

"I have thought of nothing else for days," he confessed. "That and the harm I could have caused you. I remember, very clearly, my aggressive behavior toward you in our bedchamber. It shames me."

Thomas dropped his vision to the floor not wanting to see the hurt in her eyes.

"Promise me that you will guard yourself against the madness. Promise me, Thomas. I could not bear to lose you," she begged.

"Lara, I will," he promised. "I made the same promise to our daughter. She visited me here in this chamber and saw me chained to the wall. There was no fear or pity in her eyes when she looked at me; however, she did give me a scolding." He began to laugh and saw the start of a smile upon Lara's face that she quickly covered with her hand. "She brought me a pitcher of animal blood and insisted I drink a full goblet in front of her. Lara, she is amazing. Our daughter is amazing."

"She is," Lara replied, as she reached into her pocket and retrieved a key. Taking his wrist, she inserted the key and released the cuff. Letting it drop, she reached for his other wrist.

"It pained me to confine you to the Holding Room. It pains me to see you wearing these cuffs meant for a vampire filled with madness," she whispered.

Hearing the cuff hit the stone floor and seeing his hands free, Thomas embraced Lara and held her tightly against his body. With his face embedded in her hair, he inhaled the fresh scent of lemon and mint and felt his body begin to relax. With her face against his chest, he could feel a familiar warmth begin to weave its way back through his body.

"I love you . . . I will always love you," he whispered, as he felt her arms wrap around his waist.

"I love you too," she replied. "Please, let's return to our bedchamber."

He took hold of her shoulders and gently pushed her back to look into her eyes.

"I propose we walk instead of flash this time. It would please me to be awake when we enter our bedchamber," he smiled. "I have already spent too many days without the sight of you."

As Thomas opened the door to leave the Holding Room, he was greeted by his brother.

"Tate?" he stood surprised to see him. "Are you here to escort me back to my bedchamber? I assure you, I am fine. You need not fear that I will bring harm to anyone."

"No brother," he replied. "I had hoped to find the Lady Lara. Now that you are ready to leave your confinement, I would ask that you both meet me in the Council Chamber."

"Has something happened?" gasped Lara.

"Woodward has brought me some news we should discuss," Tate replied. "We will speak about it once Thomas has readied himself for an audience. Off with you both, and come to the Council Chamber straight away."

* * *

Thomas held Lara's hand as they entered the Council

Chamber to find Tate, Baxter, and Woodward standing behind their chairs. After helping Lara with her chair, Thomas took his own seat followed by Baxter and Woodward. Tate paced back and forth at the far end of the table before he finally took his own seat.

"Why have you called us here?" asked Lara.

"My Lady, may I speak?" asked Woodward.

"Of course," she replied.

"You already know that Laralynn has shown interest in learning the bow and going on a hunt with Patrick and myself," he paused for a moment to see Lady Lara nod in understanding. "She had shown much progress with the bow, and Baxter determined she was skilled enough for her first hunt."

He could tell by the look on Lady Lara's face that she thought something had happened to her daughter.

"The Lady Laralynn is unharmed," he declared. "Please set your mind at ease."

"He tells the truth, My Lady," assured Baxter.

"Then, what is it?" she asked, as she looked back at Woodward.

"A deer was caught in a trap. Its leg was broken," he explained. "Laralynn would not let us ease its misery. She wanted to try and help it. We tried to explain to her that it would not survive with a broken leg. She demanded water and tried to offer the water to the deer. She showed no fear as she knelt by its side. She felt it take its last breath."

"Her actions warranted us meeting you in private?" asked Thomas. "She is a kind hearted child. Of that, I have personally witnessed."

"Lord Thomas," interrupted Baxter. "Let him finish."

Thomas looked back at Woodward waiting for him to continue.

"She poured the water from her hand onto the deer's broken leg," he paused for a moment and took a deep breath. "If I had not seen it with my own eyes, I would not have believed it. The deer's leg healed, and it stood on its own and ran into the forest.

My Lady, the deer had died. I was preparing to gut the deer and bring it back to Evergreen. The Lady Laralynn brought the deer back to life."

A gasp from Thomas made Lara flinch.

"Did my daughter witness this?" she asked.

"No, I had already flashed her back to the Command Center," Baxter replied. "She was upset over the death of the deer. I didn't feel she needed to see Woodward gut the poor creature."

"For that, I thank you," she replied. "Is there anything else?"

"No, My Lady," replied Woodward.

"You may go," she said. "Thank you for bringing this to our attention. I trust you will not speak of this to anyone until we have a chance to speak with our daughter."

"You have my word, My Lady," he declared. Standing, he made a slight bow and left the Council Chamber.

"I think it is time to take Laralynn to the Room of Powers," Lara sighed. "Knowing that she can flash and appears to be a healer, I must find out what other powers she has acquired."

"She can flash?" asked Thomas. "Why did no one tell me of this?"

Tate glared at his brother and shook his head, "You don't remember?"

It didn't take long for Thomas to remember that Tate had told him during his visit to the Holding Room, and he wondered what else he had forgotten.

"Thomas, we will speak with our daughter before we take her to the Room of Powers," said Lara. "This is all my fault. I thought she was human since I birthed her as a human. Since she was conceived while I was a vampire, our blood has had something to do with all of this."

"Are you sure this is not Velsa's doing?" barked Thomas. "I don't trust the old hag. Look what she did to her own sister."

"It was I that made the bargain, Thomas," she replied. "I am to blame, only me."

"You are not to blame if she has spelled our daughter," he

argued. "You never made a bargain to spell our daughter. You only bargained to protect her. Flashing and healing are something quite different."

"The Wispet Queen will tell us if she has more gifts," she said, as she stroked his arm. "When we know of her gifts, we can help her understand them. Baxter, will you ask Meadow to meet us in our daughter's bedchamber."

"Yes, My Lady," he replied. "I shall bring her shortly."

* * *

Meadow led the way to the Room of Powers. Laralynn had listened to everything Meadow and her mother had told her, and she was eager to meet the Wispet Queen. Sensing her father's uneasiness as they walked, she took his hand in her own and gave it a light squeeze.

"I am not afraid, father," she whispered. "I am excited."

"You are an amazing young lady," he said and kissed the top of her head.

As the hallway turned, Laralynn could see the large black metal hinges of the wooden door that protected the Room of Powers. Standing before it, she was surprised to hear the faint sound of voices whispering her name.

"This is the Room of Powers," her mother explained. "It contains all the powers that could be gifted to a vampire. Since you have shown signs of special powers, we are here to find out what other powers, if any, have been gifted to you." Lara looked at her daughter and gently stroked her cheek. "Are you ready?"

"Yes, mother," she replied. "I am ready."

Lara inserted the key into the lock. As she turned the key, everyone could hear tiny voices beckoning them forward.

"The sounds you hear are from the Wispets that protect the Room of Powers. They are guardians of the gifts and take care of the powers, making certain they stay strong. Please know that the Wispets are not prisoners here in this room and can leave through a portal inside the chamber at any time they choose.

They come and go, but are always present when the Wispet Queen performs the Gifting Ceremony."

After Lara unlocked the door, Thomas pulled it open allowing everyone to enter. Closing the door behind him, he stood next to Lara and Meadow.

Laralynn looked about the dimly lit room and noticed a pillar with a strange engraving. Before she could touch it, a warm light began to glow above the pillar, and an image of a woman with lavender hair began to appear. Laralynn knew she was the Wispet Queen and made a deep curtsy to show her respect.

"Step forward Laralynn," the Wispet Queen softly asked. "Step forward and place your hands upon the pillar."

Laralynn did as she was asked and placed both her hands upon the pillar. She could feel the warmth beneath her fingers and wisps of gentle heat swirling around her arms. The globes around the room began to blink and rattle. Four globes slowly drifted toward the pillar and snuggled next to each other before settling upon it. As the Wispet Queen lifted her hand to touch the first globe, four more globes drifted from the shelf and hovered above the four globes sitting on the pillar. Their bright lights slowly faded until the light was completely gone.

"Why did their lights go out?" asked Laralynn, fearing something dreadful was about to happen.

"My dear Laralynn," the Wispet Queen whispered. "The globes that have gone dark will be gifted to you in the future. There is something blocking their ability to offer their powers to you. It may be your age, a skill that you must master, or a spell that blocks these powers from being gifted. It may even be because you are human and not a vampire. Do not worry over this. Powers are often gifted later in one's life. They are often gifted when the need arises. You are still very young."

Looking for Laralynn's understanding, she waited until she saw her smile.

"Are you ready?" the Wispet Queen asked.

"Yes, My Queen," she replied, not knowing how she should address her.

The Wispet Queen waved her hand, and they watched the dark globes return to their place upon the shelf. A soft sigh was heard from the far corner of the room. Laralynn looked over her shoulder to see where it came from and noticed a very small rose colored globe. It lifted itself from the shelf and then settled back down before it lifted up again.

"Don't be afraid, little one. Come join the others," the Wispet Queen said.

Everyone watched as the rose colored globe slowly made its way over to the pillar and settled down next to the others. The globes all began to chatter among themselves until a soft hush was offered from the Wispet Queen, causing them to still.

The Wispet Queen touched the first clear globe, and Laralynn watched as it brightened but remained clear. A strange word appeared above the surface of the pillar. "Touch of Truth," she said, as the word disappeared, and the globe's light faded.

She tapped the next globe lightly, and it turned a bright red. Again, a word appeared above the pillar that Laralynn could not read. "Healing Hands," she announced, as the light in the globe slowly dimmed.

Lightly touching the next globe, it began to blink. One moment it was aqua, and the next moment it was gone. Continuing to blink, a word appeared above the pillar. "Flash," the queen announced, as Laralynn watched the word disappear into the globe and the light fade.

As the queen touched the next globe, a sound similar to a waterfall filled the room, and the globe filled with swirling bubbles. Words floated above the pillar, and the queen announced, "Air and Water." As she did, the sound of rushing water quieted, and the bubbles disappeared.

The remaining globe was the small rose colored globe that was the last to join the others. As the Wispet Queen reached for the tiny globe, it began to shimmer. She carefully picked it up and gently stroked the small globe. A small group of words appeared inside the globe. "Speaking with Animals," she announced.

Hearing the last gift announced, the globes lifted from the pillar and gathered around the tiny globe the queen held in her hand. As if it knew that the others were waiting for it, it lifted from her hand and joined them. Laralynn watched as they all returned to their place on the shelves.

"These gifts have been given," declared the Wispet Queen, as she looked directly into Laralynn's eyes. "Use them well."

The Wispet Queen faded from view as chatter and laughter filled the room for a moment and then diminished, returning the room to silence and dim candlelight.

"We are finished here," her mother said.

Laralynn could feel the pillar cool beneath her hands. As she lifted her hands she studied the inscription on its surface.

"Mother?" asked Laralynn. "What does this inscription mean?"

"Keep with Honor - Forfeit with Shame," she replied. "Come, let's talk about what we have learned. We have much to discuss."

Laralynn followed her mother from the Room of Powers. As they walked through the hallway, she again took hold of her father's hand.

"Will I be able to use my gifts?" she asked, as she looked for her father's response.

"First, you must learn how to use them," he replied. "Practice them, and use them wisely. Remember, they are gifts. Gifts can be taken away if misused."

"What do you think the dark globes will do?" she asked.

"I don't know," he replied. "It is a mystery to be discovered."

Chapter 18

"Lady Laralynn . . . what did you think of the Room of Powers?" Elda asked, very curious about a human's reaction to the Gifting Ceremony. "Were you frightened?"

"My stars, no," she replied instantly. "It was wonderful. I found it to be magical."

"You were the first human to receive gifts from the Wispet Queen, and the first human to stand within its walls. I found it strange that you would be taken there so soon," she offered not hiding her irritation.

Laralynn could hear Elda's dissatisfaction with her visit to the sacred room, but she tried to ignore it. She wanted to be friends with Elda and hoped this wouldn't drive a wedge between them. Before she could respond, shouting could be heard coming from the Command Center. Without hesitation, they both ran toward what sounded like an argument. Entering the Command Center, they found Baxter pinned to the wall with Oliver's hand wrapped around Baxter's neck, and Baxter clutching at Oliver's fingers.

"It isn't funny," shouted Oliver. "I want no part of the little witch. She cursed me."

"I was only joking," choked Baxter.

"You make fun of the sweet lass that warms my bones. . .

again, and I will slit . . . your throat," he replied, as he struggled to hold Baxter against the wall.

"What is all this about?" Elda shouted, as she grabbed hold of Oliver's arm. "Put Baxter down! Put him down, right now!"

"And who's going to make me, if I don't? You?" he smirked.

With one swift kick of her boot, Elda took Oliver's legs out from under him. Both Oliver and Baxter ended up sprawled on the floor.

"Did that answer your questions?" she shouted. "Now, what the hell is going on?"

"He was laughing about what happened at the tavern," Oliver said, as he thrust his leg out trying to kick Baxter in the shoulder. "The whole thing isn't funny. I'm cursed. The little witch cursed me, and it broke the heart of my favorite lass."

Baxter stood and stepped back away from Oliver as he rubbed his neck.

"I was only laughing because I saw the same reaction from Astra. She wants nothing to do with a mate," he tried to explain. "She had tears running down her face when she saw the mark upon her hand; however, unlike you, she doesn't know who is her intended mate."

"She didn't do it on purpose?" he asked.

"Astra was devastated when she saw the mark," interjected Laralynn. "I saw her reaction when she saw the mark upon her hand. She wanted no part of it. She had no idea who was her intended mate."

Oliver's brows lowered as he struggled to stand.

"If she doesn't want a mate, do you think she can undo the curse?" he asked.

"I doubt it. She would have quickly done so if she could have," replied Laralynn.

"So what is the big deal?" muttered Elda. "Go visit the little witch. You might find out that you like her."

"That mark on your hand will prevent you from being with another lass," warned Baxter. "You may as well see what happens. Pay her a visit. After all, you did pledge your service for her protection."

"I will think on it," he muttered. "A pledge of service and protection is all I am prepared to offer her. My affection for the lass is too strong to think of another."

"Can we get to work?" Elda looked at Baxter and then at Oliver. "I have brought Laralynn here to practice her gifts."

"I forgot about her gifts? What happened in the Room of Powers?" asked Baxter. "Lady Lara made me leave after I brought Meadow to your bedchamber."

"Baxter, it was amazing," she said, as she clasped her hands behind her back. "The Wispet Queen was so beautiful and everything was magical. I was given so many wonderful gifts."

"I know that you can flash. What other gifts did you receive?" as he waited for her answer, he noticed Elda purse her lips and cross her arms over her chest.

"I received Healing Hands, Hands of Truth, Air and Water, and Speaking with Animals. There were four globes that were dark and did not reveal a gift," she replied, trying to ignore the huffing noise that Elda was making.

"Dark globes?" Oliver questioned. "I have never heard of such a thing."

"It is probably because she is human," Elda snapped. "She should have waited until she was turned."

"Why are you acting like you are mad over a few gifts?" asked Oliver.

"Humans have never been allowed in the Room of Powers," she replied. "She probably got dark globes because she shouldn't have gone there."

Laralynn gasped at Elda's comment. As tears began to gather in her eyes, she turned and ran from the Command Center.

"Shame on you," scolded Oliver. "That was no way to treat Lady Laralynn. It isn't her fault that she has been gifted. Her mother and father are vampires, and she has probably gained her gifts through their blood."

"But it goes against," she stopped mid-sentence as Baxter interrupted her.

"Goes against what?" he asked. "Gifts are not limited to vampires. We have a witch here in the castle and Tate's mate is a hawk shifter. Lady Laralynn received the gift of flashing without entering the Room of Powers. Her powers would have eventually been exposed. Lady Lara felt it was important enough to take her to that sacred room. We must honor her decision."

Elda slowly unfolded her arms and shook her head.

"It all seemed so wrong at the time. That room has always been a special place for vampires, but I see your point. I owe Lady Laralynn an apology, don't I?" she confessed. "She probably thinks I hate her."

"I would go make things right if I were you," Oliver sternly suggested, as he waited to see Elda nod her head in agreement.

"Where do you think she has gone?" she asked.

"She is probably in the stable. She likes to spend time with Starlight," said Baxter.

* * *

Tears streamed down Laralynn's face as she opened the gate to Starlight's stall. Throwing her arms around the mare's neck, she felt a gentle nuzzle from her nose, and it made her smile.

"Let's go for a ride, Starlight," she whispered. "I need to escape the hate that Elda was showing me."

Not finding the saddle or reins, she decided to ride without them. Grabbing a hand full of silky mane, Laralynn guided the grey mare out of her stall toward the stable door and pushed it open. Leading Starlight over to the wooden rails, she stepped up on the lowest rail and threw her leg over the mare's back.

"My Lady, where are you off to?" Tolin startled her.

"I am going for a ride," she said, holding her head high.

"Where is your escort?" Tolin looked about for her father or someone from the army.

"I'm riding alone," she loudly declared.

"I am sorry, My Lady. I can't allow you to ride without an

escort. It is too dangerous to ride alone," he said, as he reached up to help her down from her horse. "I will see that Starlight is returned to her stall."

With her arms crossed over her chest and her back to Tolin, she stomped her foot in anger. She could hear him leading the mare back to the stable, ending her chance to escape.

"I have to get away from here," she mumbled.

"My Lady, do you need something?" Tolin turned to see that she was gone.

Elda hurried from the Command Center to the stable. It was obvious that someone had entered the stable and left the door open. As she entered through the open door, she saw the door at the far end of the stable was also open. It wasn't long before she discovered why. Starlight's stall was empty, and Lady Laralynn was nowhere to be found.

"Tolin! Tolin, have you seen the Lady Laralynn?" Elda shouted from the stable door seeing him leading Starlight back to the stable.

"She was just here. She must have wandered off," he replied.

* * *

Laralynn was startled to find herself standing alone in a small clearing in the forest. She had wanted to get away, but she was unprepared for the fact she had actually flashed herself to another location. Looking about to get her bearings, she realized that this was the same clearing where the injured deer had been found. The chatter of small forest creatures filled the air. As she listened, she remembered the gift of speaking with animals given to her by the Wispet Queen and wondered if she could really speak with them. Seeing a squirrel dash up the trunk of a nearby tree, she watched it stop and look her way.

"I am Laralynn. Can you hear me?" she called out to the squirrel, not expecting a reply.

"Of course, it is a pleasure to meet you," he replied into her mind.

Laralynn's hand cupped her mouth as her laughter filled the forest. Expecting the squirrel to scamper away after hearing her voice, she was surprised it stayed and even more surprised that it responded.

"We saw you save the deer," it said, while dashing back down the trunk and leaping upon the nearest boulder. "It was a kind thing you did."

"You are mistaken. The deer died. I felt her take her last breath," she whispered. "I tried to help her, but she was badly hurt."

"Not long after you were taken away, the deer stood on its own and ran away," it replied. The squirrel suddenly stopped and stood on its hind quarters. "Laralynn, you must run away. There is danger in the forest. Run!"

Before she could respond, Laralynn heard a woman's voice. Turning around, she saw a beautiful woman with long red hair standing before her.

"You startled me," gasped Laralynn, as she saw the woman raise an eyebrow and smirk.

"What are you doing in the forest all alone?" the woman asked. "There are many dangers in the forest, and I see that you do not carry a blade to protect yourself. You are very foolish."

"I might ask the same of you. I see that you do not carry a blade or a bow," she snapped in reply. "Are you not afraid of the dangers you speak of?"

"I have ways to protect myself," she smiled and took a step closer to Laralynn. "You see my dear, I am a vampire, and you are a mere human."

"A vampire? Do you know my mother and father?" she asked. "They are also vampires."

"Your parents are vampires and could not produce a vampire child?" she chuckled. She had never heard of vampires with the ability to conceive children, but if they could, they would surely have a vampire child. Curious as to why two vampires gave birth to a human child, she wanted to know more. "Who are your parents, child?"

"My parents are Lord and Lady Evergreen," she proudly stated. "Do you know of them?"

She felt herself sway a bit upon hearing the child's reply. Reaching for her throat, she muttered a few words under her breath and started to laugh.

"What is so funny?" Laralynn asked. "Why do you laugh?"

"Let me introduce myself properly," she declared, as she performed a deep curtsey. "My name is Magna Evergreen, and your mother is my sister. Isn't this delightful. I am your Aunt Magna."

"My Aunt?" she questioned.

"Yes, my dear," she cooed. "Come give your aunt a hug and a kiss."

This is perfect, she thought. I shall take Lara's child back to Crimson Claw with me. Seth and I will have so much fun with this pretty young morsel.

"RUN!" yelled the squirrel into Laralynn's mind.

Hearing the loud demand made Laralynn flinch, and before she knew it, she found herself standing in the safety of her bedchamber. She closed her eyes and tried to calm her breathing until another voice startled her.

"Where have you been, young lady?" her mother sternly asked. "We have been searching all over the grounds for you."

"Elda was . . . unkind to me," she stuttered. "I ran to the stable to take Starlight for a ride, but Tolin wouldn't let me ride without an escort."

Lara moved swiftly to embrace her daughter. She could feel her daughter's heart pounding. Kissing her forehead, she tried to comfort her.

"Tolin was only trying to protect you. Elda came to me, and she told me what happened," she whispered. "She wants to apologize and ask for your forgiveness."

"She does? I am sorry, mother," she lowered her eyes to the floor. "I wanted to get away from how she made me feel, and I just flashed. I was in the forest."

"Alone?" gasped her mother.

"Well, I was at first. I met someone," she replied.

"You met someone? Who?" she asked, as she gently pulled back from her daughter.

"I met your sister, Magna," she softly replied. "Why has she not come to visit?"

Lara tightened her arms around her daughter before she gently released her shoulders and took her hand leading her to the chairs that faced the hearth.

"Come sit with me. I have much to tell you," she softly requested.

Chapter 19

After hearing the tragic story of what happened to Magna in the dungeon of Black Thistle Castle, her crimes against humans, and her horrible attack upon her mother and father, Laralynn knew she had to learn how to protect herself. Without any gifts that she could use to defend herself, she decided training sessions in the Command Center were needed, and she knew exactly who she wanted to help her.

Laralynn stood in the doorway of the Command Center watching Baxter. He stood bare chested observing the skills of two men wielding swords and yelling instructions. The scar from the attack that took his human life was clearly visible. It seemed to glisten in the light from the torches that lined the stone walls.

She could see Elda off in the corner wrestling a brut of a man to the floor that was twice her size. After pinning his shoulders to the floor, she jumped up and eagerly offered her hand to help him stand. Returning to their stance, he grabbed her shoulders and attempted to throw her down. Once again, he landed on his back with Elda's knee on his chest. There was no doubt that Elda was an asset to the army.

They had all increased their practice sessions after word had been forwarded that Magna had stumbled upon Laralynn in the forest. The kidnapping of her father had shown them just how easily she could penetrate Evergreen's boundaries. Now that she had become whole, the renewed threat she posed was ever present in everyone's mind.

"Do you have your eye on someone special?" asked Tate.

"Uncle, I didn't hear you approaching," she gasped. Seeing Baxter had noticed her, she shyly lowered her eyes to the floor. "You see; you have given me away."

Tate smiled and gently cupped Laralynn's chin with his hand.

"Your mother tells me that you are eager to learn the ways of the army. Is this true?" he asked.

"I don't have gifts to use against those that would harm me. I need to learn how to protect myself and our people," she replied. "Baxter has taught me the bow, and I was hoping he could teach me how to use a dagger and a sword."

"You were hoping I could teach you what, My Lady?" asked Baxter.

"Does everyone have to sneak up on me?" she choked through another gasp. Laralynn could feel her face flush and looked away to see Elda coming toward her.

"Laralynn wants to learn to use a dagger," Tate answered Baxter's question.

"To learn the dagger . . . I would suggest either Oliver or Elda. They are both masters with the weapon," he said directly to Laralynn. "Since Elda is here, you can start now."

She knew the disappointment she felt was obvious to everyone, and she tried to hide it with a smile the best she could.

"Lady Laralynn, I would be honored to teach you the dagger," she cautiously declared. "I had the privilege of teaching your father and Tate many skills. I'll teach you some tricks I haven't shown them or any of the men. After-all, women don't want to give away all their secrets."

She heard Laralynn begin to laugh before she saw her quickly draw her hand to cover her mouth.

"Well, off with you," Tate gave her a gentle shove toward

Elda. "If you become half as gifted with a dagger as your mother, you will be far better than most in the army."

He saw Laralynn's mouth drop open in surprise.

It was obvious that her mother had been less than forthright about her talents. Lady Lara was skilled with several weapons. There were even rumors she had received almost every gift in the Room of Powers, but was held by a promise to keep them secret until her need to use them. It appeared that Laralynn was following in her mother's footsteps. She had her own secret gifts not yet presented to her by the Wispet Queen.

* * *

"My Lady, let me say that I am truly sorry for my behavior, and I ask for your forgiveness," Elda stood with her shoulders back and her fist over her chest as she spoke. "I put you in terrible danger. For that, I am ashamed."

Laralynn watched as Elda knelt before her.

"I pledge my service for your protection," she swore with her head bowed. "I will forfeit my life for yours without question, if the need should arise."

"Elda, please stand," she begged. "I forgive you. I accept your pledge and am honored to receive it."

Elda stood and offered Laralynn her hand and was pleased to receive hers in return.

"Now, teach me to use a dagger. I fear if I don't learn, I will surely be missing a finger or my toes in an attempt to protect myself," she began to laugh.

Pulling her dagger from its sheath, Elda laid the sharp blade against her palm.

"As you can see, the dagger has a narrow blade. It can cut from either side and has a tapered point," she explained, as she handed it to Laralynn.

"It is lighter than I thought it would be," she admitted.

"The dagger would be used if you lost your sword, or you wanted to carry a hidden weapon. I often carry a small one hidden on the inside of my boot. You will find most of the army does the same. You will appear unarmed without your bow or sword across your back, but have the security of the dagger if needed," she replied.

"Do I throw it?" she asked.

"Only if you are sure of the kill. Once you throw it, you will be without a weapon. You are better served to wait until your enemy is close. Stabbing or slashing with your blade may harm your enemy and allow you to keep the dagger in your hand for another strike."

"What's this? Do we have a new member of the army?" asked Thomas, as he stood with his arms crossed over his chest.

"If the army will have me," she laughed. "Elda is teaching me how to protect myself."

"I am proud of you. There are few in the army that are willing to take a beating from Elda. She gave me a few bruises, as I recall. You will learn much from her," he assured his daughter.

"My Lord, I thank you for your praise," Elda replied.

"I won't intrude on your practice any longer. Laralynn, I was looking for your mother. Have you seen her?" he asked, knowing full well where he could find her.

"She told me she would be in the library if I needed her," she replied.

Thomas stood watching his daughter for a few moments more and then turned to leave.

Elda pulled a dagger from her boot and took a defensive stance. Laralynn stepped back and dropped her dagger.

"My Lady, don't show fear to your attacker. Keep your dagger in your hand," she sternly said. "You must end him before he ends you."

Laralynn bent down to pick up her dagger and tried to mimic Elda's stance.

"Now, try to stab or slash me with your blade," Elda demanded. "Don't worry; you won't hurt me."

With every attempt, Elda easily avoided her attack and left

Laralynn completely frustrated.

"You are much too fast," she complained. "How am I supposed to attack you?"

"You must remember that not every enemy will be a human. You must also be able to defend yourself against a vampire or any immortal," she replied, as she quickly moved away from the thrust of Laralynn's blade.

"Elda, I wish I was a vamp . . . a little faster," she stuttered. "I will never be able to catch you."

"You will get faster with practice," Elda replied, ignoring her obvious comment.

Continuing her attempts to attack Elda, it was not until she used her gift of flashing that she was able to counter Elda's attacks and received praise for her efforts.

After what seemed like hours of stabbing and slashing, Laralynn collapsed to the ground exhausted.

"We have practiced enough for today. Get some rest, and we will practice again tomorrow," Elda said.

"Will I be able to move tomorrow?" she moaned. "I promised Tolin I would take care of Starlight after my practice. I doubt I will be able to lift my arms to brush her coat."

Elda sheathed her dagger and knelt down next to Laralynn.

"My Lady, it will get easier," she said. "You should know that you are a much better student than your father. You are light on your feet and quickly figured out how to use your gift to avoid my attacks." Standing she turned to leave. After a few steps, she stopped and stifled a laugh by biting her bottom lip. "Your father spent much of our practices on his backside. He was rather clumsy."

One look at Laralynn's expression made Elda burst out laughing, and fearing a well-placed dagger, she quickly ran for the Command Center.

Covering her mouth with her hands, Laralynn tried to keep herself from laughing as she fell back against the grass with visions of her father sprawled at Elda's feet.

* * *

Laralynn stood brushing Starlight's coat when she heard the stable door open and then close. She quietly moved keeping the mare between her and the gate. The sound of boots could be heard echoing through the stable. Hoping they belonged to Baxter, she listened carefully. Recognizing the loud creaking of Copper's stall, she stepped from behind the mare.

"Who's there," Laralynn shouted, knowing it must be Baxter.

"My Lady, it's Baxter," he replied.

Closing the noisy gate, he made his way to Starlight's stall to find Laralynn. As he approached the stall, she opened the gate for him to enter.

"I'm sorry if I frightened you," he said.

"You didn't frighten me," she replied, as she closed the gate behind him. "I'm glad you are here. Come sit by me. I want you to tell me about yourself."

Laralynn sat down on the fresh straw and patted the space beside her. Baxter sat down and leaned against the wooden siding.

"First, you agree we are friends?" she asked. Seeing his smile, she continued. "I would like it very much if you would call me Laralynn when we are alone. I know that the preferred way for you to address me is My Lady or Lady Laralynn, but it makes me feel uncomfortable."

"If you prefer, but only when we are alone," he replied.

"When we are alone," she repeated.

"What do you want to know?" he nervously asked, as he picked up a piece of straw and started to tear it into thin strips. "There really isn't much to tell."

"Have you always lived at Evergreen? Did you always want to be in the army?" she asked.

Wanting to ask more, she held her tongue to give him time to answer.

"I grew up in Primrose Pond just like you, and I hunted

rabbits for my mother's cooking pot and cut firewood with my father for the hearth. I remember plucking feathers for my mother to stuff our pillows. I plucked so many, I never wanted to see another duck." He heard her laugh, and he sat for a moment listening to the sweet sound before he continued. "I used to cross the waterway at Cobb Cove to find work in Peaks View. There, I helped the fishermen clean their fish. It was smelly work, but it kept me fed. I also held sheep for the farmers while they sheared their wool. The work was easy but hard on my back, and I decided it was best to learn a new skill. That is when I met a burly old man that taught me how to lay thatch upon the roofs of the local cottages. It was hard work and satisfying; however, it did little to light the fire within my soul." He watched Laralynn shuffle about to sit facing him as he continued his story. "One day when I was setting a trap for my own meal, a hunter crossed my path carrying a crossbow across his back. He saw that I was interested in his weapon and let me follow him on his hunt. We ran across an unsuspecting deer, and the hunter aimed the weapon and released the wooden bolt, instantly ending its life. While sharing his warm meal, he let me hold the weapon. The weight of it within my hands made my heart race. The next morning, I headed to Evergreen Castle and begged Commander Preston to allow me to join the army. I have been a member of the army ever since that day."

"Since I have been here, I feel like I am always making mistakes," she muttered. "Have you made many mistakes?"

"Everyone makes mistakes, including me," he admitted. "My worst mistake was turning my back to an enemy."

"The day you took the arrow?" she whispered, as she gently touched his hand.

He felt the light touch of her fingers and a sudden warmth pulse within his arm just before she pulled her hand away. He sat dazed for a moment before he remembered her question.

"Yes, the day I took an arrow," he replied. "It was my fault. I focused on the man before me and forgot to search the surrounding area for anyone else. By being so careless, I put my friends in danger and caused Oliver great suffering over his decision to turn me."

"He changed your life, and you changed mine," she said. "If you had not found me, I would never have met my father or watched my mother awaken. I would have accepted Jack's proposal and started a new life at Crimson Claw Castle. I would have never met you."

"Who is Jack?" he asked, confused by her reasoning.

"I met him at the Festival of the Ribbons in Primrose Pond. We would secretly meet in the evening by the pond and talk. I kept our meetings from my mother," she confessed. "I thought I had fallen in love with him. One evening he told me that he was anxious for my sixteenth birthday so that we could wed. His statement surprised me, but what he said next surprised me even more. He told me he was the son of the Lord of Crimson Claw Castle. I asked him why he had lied to me, and kept his father a secret. He said that he didn't want me to like him because of his wealth. I was hurt because he lied. I pushed him away and wanted time to think. He promised he would return on my sixteenth birthday and ask my mother for my hand. The night of my birthday, my mother died and everything changed."

Baxter sat stunned by her story.

"Laralynn, there has never been anyone named Jack that lived at Crimson Claw Castle. That castle has remained empty for well over one hundred years. No one claimed it until Jario began living there," he explained, as he thought back to the night he stood guard outside of Lady Lara's cottage. "I remember seeing Nollie run from the cottage and then seeing her stopped by a young man. That was when I heard her tell him of Lady Lara's death. Nollie ran for help, but the young man opened the gate and headed for the cottage door. He raised his hand to knock but never pressed his hand to the door. It was as if he had been prevented from knocking. He stood for a moment and suddenly turned to leave. He looked about as if he was afraid someone was watching him. He could have sensed me behind the trees."

"That must have been Jack. He told me he would return on my birthday," she added.

"I think that young man you call Jack was really the vampire, Jario," he gasped. "He was gifted the ability to change his appearance by Gautier in appreciation for breaking the curse that held Kayleigh and himself trapped from each other. The Evergreen Army knew he had been searching for your mother, and he found you instead."

"I was so foolish," she began to cry. "I thought I loved him. He told me nothing but lies."

Baxter wrapped his arms around her and felt her face press against his chest. As he gently rocked her, the warmth he felt from her touch returned and raced through his body.

"It isn't your fault," he whispered, trying to comfort her. "He took advantage of your innocence. He will never hurt you again."

"Just hold me, Baxter," she whispered. "It feels so warm in your arms."

Baxter could feel her heart beating against his chest. He knew now that she belonged to him and no one else. He would protect her from harm and wait patiently for her to love him.

"I will protect you, Laralynn," he sighed, as he kissed the top of her head. "I will always protect you."

Chapter 20

The night's sky was black as pitch as she searched for Velsa's cottage. There wasn't a hint of smoke from the witch's chimney or flickering candlelight from her tiny windows to help Magna find her way. Frustrated, she was about to scream Velsa's name when she felt something brush against her face.

"Who is it?" she shrieked. "Who dares to touch my face without permission?"

The sound of crushing pine needles was all she heard, as the sound seemed to surround her.

"Velsa, is that you?" she whispered. Nothing but silence greeted her plea. "What game are you playing? I demand that you show yourself!"

Again, she felt a light touch as her hair was brushed over her shoulder, and a faint wisp of cool air met her ear.

"I will leave this place unless you show yourself," she demanded again.

"As you wish," a man's voice politely replied.

The image of a man stood before her. His features were hidden by the darkness.

"Do I know you?" asked Magna.

"Yes," he replied. "I know you, as well."

"Come closer so that I may look upon your face," she beckoned him forward as she strained to see his face clearly.

"I find that you do not remember me, and it cuts me to the quick," his voice swirled about her head making her feel dizzy. "Has there been so many others that I am easily replaced?"

"Tell me who you are!" she screamed. "Tell me who you are! I have no time for games."

"In time, Magna," he replied, as his image began to disappear. "In time."

Magna stood looking at the spot where she had seen the man's faint image. All that was left was the darkness of the forest. Confused, she collapsed to the damp ground and tried to remember anyone she would have met with such a power. Unfortunately, too many men had crossed her path. No one stood out in her mind. They were all men she had entertained in her dungeon or at sea on the Abigale Star where she had met Seth. This immortal had strong powers. She could feel the thick air pulse around him and around herself.

"Magna," Velsa choked out her name. "What are you doing?"

Magna jumped to her feet and rushed to her side.

"Did you see the man that stood in the forest?" she grabbed Velsa's arms and stared into her eyes. "Did you see him?"

"I saw no one," she replied. "I feel no spirits lingering in the forest, not even yours. Oh my, I see that you are finally whole."

"I am whole, but this is not my concern," she whimpered.

A slight breeze blew between the trees making Magna reach for her face anticipating the feel of the mystery man's caress. Feeling nothing, she looked back at Velsa to see if she had felt anything, but she saw nothing but a scowl.

"Come, I will give you a cup of tea to calm your nerves. From the look on your face, you need calming. I have never known a man to fluster you so," she laughed. "It is usually you that does the flustering."

Looking beyond Velsa, she could see her cottage with the windows filled with flickering candlelight. Shaking her head, she felt Velsa wrap her arm around her waist and lead her through the cottage door. She was greeted by the heat coming from the fire in the hearth and the strong odor of the pungent herbs that hung from the ceiling.

As she sat down on the cot, she looked up at Velsa and asked, "Who was it? Velsa, who was the man from my past that invaded my privacy?"

A timid rapping at the door was not heard due to Magna's repeated questions. A loud bang on the door drew Velsa's attention.

"It's Lady Lara. You must leave," Velsa ordered. "Be gone!"

Without hesitation, Magna vanished leaving behind her wisp of red smoke. Velsa franticly waved her hands, and the smoke disappeared.

"Enter," Velsa shouted, and watched Lady Lara enter her cottage and close the door behind her. "What brings you to my cottage in the middle of the night?"

Lara sensed a visitor had just left and looked about the cottage for any hidden danger. Finding nothing but a familiar scent lingering in the air, it took her only a moment to determine the owner was her sister. She focused back on Velsa as she watched her smile and clasp her hands at her waist.

"Magna has gone," Velsa offered, knowing full well that Lara knew of her recent departure. "I ask again, what brings you to my cottage in the middle of the night?"

"I have not come for a bargain, but I have come to make a simple request," she replied.

"You know that I do nothing without getting something in return," she laughed. "You must remember your last visit. Did you not learn that lesson already?"

"I learned it very well, but please, hear me out," she begged.

"Go on," Velsa sighed, as she plopped down in her rocking chair.

"The move from Primrose Pond to Evergreen has been difficult for Laralynn. She has tried very hard to make Evergreen her home, and she has been struggling to find her way. She misses her friends and the freedom the small village offered her. I plan on taking her to Primrose Pond to visit them. I would like it very much if you would also be there. I know that she misses you and enjoys your company," she said, as she anxiously waited for Velsa's reply.

"It is true. She is special to me," Velsa confessed. "I would not admit it to anyone else, but I have missed her too. I will comply with your request. A visit with Laralynn will be payment enough, with one exception."

Knowing that everything came with a price, Lara pursed her lips and stared at the old witch. She could see the smirk on her face, and it was unnerving.

"What do you demand?" she asked.

"That you allow Laralynn to visit me here at my cottage," she replied. "Whenever she wants and allow her to come alone."

Lara gasped and brought her hand to her throat before she began to shake her head.

"She is too young to ride without an escort. I cannot allow this," Lara snapped.

"You keep secrets from me. I know Laralynn can flash. I have heard it on the wind," she replied.

"She can flash, but she is not able to control it yet," she complained, as she began to pace the small confined space.

"You need only bring her here once, and she will be able to find her way back here. No harm will come to her," she insisted. "I give you my word. If you insist, I will make a blood promise."

Lara was surprised to hear Velsa offer a blood promise. She knew that it was the most binding of all the promises she could make.

"I accept your terms," she replied.

Velsa stood and snatched her blade from her cluttered table. Pulling back her sleeve, she drew the point of the blade over her wrist. After tossing the blade back onto the table, she cupped her hand beneath her wrist and watched the blood drip into the palm of her hand.

"I make this promise sealed with my blood that no harm will come to Laralynn. She will be protected in my presence. She will be protected in her journey to and from my cottage. I make this promise before her mother. I give her the right to take my life if I should break this promise. If I should fail, she need only utter "Justice" and my life will be forfeited," she loudly proclaimed.

The blood rose up and hovered above Velsa's palm. Picking up a vial, she removed the cap and held the open vial out towards the blood. Slowly, the blood filled the vial. Replacing the cap, she then handed the vial to Lara.

"I have given you a blood promise. I expect you to keep your word, as well. Be gone with you," Velsa whispered, while flicking her hand toward the door and turning her back to her. "Wait, tell me when I should meet with you."

"The first day of the Festival of Ribbons," she laughed. "We will see you the first day of the Festival, and I thank you for your blood promise."

Velsa nodded, and Lara vanished.

"She misses me," she whispered. "The child misses me."

No sooner had Lara left Velsa's cottage than Magna returned.

"Honestly, you must do something about that wretched smoke," Velsa complained. "Might you leave it at the door the next time you visit?"

"If I must," she muttered, as she sat down on the cot and proceeded to remove her boots. Looking back over at Velsa, she tilted her head and pointed her finger at her face. "Why didn't you tell me that my sister had a child?"

"What?" she gasped. "Were you listening?"

"You heard me. Why didn't you tell me that my sister had a child?" she repeated.

"I had no reason to tell you. She is of no interest to you," Velsa snapped.

"She is of interest to me," she replied. "After all, she is my niece and quite lovely. To my surprise, I discovered she is human. Can you imagine? My sister couldn't even conceive a vampire child."

"So, you've seen her?" she asked.

"I have seen her, and she has seen me. I introduced myself to her," she laughed. "She was surprised to find out I was her mother's sister. To my surprise, I discovered that she has been gifted. I saw her flash. It was very timely; I might add."

"Why should that surprise you?" Velsa chuckled. "Lara has many gifts, and it seems that some of them might have been passed on to her daughter."

"You know more than you are telling me. What are you hiding?" Magna demanded.

"I hide nothing," she hissed, as she stood from her chair and glared down at Magna. "I will offer you a warning. Leave Laralynn alone! She is not to be harmed. I know all about your appetite for drinking human blood and torturing your victims."

"And if I disobey your warning, what then?" she yawned, patting her mouth with her fingertips. "Are you going to hurt me?"

"I will do worse than hurt you," Velsa screamed through her clenched teeth.

Purple sparks began to fly from Velsa's fists. Magna ducked trying to avoid the burning flecks of ash that flew about her head. When she saw Velsa raise her hand to point in her direction, Magna had had enough. She grabbed her boots and quickly vanished making sure to leave a generous amount of red smoke to annoy the old hag.

Relieved that Magna was gone, she sat back down in her chair and tried to calm herself.

"I would like to pull every red strand of hair from that vampire's head," she muttered, as she waved her hand to rid her surroundings of Magna's red smoke.

Closing her eyes, she envisioned the vampire without hair and started to laugh.

Chapter 21

Elda's curious nature kept her thinking about the silver haired vampire she had seen at the tavern. Since Lord Thomas was the only one that had seen him, other than Lady Lara, she had decided to ask him to go on patrol with her. To her surprise, he agreed.

The evening was cool and a thick layer of fog surrounded the village as they approached the tavern on foot. Music filled the air, as well as, the scent of rabbit stew. There was only one horse tethered to the post, and a wagon hitched to a mule.

"It seems much too quiet," cautioned Thomas. "A ship in the harbor usually makes for a rowdy tavern."

"You know Lulu," laughed Elda. "She doesn't mind swinging a tray against their heads to keep the order. She is a tough old bird, but I would suspect their mouths are being stuffed full of the rabbit stew that I smell."

"That she is. I believe I received her wrath a few times before Lara found me," he admitted. "I had no need for the taste of her stew. I hate to admit it, but my focus was purely that of ale and the blood from young women."

The tavern was full of the ship's crew playing cards, and as expected, they were happily partaking of Lulu's rabbit stew. A few buxom ladies sat among the men doing their best to encourage another round of ale. Seeing Zeb at the bar, Elda and Thomas gave him a wave and were greeted by a mug of ale held high in the air. Leaning back against the bar with his mug in hand, Thomas looked about the smoky room for the vampire they knew as Balgair. Not seeing him or anyone else he recognized, he turned back around to have Zeb refill his mug.

Hearing a man pounding his fist on his table, Elda looked over her shoulder to see a woman entering the tavern. Another man with a protruding belly barely covered by his soiled tunic began whistling at the woman as she made her way to an empty table. She seemed unflustered by the attention as she sat down lifting her woolen skirt while crossing her leg over her knee. The men all stared at her red stockings and tightly laced black boots that were clearly visible under the table. She removed her shawl and draped it over the back of the chair next to her. Waving her hand to get Lulu's attention, she brushed her dark brown hair over her shoulder exposing the top of her plump breasts.

Thomas leaned close to Elda and whispered, "If I didn't know better, I would think I was watching Magna."

"The men certainly seem bewitched by her," she replied. "It will be fun to see which one of them has the courage to approach her."

Almost before Elda could finish her response, a tall bearded man stood from his table and sheepishly approached the woman. Surprisingly, the woman allowed him to sit at her table. Thomas and Elda watched as they drank mug after mug of ale and eventually stumbled up the stairs.

"That didn't take long," Elda jabbed Thomas in the ribs.

Men came and went as the evening passed. Fearing Balgair was long gone, they downed the last of their ale and threw a few coins on the bar. Just as they were ready to leave, the door opened and in walked the vampire they sought.

"Do you believe our luck?" Thomas whispered. "He just walked in the door."

Without hesitation, the vampire walked directly toward them.

Elda bent and pulled her dagger from her boot, but saw him raise an eyebrow and slowly shake his head. A sudden calm filled the air around them.

"There is no need for weapons, my dear," he softly said. "I know that you have been waiting for me. Here I am. You need not hunt for me any longer."

Thomas quickly grabbed his tunic tightening the fabric with his fingers around the vampire's neck. Jerking him forward, he could smell the scent of sage and smoke as they faced each other nose to nose.

"You took my mate from me, you bastard. You put her in danger by helping the traitor, Jario," he growled.

Thomas knew the vampire's powers far outmatched his own and those of Elda's. He needed to arrest him, but without Meadow's help, he knew it was pointless.

"It is true; you are no match for me," he calmly replied. "If you will allow me, I will make you a bargain that will please both of us?"

"What bargain could dismiss what you have done?" he snarled.

"If you can forgive my crime against your mate, I will give you the name of the vampire that killed your family," Balgair calmly offered.

Thomas released his tunic and dropped his arm to his side. He stared in disbelief at what he had just heard. He could feel Elda take hold of his arm as his body swayed back against the bar. The vampire looked directly into his eyes, and Thomas was unable to move as he listened to Balgair speak.

"Have you forgotten the many nights you returned stumbling drunk to the charred remains of your home? Have you forgotten the hatred you felt for those that killed your parents and your sisters? Have you forgotten how often you wanted to die and prayed for death? I could have ended your pain on that dirt road, but I asked you if you wanted to live. Your answer was yes, and I gave you a chance to live for eternity," he placed his hand upon Thomas' chest and continued to speak. "I have turned many humans and collected many powers from vampires throughout the centuries. If you could read your mate's mind, you would know that she too was turned by me. If I had not done so, you would have never met her. I knew of your search for me, and I came willingly to this tavern to meet you face to face. I ask you to forgive me and let this bargain be made between us. I believe it is fair and an even trade. Do you agree?"

As Balgair withdrew his hand, he could feel his body relax. The chance to find the vampire that killed his family far outweighed his crime against Lara. Lara still lived, but his family was brutally taken from him and rested in their cold graves.

"Yes, I will accept your bargain," he declared, after silently pondering the vampire's proposal. "Wait! How do I know that you speak the truth?"

"Let me prove it to you," he said, as he placed his hands on either side of Thomas' head.

At first, his mind gave him nothing but darkness, but slowly, a vision unfolded before him. The cottage that he once called home came into view. A painful vision of their brutal deaths was revealed to him. A tall man with long black hair stood watching the flames eat away at the thatched roof, and the black smoke billow into the sky. As he turned around to leave, Thomas saw his face. A face he would never forget. As the vision faded, he felt a tear run across his cheek.

Balgair removed his hands from his head and waited for Thomas to respond.

"What is his name?" growled Thomas. "What is the murderer's name?"

"His name is Francisco, but he is known to most as Franco," he replied. "I have felt his presence on this island. I believe that he is still here."

"Is he powerful?" asked Elda. "Will we need the help from a witch to subdue him?"

"He is not so strong that a witch is needed," he replied. "Fire or a blade to the heart will be all that is needed to end this vampire. Have you any more questions?"

Thomas looked at Elda and saw her shrug her shoulders.

"It appears we are finished and I will take my leave," announced Balgair.

He politely nodded to Elda and vanished. Nothing remained but a silver mist that gently settled to the floor.

"Let's get out of here," blurted Thomas. "I need to feel the cool air upon my face. I need to hold Lara in my arms."

Elda replaced her dagger and caught sight of the woman they had seen earlier. She held tightly to the wooden bannister with a strange look upon her face. Not wanting to be left behind, Elda forgot about the woman and hurried after Thomas.

The woman had heard everything the silver-haired man had said and saw him vanish. She rubbed her hands over her arms trying to remove the sudden chill and quickly grabbed the bannister to keep herself from falling. Putting one foot in front of the other, she slowly made her way down the stairs and toward the tavern door. She never heard the men whistle for her attention as she opened the door and stepped out into the thick fog. Forgetting to close the door behind her, she kept walking until she felt the damp tall grass beneath her feet. Stopping, she looked down at the wet hem of her skirt, and lifted her hand to her throat. She felt panic as the red smoke swirled around her body. As she vanished, his bitter name crept from her lips, "Franco".

* * *

She sat in the darkness of her bedchamber reliving every detail of the day she met Franco at Black Thistle Castle. He was a tall mysterious stranger dressed in black, and she was a mischievous young woman drawn to the thistles and ruins of Black Thistle Castle. She had played a foolish game of pretend that afternoon that led to her turning and the loss of her virginity. For his betrayal, she made a vow to give him his final death. She had the means to give him a gruesome death, and if she found him, she would see that it was a slow gruesome death.

Her excitement over Franco's death caused a fire to rage in her throat calling for the taste of blood and the thrill of torture. She knew it would be unwise of her to entertain the men in the castle's army or the dungeon. Lord Seth would undoubtedly object to her wicked addiction with someone other than himself. The taverns were her only option. While fulfilling her desire for blood, she would be able to hunt for Franco. If she found him, she would stoke the flames that they once shared and surprise him with his final death. Pleased with herself, she leaned back against her pillows.

Fantasizing about all she would do to the vampire, she didn't hear her door open. Seth stood at the foot of her bed before she realized he had entered her chamber.

"What has you so distracted?" his booming voice startled her.

"Why, thoughts of you, My Lord," she quickly responded, diverting her attention to the vampire that stood before her.

"I found your chamber empty this evening. I have warned you about leaving without my approval," he barked.

"You know that I still desire the taste of human blood," she replied. "I simply left to feed and returned once I was sated."

"Do not test me, Magna," he snapped. "A trail of dead bodies leading to my door will not be tolerated. I have not shown any desire to threaten anyone on this island and none threaten me. I prefer to keep it that way."

"I drank from one willing sailor that will probably set sail tomorrow," she grinned. "My marks were healed, and he has forgotten all of it."

Seth stormed to the side of her bed and grabbed her throat before she had a chance to move. Lifting her from the bed, he stared deep into her eyes.

"Let me remind you of our bargain. I have agreed to allow you to stay within my castle. In exchange, your body belongs to me," he growled. "Do you understand?" He saw Magna's attempt to reply but heard nothing more than a grunt. "If I discover you have betrayed our agreement, I will rip the heart from your chest and throw your body to the dogs. What is left of you will scorch in the midday sun until you are nothing but ash. I still remember the night you betrayed me with the Captain on the Abigail Star. You are lucky I gave you another chance and did not give you your final death as you sat paralyzed in my dungeon. Had it not been for your quick action in saving my precious mermaid from the Captain's harpoon, I would have ended you."

Seth released her neck and backed away from the bed. Fangs descended, he watched her lift her wrist toward him.

"My Lord, take my blood. See the truth. I only took his blood," she choked out the words.

"The thought of it sickens me. I can no longer look at you," he muttered, as he turned and stormed from her chamber.

Magna collapsed upon her bed pillows grateful for his departure.

I must figure out a way to leave this castle and find Franco, she thought, as she rubbed her neck. I know, I'll invite Velsa here to create my thistle garden and make the needed bargain to hide my movements.

Happy with her plan, she decided a goblet of sweet berry wine and bread drenched in honey would calm her nerves.

"Claudia," she shouted.

Chapter 22

The whimsical music from the wooden flutes and people cheering were the first things Laralynn heard as she stepped from the cool shade of the trees. She anxiously looked about for her friends. As she ran toward the crowd searching for Nollie and Lettie, Baxter followed closely behind her.

"It is good to see a smile upon her face," Lara said. "I'm glad I decided to bring her back for a visit; however, I wish I could have brought her father. He would have enjoyed seeing her with her friends."

"We could have taken the horses, My Lady," Oliver replied. "I'm sure he would have enjoyed the festivities."

"I would have been forced to ride at night to protect myself from the sun's rays. My gift of flashing keeps me safe," she said, as she looked for a place to sit. She removed her cape and spread it across a thick layer of pine needles before seating herself. "The sun was not the only reason I decided to use my gift. I prefer not to spend too much time away from the castle since my sister still roams this island. The reach of Meadow's protection spell does not go much beyond the edge of Evergreen's forest. I have warned Baxter, and I do the same to you. Be alert. If you see the red smoke of my sister, guard Laralynn with your life."

"Always, My Lady," he fisted his hand over his chest.

"Now, find me an apple and one for yourself. I'm sure Lord Fallon has sent a wagon full of the juicy delights," she cheerfully demanded.

Oliver had only been gone a moment when she heard Aslev call her name.

"It is a pity the sun prevents you from partaking of the merry festivities," she teased.

"I have enough shade to keep me safe and a perfectly good view of those that entertain the crowd," she replied. Looking up at Aslev, she saw the frown upon her face. "I'm glad that you could come. Laralynn will be pleased to see you."

"It was for Laralynn and nothing more," she snapped. "I am anxious for her to visit me at my cottage."

"In time," Lara replied. "We have just arrived. Sit down. Give her time to enjoy her friends."

"I think I will mingle among the people for a while and listen to the gossip. It is a good day to walk in the sunshine," she chuckled, as she walked away.

* * *

Laralynn had found her friends standing in line at Lord Fallon's apple wagon. Their shrill screams of surprise pierced the ears of many that stood around them. Giggling and grabbing their apples, they dashed off to find Ian and Hazel. As they entered the market, a young woman was standing at the counter filling her basket.

"Laralynn! Oh Laralynn! I have missed you," Hazel cried, as she scurried around the counter and threw her arms around her giving her a tight hug. "Is Lady Lara with you?"

"Yes, she is sitting in the shade. I will tell her you asked of her," she replied.

"There is no need, I will go find her myself," she said, as she headed toward the open door. "I won't be long. Close the door when you leave."

Looking back at the young woman that now faced her grinning, she immediately recognized her.

"Astra," she called. "It is so good to see you. Come meet my friends."

"Lady Laralynn," she replied and made a small curtsey.

"Please, there is no need for that," she replied, as she put her arm through hers. "I am here to enjoy my friends. I want to be just like everyone else, today."

Nollie and Lettie stood holding hands as they waited for Laralynn and Astra to join them.

"Astra, this is Nollie and her sister Lettie. They are my dearest friends. I grew up with them. We rarely went a day without spending time together or getting in trouble," she giggled. "We are like sisters."

"It is very nice to meet you," Astra smiled, as she extended her hand.

"It is nice to meet you too," Nollie replied. "I don't believe that I have seen you in the village. Do you live here in Primrose Pond?"

"My cottage is at the end of the dirt road that leads south away from the village. You can see it from the road. It is a small cottage just beyond the shelter of the trees," she explained. "You must come for a visit. I have been a little lonely since arriving. It would be nice to have someone join me for a cup of tea and a little conversation."

"Lettie and I would like that very much," she replied. "We'll bring the honey for your tea. We have a hive that is doing quite well."

"Astra, it has been awhile since you visited us at Evergreen" she said. "Come see my mother. I'm sure she would like to see you again."

"Of course," she replied.

The young women exited the market and closed the door as Hazel had requested. Stepping down from the porch, they headed toward the shade of the trees. Baxter stood close enough to watch Laralynn but far enough away to give her privacy with her friends. He was pleased to see Astra until he realized they were heading straight for Oliver. Baxter quickly dodged between several people milling around the platform and took his place beside Oliver. Hazel and Lady Lara were just saying their good-byes when the young women approached, and he could see the surprise on Oliver's face when he noticed Astra.

"Mother, look who I found," Laralynn pointed to Astra, Nollie and Lettie.

"Girls, how lovely to see you again," she said, as she took the time to kiss each of them upon the forehead. "How is your mother? I miss her company."

"She is well. She sits with Beatrix today. Her child is due most any time," Nollie said. "It will be my turn to sit with her tomorrow if the child has not arrived."

"If I can be of any help, you need only ask," offered Lara.

"It should be an easy birth. This will make six young ones," she replied.

Baxter looked over at Oliver and saw him clenching his fists. He watched him slowly move his right hand around to rest upon his lower back. The mark upon his hand was glowing, and he suddenly flinched as he heard Astra call his name.

"Astra, are you enjoying your new home and the people of Primrose?" he asked, trying to control himself and sound unfazed by her presence.

"It has been an adjustment but a welcomed one. Anywhere away from that mountain is good enough for me," she declared. "Sleeping in a soft bed has been a delightful experience."

Oliver felt his hand getting warmer and noticed Astra rubbing the palm of her hand against her skirt. He knew he had to speak to her about the mark upon his hand, but the thought of it terrified him. Trying to get up the courage, he fidgeted his weight from one leg to another. Finally, he decided he had to do it.

"My Lady, would it offend you if I spoke privately with Astra?" he asked.

"Of course not, Oliver," she replied.

"Astra, might I . . . might I have a word with you?" he stuttered.

Oliver could hear the girls giggling as they all looked at Astra for her reply.

Confused, Astra agreed and followed Oliver to a cluster of large rocks far enough away from everyone to allow for a private conversation. Astra seated herself and looked up at Oliver. She could tell something was wrong, but she had no idea what he wanted to say to her.

"I don't really know how to say this . . . so . . . I'll just come out with it," he said. "Last we met, do you remember shaking my hand?" He saw her nod her head and smile.

Why did she have to have such a beautiful smile, he thought?

"After you left the Command Center, I noticed something strange. A mark was left upon my hand."

He pulled his hand from behind his back and presented the glowing mark upon his palm for her to see.

Astra drew her hand to her mouth and gasped. Tears began to fall from her eyes as she wrapped her arms around her body trying to stop the shaking. Not knowing what else to do, Oliver knelt down to try and comfort her. He reached for her hand and placed it in his open palm, covering it with his own.

"Hush," he whispered. "There is no need to cry."

Feeling a sudden warmth radiating from her hand, he turned her hand over to find a glowing mark. Holding out his hand next to hers, the mark he saw was a mirror image of his own.

"It can't be! It's you, Oliver? You are my intended one?" she cried.

"I don't know if I should be relieved that you are upset or insulted that my ego has been wounded," he laughed, trying to ease the tension.

"It was not my doing. You must believe me," she tried to reassure him. "It just happened. I was not the cause of it."

"I believe you. Now, how do we fix this? How do we undo this curse?" he searched her eyes for an answer. "There must be a way."

"Oliver, I can't undo it," she sniffled. "This mark only appears when you have found your intended mate. It will not allow you to change your destiny."

"Well, I have already found that out," he shrugged. "It stopped me as I was about to climb the stairs at the tavern. I have been quite friendly with a lass in Echo Bluff. She saw the mark, knew what it meant, and backed away from me. It broke her heart."

"What?" she blurted, feeling a sudden twinge of jealousy. "I don't care to hear about your broken-hearted lass or what you were about to do in the tavern."

"Astra, are you jealous?" he smirked. "You are quite beautiful with your cheeks flushed and a hint of fire in your eyes."

"You think I'm beautiful?" she softly asked. "No one has ever told me that I'm beautiful."

"I pride myself in judging the beauty of a lass, and I find you very beautiful," he said, not ashamed in the least that he sounded as though he was bragging.

Astra lowered her face and closed her eyes. His words pulled at her heart and kept her from thinking clearly. She suddenly felt extremely tired.

"Oliver, please forgive me, but I would like to return to my cottage. I find that I am very tired and need to rest," she said, as she looked up to see disappointment on his face. "We have both learned much today."

Oliver stood and took Astra's hands to help her stand. She was a wee thing, and he towered over her.

"Might I see you safely to your cottage," he asked.

"I would like that," she replied. "After all, you did pledge your service for my protection."

Oliver placed her hand upon his arm, and they slowly made their way to the path that led to her cottage.

* * *

Everyone stood watching Oliver kneeling before Astra. It was obvious she was crying, and Oliver was trying to comfort her. Baxter feared the worst but was the most surprised to see Oliver leading Astra toward her cottage.

"They like each other," Laralynn said, as she bounced on her toes.

"Let's not draw any conclusions," her mother replied. "They need to get to know each other. Don't forget that Astra has just returned from her imprisonment on the mountain. She may not be ready to accept Oliver."

"I didn't think Oliver was ready to accept Astra," added Baxter. "It appears he has changed his mind."

"What is everyone looking at?" asked Aslev, as she looked in the direction of their stares.

Hearing Aslev's voice, Laralynn turned and threw her arms around her waist causing Aslev to take a few steps backward to keep from falling over.

"Oh, I have missed you," she sighed. "I'm so glad that you are here."

"I have missed you too," she whispered, as she leaned down to kiss the top of her head. "You must come to my cottage and visit me. I'm sure your mother will allow it."

"Aslev, I would love to visit you," she said. "I have so much to tell you."

"I don't want to interrupt your time with your friends," she said, as she smiled at Nollie and Lettie. "Go! Enjoy your day at the festival. You can visit me another day. Have your mother bring you to my cottage. She knows the way."

"I would be happy to bring Laralynn for a visit," Lara replied. "We will make a visit once the festival is over."

"I will be expecting you," she declared. "We can have clover tea with some warm teacakes. Now, go enjoy the music. They are about to throw the ribbons. I'm sure you want to catch a few of them."

"It was nice to see you, Aslev," Laralynn replied. "I will see you again soon!"

The girls waved their good-byes and ran for the village square.

"Don't let me down," Aslev cautioned. "Lady Lara, I will expect you soon."

Before Lara could respond, Aslev vanished.

"My Lady, I sense trouble," Baxter warned.

"So do I, so do I" Lara replied.

* * *

Velsa hid behind a tree and waited until Astra entered her cottage and Oliver was well down the road before she made her way to Astra's cottage door. She could feel the magic barrier and knew that she wouldn't be able to enter without Astra's consent. Her sister had managed to conceal her escape from the mountain and from the voices on the wind that had kept her informed of such matters. By that feat alone, it was clear her magic had returned, and it was strong. It was much stronger. Frustrated that she had been kept in the dark about her sister's return, she gently knocked on the door and waited to see the stunned look upon Astra's face.

"Oliver, is that you?" she called, as she approached the door. "Did you forget to tell me something?"

"I'm afraid not, my dear," she snickered. "It is your loving sister."

Astra froze at the sound of her sister's voice. She hadn't heard that voice since the night she had cursed her to the mountain. Her hands began to shake, and she wanted to scream for help until something inside of her calmed her down. It was as if a warm embrace had given her body and mind the comfort she needed. Making her way to the door, she opened it and stared at the woman that had ruined her life.

"What brings you to my door?" she calmly asked. "Have you no one else to bother?"

"I wanted to welcome you to Primrose Pond," she replied, as she tried to fake a smile. "I would have come sooner, but you didn't let me know that you had returned."

"I wanted to quietly settle into the village and have time to forget my time on the mountain. I seem to recall that we didn't part on good terms. Advising you of my return seemed a little foolish," she explained.

"What you did was foolish. That foolish deed put yourself upon the mountain," she snapped. "I am here to warn you to stay out of my way. Do not interfere in my relationship with Laralynn or anyone else. If you do, you will find yourself back on the mountain without a way to escape."

"I will stay out of your way . . . if you stay out of mine and those I care about," she firmly stated and slammed the door.

She heard Velsa mumbling to herself and waited for some kind of retaliation, but it never came. Proud of herself for standing up to her sister, she plopped down in her chair and took a deep breath. Closing her eyes to calm her nerves, her mind wandered back to her walk with Oliver.

"Oh Oliver, you are a delightful surprise," she whispered. "A delightful surprise."

* * *

The last day of the festival had ended and Laralynn bid her dear friends good-bye with an invitation to come visit her at Evergreen Castle.

"Don't stay away so long. Come visit us. We'll all go have tea with Astra," Nollie said through tear filled eyes. "I will miss you."

"We still haven't found the fairies at the pond. We'll need your help," Lettie reminded her. "You'll have to come back for a visit."

"I'll come back soon," she sniffled, trying to hold back the tears. "We'll do all the things we use to do."

She hugged them one more time and took her place next to her mother. As Oliver headed toward the path, she waved good-bye one last time. Following behind her mother, she turned to see Baxter step in behind her. After they had moved well within the cover of the trees, Lara asked for everyone to stop.

"I made a promise to Aslev that I would bring Laralynn for a visit," she announced, as she looked at Baxter and Oliver. "It would be wise if you stayed near. Now that we know Magna has been seen in the forest, she could be anywhere. Please stay clear of Aslev's cottage. Now, join hands. It is too far to walk."

Reappearing in a thick cluster of trees, Laralynn quickly looked for her cottage. Finding nothing but hollow tree trunks and bushes with sharp thorns, she feared her mother had brought her to the wrong place.

"Velsa, I have brought my daughter for a visit," she sent her voice to *Velsa's door.*

Hearing Lady Lara's voice, Velsa looked about her cottage. It was in its usual state with clutter piled everywhere. She quickly snapped her fingers and hid the clutter. With a wave of her arm, a hand-braided rug now covered the floor, a small table with chairs were dressed with a vase full of wildflowers, and her cot was covered with a linen cushion stuffed with feathers. With the clap of her hands, the herbs and bones that hung from the ceiling were gone, a small fire crackled in the hearth, and a pan of teacakes steamed in the pot over the fire. Ridding herself of her old tattered black dress, she conjured a brown woolen dress and crisp linen apron. Tying the end of her braid, she readied herself to great Laralynn and let her cottage be known.

"I see something through the trees," shouted Laralynn. "Is that her cottage?"

Seeing her mother nod, Laralynn ran to the door and raised her hand to knock. Before her hand could touch the door, Aslev pulled the door open.

"What a wonderful surprise," she laughed, beckoning Laralynn inside. "You are just in time. I am ready to take the steamed teacakes from the hearth."

She looked at Lady Lara and over her shoulder to see that Baxter and Oliver stood near the trees. Frowning, she stepped back to allow her to enter.

"I thought it best to bring an escort," she whispered. "It is Magna that I fear not you."

Aslev raised a brow and shook her head as she made her way to the cooking pot.

"Please sit down and make yourself comfortable. Laralynn, tell me all about living at Evergreen," she begged. "It must be so different from living in the cottage you shared with your mother."

"It is much different, but I have learned so many different things," she said, as she inhaled the sweet aroma coming from the cooking pot. "I've learned to wield a dagger, and Baxter has taught me the bow. I have danced with my father, which was wonderful. Lord Hamish of Cumberland Castle brought me a gift of a beautiful grey mare that I named Starlight. I have learned to feed, groom, and ride her. Mother still insists that I have an escort when I ride."

"You have been busy," she replied, as she placed the pan of teacakes on the table. "What has been your favorite thing?"

"It has to be meeting the Wispet Queen. She was so beautiful," she replied. "My mother took me to the Room of Powers to see her. It was magical."

"What did you discover?" she asked, as she glared at Lady Lara.

"I was gifted with Flashing, Healing Hands, Hands of Truth, Air and Water, and Speaking with Animals," she grinned. "Isn't it amazing? I haven't tried Hands of Truth. Would you like to try it with me?"

"Why not try it with your mother after our treat?" she laughed. "Our teacakes are going to get cold if we don't eat them."

Aslev diverted the conversation to simpler things while they drank clover tea with honey and ate the sweet teacakes. She had learned much from this visit, enough to know Laralynn could be a threat to her plans. She had to be very careful when their hands touched. Hands of Truth could give her identity away and possibly her desire to take Kayleigh's tail.

All in all, it was an enjoyable visit. Aslev walked to the door and bid them good-bye. She stood at the door and waved until they had gone from sight. Chills ran down her spine as she thought of Laralynn's gifts.

Stay clear of the young girl's hands, she reminded herself. They are full of danger.

Chapter 23

Magna stood before Lord Seth and anxiously waited for his answer. It frustrated her that she had to ask permission to leave the castle. Having to ask permission was almost worse than her imprisonment at Black Thistle Castle. If she had her way, she would be the ruler of Crimson Claw Castle, have free-rein with the prisoners in the dungeon, and he would feel the wrath of her claws.

"I told you I would allow a small patch of thistles. Go and bring back the witch," he said in a dismissive tone. "I am quite curious to meet the witch that won the War of the Witches and destroyed Black Thistle Castle. I'd like to know if the woman is as magnificent as the tale." Seeing that she had not moved, he waved his hand toward the door. "Be off with you. I have more important matters to occupy my time."

She vanished before he could change his mind and appeared in the forest near where she believed Velsa's cottage to be located. Looking about for any sign of it, she chewed on her bottom lip until the taste of her own blood swirled over her tongue. She was starting to hate the way Seth treated her and how one simple phrase could make her jealous.

Wait until he sees Velsa, she thought. Magnificent? Phffft! That ugly cow. He'll be surprised.

"Velsa, for the love of the stars in the night's sky, where have you put your dreadful little cottage?" she shouted. "I'm walking in circles."

She suddenly felt something or someone grab her arms, secure them tightly to her side, and force her body forward. She streaked through the trees swerving at the very last moment to avoid the low branches of the thick forest or the moss covered boulders. Unable to break from its tight hold or stop her movement, she feared she would be impaled upon the sharp point of a broken branch or smashed against a sturdy tree trunk. Seeing the cottage door racing toward her, she shrieked for mercy and immediately stopped before smashing head first into its door. She felt her arm raise and her hand bang against the door. The door swung open, and she was forced inside.

"My dreadful little cottage," snapped Velsa, as she lifted her hand and pointed her finger toward Magna. "Surely you were not speaking of my cottage."

Magna forced a smile and tried not to appear intimidated by the witch.

"I've come . . . I've come to invite you to Crimson Claw Castle," she nervously choked out the words. "I miss my dear thistles, and I was hoping that you would come to the castle and create a patch of them for me." Before Velsa could respond with a fist full of sparks, Magna quickly continued. "Wait! There is more. Lord Seth would like to meet you. He has invited you to the castle."

As she lowered her hand, a curious grin spread across Velsa's face. It had been some time since anyone had invited her to meet the lord of a castle. She felt a slight flush cover her face and a parched feeling in her throat.

"I accept the invitation," she replied. "If I find the meeting pleasurable, I will forego the need to make a bargain with you for the creation of your dear thistles. They will simply be my gift to you."

She felt the moment she was released from Velsa's hold. Her arms relaxed, and she shook her hands to get the feeling back in them.

"You nearly killed me out there," she whined. "Why don't you leave your cottage in plain sight?"

"I don't care for uninvited guests," she snapped.

Magna's hair fluttered around her face as a slight breeze entered through the open door. Pulling the strands down away from her eyes, she noticed the sudden movement of Velsa's eyes toward the door. She could feel a streak of cold air running down her back, and it made her shiver. Slowly she turned to face the door. Standing in the doorway was a tall man dressed in black.

"Ladies, you left the door open," he smirked. "You must be more cautious. You never know what evil will take advantage of an open door."

Immediately purple sparks filled the room.

"Now, now," he calmly stated, as he raised his hand to deflect them. "There is no need for this colorful display of aggression. I simply came for a visit. Who wouldn't want to visit two lovely ladies?"

"Why would I allow you to enter through my door? We have never met," Velsa shouted. "You best leave before I turn you into a scrawny rat and squash you with the heel of my boot."

"There is no need for that, my dear. Magna and I are old friends," he explained, as he watched the strained expression on her face. "Maybe I should rephrase that statement. Magna and I are intimate friends. You see, I was her first. It was wickedly delightful."

Magna knew him the moment she turned around. She clenched her teeth to keep from screaming. Holding her fisted hands behind her back, she tried to calm herself. Her search was over. Franco stood right in front of her. She had to stay calm and follow her plan. She needed to make him want her again.

"Magna," barked Velsa. "Magna, is this true? Do you know this vampire?"

"Yes," she replied, never turning around and keeping her eyes locked on his. "We secretly made vows to one another in the dungeon of Black Thistle Castle. It was only a game. A game that resulted in my turning and the loss of my virginity."

"A minor detail," he chuckled. "I find my indiscretion has made you even more beautiful."

Feeling the moment was right to capture his attention, she took a step toward him.

"It gave me a life filled with the lust for blood and passion," she said, as she drew her hand over his arm. "Had you not turned me, I would be dead and buried. This meeting would have never taken place."

Franco inhaled the scent of smoldering coals and felt his fangs descend.

"Your timing could not be worse," Velsa blurted, trying to gain their attention. "Magna and I were on our way to Crimson Claw Castle."

"That is true," Magna replied. "Franco, can we meet another time and place?"

She could see his disappointment and waited for his reply.

"If you must," he whispered. "If you must."

"I frequent Hunter's Point and Echo Bluff. I'm sure I will see you again, but we must leave for the castle. Lord Seth is expecting us," she declared.

She noticed his eyes turn black once she mentioned Seth's name and wondered if they had a history. Franco slowly backed toward the door and bent slightly at the waist.

"Until another time," he said. "Do not make me wait too long, or I will come for you."

He was gone as silently as he had arrived.

Turning toward Velsa, she saw that she had completely forgotten Franco. She had changed her appearance and dressed for the occasion of meeting the lord of the castle.

"Shall we go?" she asked, as she offered Magna her hand.

Magna nodded and took her hand. She could hear the door slam just before they vanished.

* * *

As they reappeared in the Great Hall, Velsa fell to the floor with her feet tangled in the heavy layers of her gown. It was all Magna could do to keep from laughing at her vulgar shrieks of anger and her flailing arms.

The sound of hurried footsteps was followed by the sudden outstretched hand to assist Velsa to her feet.

"Are you hurt?" Seth asked with concern.

"Nothing more than my pride," she replied, as she adjusted the thin strips of satin at her shoulders. "Thank you for your assistance. It is rare to find a lord that is kind and a gentleman."

Magna wanted to gag as she listened to Velsa's sickening chatter.

"Welcome to Crimson Claw Castle," he declared with a quick bow. "I have heard many stories of the witch that won the War of the Witches. It is an honor to finally meet you."

Lifting her chin, Velsa accepted the praise Lord Seth bestowed upon her. Holding out her hand, she eagerly waited for his lips to meet the back of her hand. Feeling him take her hand in his, she gasped as the heat of his lips brushed against her skin.

"Magna, would you ask Claudia to bring us sweet wine and figs soaked in honey. We will take them in my private courtyard," he said, without looking at Magna. "I find I would like a private account of the tales told by the witch herself. You are free to roam the island to your heart's content while I entertain our visitor."

Magna stormed from the Great Hall in search of Claudia. Furious with his demand, she muttered under her breath until she realized he had given her the freedom to leave the castle. With a sudden shift in her demeanor, Magna began to whistle as her thoughts of finding Franco swirled about in her mind.

* * *

This was the third night in a row that Lord Seth had entertained Velsa and allowed her the freedom to take her leave of the castle. Magna sat at a small corner table close to the door of the tavern. She had eagerly watched the door every time it opened in hopes of seeing Franco. If he didn't arrive soon, she would have to track him down.

A rowdy bunch of heavily bearded men had filled the tavern with the smell of musk and billowing smoke from their pipes. A few of them, along with a few brave women, danced merrily to the music that rang from the musicians' instruments. Magna was fascinated by the sound coming from the Rebec's strings and the man that played it. As he swayed from side to side with the rhythm of his bow against the strings, he would wink or wiggle his eyebrows to draw her attention.

Just as the round finished and he stepped from the small stage advancing toward her, the door to the tavern opened. She gave the man a brief glance and returned her sights back on the friendly musician.

"Magna, have you been waiting long?" a familiar deep voice made her gasp.

She stood frozen in place as he took her hand and raised it to his cold lips.

"You startled me," she replied, trying to regain her composure. "I had given up hope of seeing you again."

"I am sure that I can convince you that I was worth the time you spent sitting in the corner of this tavern," he grinned. "Have you a room? I believe what I have in mind requires a certain amount of privacy. Since there is no dungeon beneath this tavern, a room would be required."

"You are very bold, Franco," she laughed. "I am not as easily persuaded as I was so long ago."

"Really, I was sure I caught the scent of arousal," he countered. "Was I mistaken?"

Ignoring his response, Magna sat down and raised her hand to offer Franco a seat beside her. She wasn't eager to have his fangs in her neck until she knew more about him.

"Obviously, you don't frequent Alltree Island, or I would have seen you before now," she said. "Even though, you did keep yourself hidden from me during our last encounter in the forest."

"No, I don't care for the voyage I must take across the ocean," he replied. "The confinement and rough water do not agree with me. I have found that the ways of the women in France are more to my liking. Have you sailed the ocean to distant lands?"

"I agree with you. The confinement in the small quarters that are provided for a voyage are not to my liking," she sighed. "Unless . . . unless an agreeable passenger sees fit to share them and their blood."

Franco stood and made his way to the bar. She saw him throw a few coins on the shiny surface and retrieve a key from the barkeeper. He made his way to the foot of the stairs and turned to look at Magna. He gave her an inviting nod and headed up the stairs. It was all Magna could do to keep from laughing. With very little encouragement, she had Franco right where she wanted him. Feeling her claws starting to extend, she stood and hurried after him. After all, a stake through the heart while lying in bed was a much better story than offering him a final death at the foot of a pine tree.

As she stepped on the landing at the top of the stairs, she saw him leaning against an open doorway with his arms crossed over his chest and wearing an arrogant grin. Hiding her claws behind her back, she swayed her hips as she moved toward him. His nostrils flared as he inhaled her scent of smoldering coals and stepped back allowing her to enter his room.

"I am glad that you have decided to join me," he smirked, as he closed the door.

"If you had arrived a moment later, you would have found me in the arms of another," she laughed, forcing her claws to retract.

"I have not even been gone a century, and already, I find you seeking the affections of someone else," he huffed. "Do you not remember that we declared our love for one another in the dungeon at your beloved castle."

"I seem to recall that I woke after losing my virginity to find myself abandoned and in an awful state," she replied. "It seems only natural that I would attempt to find another to replace you."

They paced in a circle like leery animals throwing numerous insults at each other until Franco grew tired of her games.

"Can we start again and forget my past transgressions? Your insults have pierced me to the core," he begged, as he playfully bent down on one knee. "Let's play a new game of pretend. To make up for my inappropriate behavior, I will let the lady choose."

Magna smiled and made her way to the bed. Undoing the end of her braid, she ran her fingers through her flaming red hair until it hung in waves beyond her knees. As she began to untie her corset, she noticed his eyes darken as he stood.

"There is a game I like to play," she said, as she dropped her corset on the floor. "It is Keeper of the Dungeon. I realize the setting is not to my liking, but as you know, I can pretend quite nicely."

"This sounds interesting," he hissed, moving toward her and taking hold of her arms.

"I am the dungeon's keeper and you will be my prisoner. Remove your tunic," she demanded. "You have wronged the mistress of the castle and deserve to be punished."

He laughed as he pulled his tunic over his head and threw it on the floor. He felt a slap across his face for his reward. Feeling his arousal strain against the laces of his breeches made him eager to press his mouth to hers. He grabbed her around the waist and pulled her against his body.

"I believe the prisoner has grand desires for his keeper," he whispered, before he forcefully claimed her mouth.

Magna reveled in his desire for her, and felt her claws extend once more. He invaded her mouth with his tongue, and she felt him drag his fangs against her bottom lip as he pulled back from her. She could feel the heat of desire racing uncontrollably through her body.

"You are no longer the innocent young girl I met at the castle," he teased. "I can feel your body pulsing with desire for me."

"I feel it too," she replied, as she felt her body quiver with excitement. "I have longed for your return."

She shook her head and tried to focus back on their game. Pushing him away, she straightened her back and threw back her shoulders.

"You have wronged your mistress, Franco. Are you brave enough to receive your punishment?" she snarled.

He forced himself not to laugh and then nodded his head as he spoke, "I ask for leniency and forgiveness from my mistress."

"Kneel before me, Franco. Your mistress has given me orders that I must not hesitate to fulfill," she sternly ordered.

Franco knelt and bowed his head while Magna moved to stand behind him.

"You are to receive two lashes," she barked.

He rested his hands on the floor in anticipation of his punishment.

Magna raised her arms and quickly raked her claws deep into the flesh of his back, one hand after another. He growled as he stood and turned to face her. Looking down at her hands, he saw her claws covered in his blood. Furious, he reached for her arms, but his hands only grabbed the swirling red tendrils of smoke that she had left behind.

"This is not the end of our games, Magna," he hissed. "If it is torture you desire, you shall have it."

Chapter 24

The table was stacked high with books. On one side were the books Desirae had gone through and on the other were what remained to be read. Every day since leaving Crimson Claw Castle, she had read everything she could find about the War of the Witches, and the strengths of the witches that perished in the war. She was surprised by how much had been written so many years ago.

Desirae and Alicia each carried several dusty leather bound books into the library. As they dropped them on the table, the sunlight pouring in the window offered a clear view of the dust billowing up into the air. It was as if the layer of dust had been protecting them until they could be found, and their mission was now complete.

"How do you think these books got inside the stone wall?" asked Alicia. "From the few passages you read, they were clearly written after the war of the witches ended and the castle was demolished."

Desirae ran her fingers over the edges of one of the leather covers. Carefully opening the book, she admired the flourishes of each hand written word upon the brittle parchment. Placing her hand upon the page, she could feel a connection to the witches that had perished. For a moment, she could feel the strength of her sister.

Derora, I miss you, and I promise I will avenge your death, she thought.

"I believe the witches that perished spelled these books to be filled as time passed," she replied, as she tried to hide a tear that slipped from her eye. "If only my sister could be here to tell us in person. Since she can't, we will have to draw our own conclusions to our discoveries."

"Do you think there could be more hidden books?" she asked, as she tried to rub the dust from her hands.

"If stones start falling from the walls, like they did in the Council Chamber, we are sure to find more books," she laughed. "Just take care where you walk."

Taking their seats at the table, they each took a book and began to read. Alicia faced the open door and missed seeing Killian standing guard outside in the hallway. In all their reading, they had not found anything that would allow Desirae or Gautier to break Killian from the stone that incased him. She was beginning to think he would never be free. As she thought of their short time together, she felt the comfort and hope offered by her wolf. It was a reminder to keep searching for an answer to bring Killian and his wolf back to them.

There is a loophole, somewhere, she thought. We just have to find it.

They silently read page after page until the dim light in the library caused Alicia to light the candles. The candlelight gave a warm amber glow to the book filled room.

"Desirae," Alicia whispered. "I need to rest my eyes and my mind. I've read the same few lines over and over again. I can't seem to focus to read the words."

"Go on my dear," she replied. "I think we both could use a rest."

Desirae blew out the candles and followed Alicia out of the library. After closing the door behind them, they headed down the hallway. At the far end of the hallway, they could see Lady Kayleigh approaching them.

"My Lady, is there something we can do for you?" asked Desirae.

"I was coming to bring you this book. A panel in the pantry fell to the floor, and Alicia's mother discovered this book wrapped in cloth," she said, as she handed it to Desirae. "It is curious don't you think?"

"Curious?" asked Alicia, as she looked at Lady Kayleigh for an explanation."

"Yes, almost every book has been found at a different location in the castle. This book in the pantry, others in the Council Chamber, a few others in the armory, and even one in the dungeon wall. Why so many different places?" she asked. "Why not all together?"

Desirae thought for a moment trying to make some sense of what Lady Kayleigh had said. It did seem strange that the books would be spread about the castle. Had the witches done that to prevent all of them ending up in the wrong hands? Had they randomly hidden the books without any forethought? Or, was there a meaning to the locations and the books within the locations?

"Come, let's return to the library," Desirae said, as she hurried down the hallway.

Opening the door, she snapped her fingers and the candles burst into flame. She viewed all of the books on the table and picked up a small stack.

"I want to remove all of the books from the table except the books that were discovered hidden in the walls," she stated, without explanation.

The women went to work carefully stacking the books in the corners of the library. What remained were thirteen books of different sizes. Without giving it another thought, Desirae stacked the books into four piles, one pile for each location. In the first, the only book found in the pantry. The next had two stacks of four books each from the Council Chamber. The third stack contained three books from the armory. At the far end of the table, the single book found in the dungeon sat alone.

"What do you think it means?" asked Alicia. "What do you think the witches were trying to tell us?"

"I don't know, Alicia," Desirae sighed. "I don't know, but we are going to figure this out."

The women sat around the table staring at the books. Occasionally, one of them would pick up a book, open it, and then close it before placing it back on the table.

As they all sat deep in thought, Alicia's voice startled them as she spoke, "I used to play a game with my mother. She called it, "What is the meaning"? She would say a word, and I would tell her what it meant to me. She might have said water, and I would have responded with wet or refreshing. Let's play that game."

"We don't have time for games, my dear," replied Desirae. "I know you are tired but concentrate on the book's words."

"Let's try it," encouraged Kayleigh. "We need a distraction, and maybe it will help."

"I will start with the word, pantry," Alicia said, as she waited to hear their responses.

"Storage," Desirae replied.

"Supplies," added Kayleigh.

"Supplies," Alicia repeated.

"Flour," laughed Desirae. "I don't see how this game will help us.

"Be patient," Kayleigh whispered. "Herbs!"

"Herbs," Alicia repeated.

"Sage," Desirae reluctantly contributed.

"Lavender," sighed Kayleigh. "I love lavender."

Uninterested in the game, Desirae picked up the book that had been found in the pantry and flipped it open. She gasped as she looked at the page before her.

"What is it?" Alicia asked, as she stood and walked around the table to stand beside Desirae. Seeing the drawing, she covered her mouth to keep herself from shrieking. "It's a drawing of lavender."

"Wispet Canyon was once full of the fragrant herb," offered Kayleigh.

Turning back to the first page of the book, Desirae began to read out loud from its pages. Kayleigh and Alicia listened to the dreadful account of the destruction of Wispet Canyon and all of its beautiful lavender. It was heartbreaking to hear of the banishment of the Wispet Queen and the other Wispets by Velsa's own hateful demanding words. Throughout the book, they stopped to examine beautiful drawings of the Wispet Queen, their small stone cottages, and the fields of lavender that once filled the canyon. Turning to the last page, what appeared to be a poem caught their attention. Desirae read it out loud for them.

> **Bring forth the hail and lightening.**
> **Bring forth the wind and fire.**
> **Demolish its purple beauty,**
> **that brought happiness and love.**
> **Take away all gifts of power.**
> **Take away the need for life.**
> **Let them dwell in utter obscurity,**
> **full of hatred and full of spite**

"What kind of poem is this?" asked Kayleigh. "It's hateful."

"This is the spell Velsa used to curse Wispet Canyon," declared Desirae.

"It must be very important or the witches wouldn't have included it in the book, but how can this spell help you?" asked Alicia.

"I'm not sure. I will show it to Lord Gautier. He is much more powerful than I am, and he might be able to reverse it," she replied.

Realizing that each book upon the table could hold some kind of importance, they each grabbed a book and started reading. It was clear the witches that perished on that dreadful day were doing their best to help Desirae avenge her sister. It would be up to Desirae to figure out how to do it, and Kayleigh and Alicia would help in any way they could. They had read all night and barely noticed the sun was starting to rise when the last book was closed.

"What have we learned," yawned Alicia. "I'm afraid I may have fallen asleep a few times before I finished the book from the dungeon."

"The best I can tell, the books that were found in the Council Chamber were all about power," Kayleigh replied. "They read more like journals that documented each of the witch's strengths. They all made a reference to each other and the importance of numbers to combat evil."

"What does that mean?" asked Alicia. "I still don't understand."

"I'm not certain," laughed Kayleigh. "Each witch died fighting Velsa, alone. It could mean we should band together. There are passages that give instructions to call for the help of the witches that have left this life."

"That makes sense," Desirae agreed. "In the books I read from the armory, the witches wrote about spells to combat evil."

"I'm still confused," Alicia shook her head. "We need to call the witches, create a spell to combat evil, and reverse the canyon spell. What does the dungeon have to do with any of this?"

"It was one of the only things that survived the War of the Witches," Kayleigh sighed. "It had to be strong enough to keep me hidden away from Gautier and my wolf. The dungeon and the hidden chamber were the only things that survived. The two places Velsa cursed our spirits to stay trapped alone."

"The stones are our strength, the witches are the power, the weapon is the spell we will create, and the lavender is what binds it all together," Desirae declared.

"How did you figure it all out?" asked Alicia.

"My sister, Derora, helped me," she smiled. "Let me show you. It was the last words in her journal. See . . . here it is."

Stones of strength and power of witches will be chanting the weapon bound with fragrant herbs.

"Now, we need the spell, and I know who can help us," she declared.

"Who?" asked Kayleigh and Alicia at the same time.

"Astra, Velsa's sister," she replied. "What better way to know Velsa than through her sister."

Chapter 25

Her leather vest and sleeve fit snuggly against her body after her father had secured the laces. As Laralynn brushed her fingertips over the laces under her arm, the memories of Baxter tightening her laces warmed her heart. She picked up her quiver of arrows and secured it over her shoulder. Two bows leaned against the short stone wall that bordered the steps to the Command Center. She waited until her father chose his before taking the remaining bow. This would be her first hunt with her father, and she was excited to have been asked to come along.

They had been following the tracks of a buck from early morning until the sun moved directly overhead. The forest provided the much needed shade, but it was still a stifling hot day. Laralynn could feel the dampness of her tunic beneath her vest and longed for a cool drink from a stream to quench her parched throat.

"Do you get the feeling we're walking in circles?" Laralynn whispered. "Is he trying to cover his tracks?"

"It seems that way. He appears to be leading us into a thicker crop of trees," replied Woodward. "He's looking for more protection from his surroundings."

Hearing the sound of branches rubbing against the base of a tree, Woodward raised his bow. Out waddled a flustered skunk after squeezing between a moss covered rock and the gnarled root of an aging tree. Cautiously backing up a few steps to give the worried creature room to maneuver, Laralynn took advantage of her gift and silently calmed his fears. They had no desire to tangle with a skunk. Relieved that the animal had not been more menacing, the trio continued on in search of the buck.

Seeing the sun move further toward setting and the shadows grow longer, they decided the buck had outsmarted all of them. They were about to end their search and head back to the castle when the buck charged Woodward rearing up striking his head and chest with his hooves and antlers. Before Thomas could raise his bow, the buck had vanished into the thick cover of the forest.

Woodward fell unconscious to the ground and bleeding from a large gash that ran from the center of his forehead to just beyond his ear. Blood was soaking his tunic, above and below the edge of his leather vest. Laralynn knelt down beside him and started untying the leather bindings. She carefully lifted it over the top of his head letting it rest on the ground above his head. Pulling a small dagger from her boot, she tore his tunic to expose his wound. His ribs had been broken and a bone was protruding through his chest. Laralynn looked up at her father unsure of what to do.

"If I flash him back to Evergreen, it may kill him," she cried. "What do I do, father?"

Thomas knelt down next to Woodward and took hold of his hand.

"Laralynn, stay calm. Remember, you have the gift of healing," he assured her. "Place your hand upon his wound. Your gift should heal him."

She carefully placed her hand over the protruding bone and closed her eyes. She focused her thoughts on stopping the bleeding. Try as she may, she could still feel his life's blood flowing under her palm.

"Father, his wound isn't healing. He is going to die," she

cried. Laralynn could feel the tears on her face and tried to wipe them with her hand. Looking at her father with a blood smeared face, she waited for instructions.

"Think back to healing the deer. How did you heal the deer?" he calmly asked.

"I stroked her side and poured water from my hand onto her broken leg," she replied.

"That's it! You need water to be able to heal him," he concluded. Taking his water vessel from his waist, he found it empty. Pressing his hand against Woodward's vessel, he cursed after finding it empty too.

"I drank the last of my water too," she said, shaking her head. "Is there water near?"

Thomas listened carefully for the sound of running water and searched with his vision to find the nearest source.

"There is a stream just beyond this clump of trees. I'll take our skins, fill them and return to you as soon as I can," he explained. "Do your best to stop the bleeding."

"Hurry, please hurry," she whimpered. "We can't let him die. What will Patrick do without a father?"

"I promise you, we won't let him die," he said, as he kissed the top of her head and ran into the forest.

Laralynn ripped the sleeve of her tunic free and pulled it from her arm. Wadding it up under her hand, she placed it on his chest to try and stop the bleeding. The cloth slowly began to fill with his blood. Hearing him make a strange gurgling sound, she cringed when she saw that his mouth was filling with blood. Turning his head to the side, she hoped that he would not choke on his own blood before she was able to heal him.

"Woodward, stay with me. Patrick needs you," she whispered.

She heard the snapping of twigs and looked up eager to see her father. Instead a man she had never seen before stepped from the trees. He was tall and very pale with long black hair. He tilted his head as he looked at her and then at Woodward.

"What do we have here?" he asked, as he sniffed the air and

stepped closer to Laralynn.

"He has been injured," she gasped at the coldness of his voice. "I can't stop the bleeding from his wound." She lifted the blood soaked fabric and showed the man Woodward's wound. Seeing the blood bubble up, she quickly covered it again. "I fear he will die if I can't stop the bleeding."

"He has lost a great deal of blood. So much so, it appears his life's blood is almost spent," he said, as he knelt beside her. "However, you are ripe for the picking."

"What?" she gasped, as she felt his finger rake against her skin from her bare shoulder to her elbow.

"You possess the delightful scent of fresh apples," he said, as he inhaled her scent again. "A delicate fragrance that I find very appealing."

Laralynn could feel the hairs on the back of her neck stand on end, and she knew she was in danger. She tried to remember all of the tricks Elda had taught her and how she could outsmart the man next to her.

"Outsmart me? I am older and smarter than you," he smirked. "You are but a delicate flower that can be snapped from the vine with a flick of my wrist."

Without waiting a moment more, she snatched her dagger and flashed a few feet away from Woodward and the stranger. She stood with her feet spread waiting for his attack.

"I see that I have misjudged you," he laughed, as he stood and stepped over Woodward onto the blood soaked ground. "A human with gifts stands before me. You have made the game much more interesting."

"Come near me and I will put an end to you," she blurted through clenched teeth, remembering to put fear in her enemy.

"You are very brave for a young woman," he said, as he rested his hand upon the hilt of his dagger. "Is this a game of pretend? Is this like the game of pretend Magna played? Are you waiting for me to charm you?"

"What of Magna?" she asked, as the story her mother had told her of the stranger that had turned her sister fleeted through her mind. "You are the demon that turned my mother's sister. For that crime, you will pay with your life."

His laughing caught her off guard. The next thing she knew; she could feel his breath upon her neck. He scraped his fangs against her skin causing droplets of blood to run toward the waiting tip of his tongue. As he began to lick the blood from her neck, Laralynn heard a ferocious growl just before she was knocked to the ground. She saw the flash of her father's dagger as he pushed the stranger away from her and onto the ground. The horrible sound of blade against bone and cries of pain filled the air, and then there was silence.

Laralynn crawled to her father's still body. As she tried to pull him back away from the stranger, she could see her father's dagger had penetrated the stranger's heart. Looking down at her father, she gasped when she saw the stranger's dagger lodged in his chest. Pulling it free, blood poured from the wound.

"Wake up, father," she cried. "You have to wake up. Please don't leave me."

"You killed him," Magna shouted, startling Laralynn. "You killed Franco. You had no right to kill him. He was not yours to kill."

As she walked toward Franco's body, Laralynn scooted backwards away from her and her father. After hearing the stories of what Magna was capable of, she wanted no part of her. She cautiously stood trying not to draw attention to herself as she watched Magna lean over the stranger she called Franco and brush the hair from his face.

One cautious step at a time, she crept back toward Woodward. She knelt down and put her ear to his mouth. He was still breathing but barely. Did she dare flash with him back to Evergreen? If she did, the movement could kill him. Torn with staying with her father or trying to save Woodward, she gripped Woodward's hand and prepared to flash. She could hear Magna mumbling but couldn't make out what she was saying. Looking up to see if she was still hovered over the stranger and her father, she saw her turn her head to look at her. Her eyes were red and the scent of smoldering coals filled the air.

As she slowly stood and looked down at Laralynn, she shrieked, "Laralynn . . . you are going to pay for this. I am going to take your life in payment for what you have done to Franco."

Magna pointed back to Franco with the tip of the bloody dagger she had pulled from his chest and then pointed it at Laralynn.

Knowing she had to get away, she tried to flash, but she couldn't move.

"I have a few gifts of my own, dear niece," she laughed, as she lifted her arm. "Stand up and prepare to meet your end."

Laralynn had her hands over her ears and tried to shut the words out of her mind, but it was useless. Magna's power was too strong and forced her to obey. She slowly stood and watched Magna walking toward her. Standing face to face, the strong scent of smoldering coals burned her nose and throat. The color of Magna's eyes changed from red to black. Red tendrils of smoke began to swirl about Laralynn's legs, and it burned everywhere it touched her skin.

"Now, you are all mine," she hissed. "Not to worry, I shall make your death fun before I deliver your body back to my sister."

As the red smoke swirled up about their heads, Magna dropped the bloody dagger and raised her hand to take hold of Laralynn's arm. She smiled and ran her tongue over her descended fangs enjoying the fear she saw in Laralynn's eyes. The look of satisfaction suddenly changed to a look of pure horror as Magna's shoulders jerked, and her eyes bulged with a look of severe pain. Her body began to wither before she slumped to the ground.

Laralynn watched her fall, and when she looked up, she saw an old woman before she saw the blood dripping from the lifeless heart she held in her hand.

"You are free, child," the old woman softly said. "She can no longer hurt you."

The old woman dropped Magna's heart to the ground, repeatedly crushing it with the heel of her boot, and turned to walk away without saying a word.

"Wait! Please, wait!" Laralynn cried out after her. "Who are you? I must thank you for saving my life."

"There is no need, my child," she said, without turning around "A promise made is a promise kept."

Laralynn ran to her father and took the water skin he had tied at his hip. She pulled the bit of leather from the opening and tipped it up until the water flowed onto the palm of her hand. Pouring the water from her hand onto the wound, she watched as it slowly began to heal. Not waiting to see if he opened his eyes, she ran to Woodward and poured the water from her hand onto his wounds. She was pleased to see his forehead healed quickly; however, the wound on his chest did not change. She poured more water from her hand, and this time, she saw the wound beginning to heal.

Relieved and exhausted, she moved away from the bodies that littered the ground. She felt a tightness in her chest and tried to take one deep breath after another. Desperate for air, she tore at the laces until she freed herself from her vest. Flinging it to the ground she felt her lungs heave unsuccessfully for a breath of air. As she fell to the ground, she heard herself call out Baxter's name before the darkness took her.

* * *

Velsa had heard Laralynn's fear as clearly as if it had been her own. It swept her from Seth's bedchamber and into the clearing to stand behind Magna. With the red smoke filling the air, she could feel Laralynn's pain as it burned her delicate skin. Magna's threatening words of death sealed her fate, and the blood promise forced her to take Magna's heart. The smoldering stench of Magna's blood invaded her senses as it dripped from her fingers. Dropping the lifeless heart to the ground, she gathered up her skirt with her clean hand revealing the pointed toe of her boot. Lifting her foot, she forced the heel of her boot into the center of the heart, over and over again, until it was beyond recognition.

Velsa turned and started to walk from the clearing without looking back as she tried to block out Laralynn's cries for her to stop. She wanted to stop. She wanted to stop and cradle that precious child in her arms. The bloody scene she left behind demanded her to stop, but she needed to keep this side of herself hidden from her.

Keep walking, she thought. I must not let her touch me. The truth will all unravel before her eyes if those gifted hands touch me.

She kept walking until she could no longer hear her. Taking shelter within the quiet of the cool forest, she shed a single tear for Magna and then she vanished.

Reappearing in her cottage, Velsa slammed her hand against her door, leaving a bloody handprint. Her body began to ache as she breathed in Magna's scent. Desperate to get away from it, she began ripping at her clothes until she stood naked with bits of shredded cloth scattered at her feet. Stumbling about her cottage trying to get away from what she had done, Velsa began filling her washtub with scalding water. As she lowered her body down into the steaming tub, she muffled her screams with her hands and let the burning pain erase her memories of Magna. It would be as if she never existed. Her name and her face would be gone forever.

Chapter 26

Oliver and Baxter had been sparring for the better part of the day and had just sat down to rest when Elda entered the exercise room.

"Who wants to go on patrol with me?" she asked, avoiding Baxter and looking directly at Oliver.

"He isn't going anywhere until we practice longswords. I still owe him for the last time he nicked my ear," joked Baxter.

"It was all in fun," Oliver replied. "I was just trying to make your ears appear even."

"There's nothing wrong with my ears," Baxter snapped.

"Hurry up! Get your practice over with," nagged Elda. "I won't wait forever, Oliver."

"Speaking of waiting forever, how is Astra?" laughed Baxter. "You were getting mighty friendly with her at the festival. We saw you down on your knees."

"We talked," he replied, as he picked up his longsword and circled it over his head.

"Just talked?" asked Elda. "That's all? Are you losing your touch with the ladies?"

"Yes, we just talked. Neither one of us are ready for a mate," he mumbled. "We have decided to wait and see if we miss each other."

"So, do you miss her?" Baxter asked, as he picked up his longsword and mimicked Oliver's movements trying not to laugh.

"Yes," he declared, while pointing his longsword at them. "I dare you to make fun of me, but I miss her. There is something special about that little witch."

Taking his stance, he waited for Baxter to take his position. He grinned as he watched him boldly move into position and was eager to take a nick from his other ear. Baxter returned the grin as he took a moment to tuck his hair behind his ear.

"I see you are making it easier for me," laughed Oliver.

"I dare you to try, my friend," he teased. "I dare you to try."

Raising his longsword, he hesitated and then immediately lowered his blade. Elda could tell that something was wrong and stepped forward placing her hand on his shoulder.

"What is it, Baxter? What's wrong?" she asked.

Oliver lowered his sword and waited for his answer.

"Laralynn just said my name," he replied. "Nothing more, she just said my name."

"Where is she?" asked Elda.

"I assume she is still in the forest. She went with Woodward and Lord Thomas," he replied. "They must be in trouble. You two, go find Gavenia! We need her hawk to help us find them. I'll get the horses ready."

While they ran off in search of Gavenia, Baxter headed for the stable. In no time, Elda met Baxter outside the stable with the sound of Gavenia's hawk circling overhead. Elda mounted her horse, and they both headed for the forest while trying to keep Gavenia's white hawk in sight.

Baxter tried several times to enter Laralynn's mind to no avail. Unless she opened her eyes, he wouldn't be able to find her.

"I can't reach her with my mind," he shouted. "I see nothing but darkness."

"She is probably asleep. Try reaching Lord Thomas," she yelled back at him.

"I see the same. This is bad, Elda. This is bad," he shouted, as he nudged Copper with his heels to encourage him to go faster.

The further into the forest they went, the more difficult it was for the horses to maneuver and for them to see the hawk. The slow pace had Baxter frustrated. They kept looking up for Gavenia's hawk and listening for her to call them. He was almost ready to call for additional help when he heard the hawk's repeated call. They moved as quickly as they could through the trees toward the sound. Baxter could see a patch of light up ahead through the trees. Dismounting Copper, he ran toward the clearing.

There in the dim afternoon light were bodies spread about the clearing. He knelt first by Woodward's side and saw the blood on his face and tunic. He searched for wounds, but he found none that would account for all the blood around him. Hearing Elda approaching, he ordered her to see about Lord Thomas. As he stood to search for Laralynn, he noticed the withered remains of a woman. Assuming she played some role in the scene before him, he approached the body with care. Turning her face toward him, he was shocked to find Magna with a hole in her chest and what appeared to be the remains of her heart smashed on the ground next to her.

"What happened here?" muttered Baxter, as he noticed another body next to Lord Thomas. "Where is Laralynn?"

A flutter of something golden next to a cluster of small boulders caught his eye. As he moved toward it, he realized it was Laralynn's hair and hurried to her side. She had blood smeared on her face, her tunic was torn and missing a sleeve, but she seemed unharmed.

"Laralynn, can you hear me?" he softly whispered. "Open your eyes for me."

Hearing no response, he scooped her up in his arms and carried her toward Elda and her father. He could see that Elda was helping Thomas sit up.

"Is he hurt?" asked Baxter.

"There is a great deal of blood, but I can't find a wound," she replied.

"Since it doesn't appear there is any danger, I'm going to flash Laralynn back to Evergreen. I'll be back for Woodward," he said. "Thomas will have to return by horseback unless he wants to sleep for the next week."

"I'll ride," he groaned, as he rubbed his chest. "How is my daughter? I tried to protect her. Was she harmed?"

"She doesn't appear to be hurt, but I can't wake her. I'm taking her to Flora," he replied and then vanished.

Chapter 27

Flora looked up as Baxter entered the Healing Room. She pulled the fresh bed linens up around Laralynn's chin and walked around to see after Woodward.

"How is she?" asked Baxter. "Has she opened her eyes yet?"

"No, she still sleeps," replied Flora. "Meadow and Lady Lara have tried to read her mind, but she has it closed to everyone. Like you, they found nothing but darkness."

"I'm not surprised after what we found in the clearing and what Lord Thomas has told us," he said. "It was a bloody scene."

"I found no wounds on anyone. I even called Meadow to examine them to be sure there were no magical wounds. She found nothing," she smiled. "Do not worry Baxter. She will wake in her own time."

He nodded and looked over at Woodward.

"How is Woodward?" he asked, as he heard the sound of rhythmic snoring.

"Woodward has recovered nicely, but he is weak from blood loss," she explained. "A few more days of rest and he will be able to return to his cottage. Charlotte and Patrick have been to see him several times. They are both eager for him to return home with them.

Baxter felt a hand upon his shoulder and turned to see Tate standing behind him.

"You are needed in the Council Chamber," he said. "Lady Lara has asked for you."

"Flora, I will come back later and sit with them and allow you a chance to rest," Baxter said and then left with Tate.

* * *

Everyone stood as Lord Thomas and Lady Lara entered the Council Chamber. Thomas helped Lara with her chair and then took his own. After everyone was seated Lara greeted everyone with concern lingering in her voice.

"As you know, my sister was present at the clearing with Woodward, Thomas, and Laralynn," she stated, as she paused a moment before she continued. "We do not know the role Magna played in causing Laralynn to sleep or if she had any role at all. We can only assume, based on her evil past, that she did have something to do with it."

"I for one am glad the evil bitch received her final death," Oliver blurted. "I just hope she stays dead this time."

Lara released a soft sigh and focused her attention on Oliver.

"I'm sure your feelings are shared by many at this table; however, I think they are best kept to yourself, Oliver," Lara scolded. "However, there are other matters that should concern us all."

Feeling the sting of her response, Oliver realized his words had offended her.

"My Lady, excuse my boldness," he replied. "It was wrong of me to speak of your sister in that way."

"You are excused," she quickly assured him with a smile. "My sister was once my dearest friend. It will be a memory that I will keep forever. Sadly, Franco took my sister from me, as well as, the family of Thomas and Tate. We all knew of her wicked nature after her turning, and most recently, we learned of Franco's crimes. With their final deaths, it has ended, and we are all better for it."

Oliver slowly raised his fist over his chest and silently mouthed, "I am truly sorry."

Lara nodded and looked at Thomas to address their concerns.

"With Magna's death, we are concerned there could be a new evil lurking on this island," Thomas began. "Fortunately, it spared our daughter's life; however, it knows how to provide vampires their final death." He saw the look of surprise on each of their faces. A new enemy could bring fear to everyone on the island. "Until Laralynn wakes and is able to tell us what or who she saw take Magna's life, we must be prepared for an attack on us or the humans that live among us."

"I will see the warning towers are filled for Evergreen's protection and patrols are run to protect the villages. I will send word to Lord Cumberland, Lord Gautier, and Lord Fallon," Preston stated. "We all knew that Magna had been partaking of Lord Seth's hospitality. Should I send word to him of her death?"

"What affects us, affects us all," Lara replied. "Send word to all the castles on the island. This evil could be anywhere."

"As you wish, My Lady," Preston replied.

"Have the bodies been destroyed?" asked Thomas.

"Yes, My Lord," replied Baxter. "Tate and I made the pyres and watched them burn until nothing was left but ashes. Meadow stood watch to detect any spirit that tried to escape. It has ended. They are gone."

"I thank you for your dedication to Evergreen," Lara said. "Each and every one of you is important to me and to Evergreen. Stay vigilant and protect those around you and yourselves. You are dismissed."

Everyone stood with their fists over their chests as Thomas assisted Lara with her chair. She nodded her appreciation and took Thomas' arm as he led her through the doorway.

"If only Laralynn would wake," sighed Lara. "I fear what this has done to her."

"She will wake soon, my love," he replied, as he took her hand and kissed her palm. "She will wake stronger because of what happened."

"Why do you say that?" she asked.

"Because, she is her mother's daughter," he smiled. "Now, let's go see our daughter."

* * *

Baxter waited until Lord Thomas and Lady Lara left the Healing Room before he entered. He saw Charlotte and Patrick huddled in the corner talking to Woodward. Patrick was helping his father sit up while his mother held a small bowl of broth. Wanting to give them privacy, he moved around to the far side of Laralynn's cot. Pulling a stool up as close as he could get to her, he gently brushed the strands of hair from her face. As the tips of his fingers touched her skin, he felt warmth race up his arm and realized the warm sensation was getting stronger. Lifting the edge of the linen cover, he pulled her arm free so that he could hold her hand. It was so soft and small compared to his large calloused hand. He rubbed his thumb back and forth across her smooth skin as he thought about the first time he had seen her at Ian's market. She had been a babe wrapped in Hazel's arms. Lifting her hand to his face, he inhaled the sweet scent of fresh apples as he gently kissed her fingertips.

"Baxter, is that you?" Laralynn struggled to get the words out.

"You have decided to join us," he grinned. "You have been sleeping for a long time."

"Is everyone . . . alive," she choked on the words. "My father . . . and Woodward?"

"Woodward is in the cot beside you, and your father is with your mother. Everyone has recovered, even you," he tried to reassure her. "Let me go get your mother and father."

"No, please stay with me. I don't want to be alone," she whispered. "I don't want you to go."

Baxter looked up as he heard Patrick climbing over his father's cot.

"My Lady, I will go get them for you," offered Patrick, as he hurried through the doorway.

"You are safe. There is no need to worry," Baxter said, as he squeezed her hand. "Flora has taken good care of you, and we were all waiting for you to wake."

"I remember calling your name," she shyly said, as a hint of pink covered her cheeks. "I was scared, and I didn't know what else to do. I needed help, and I called your name."

"I heard you," he smiled.

"You heard me?" she asked.

"It appears we have discovered one of your secret gifts," he laughed.

"Then, it was you that came for me?" she asked.

"Yes, and I promise I will always come for you, Laralynn," he whispered and then kissed the back of her hand. "Nothing will keep me from you."

Everyone turned toward the door as Lady Lara and Lord Thomas hurried through the doorway. Lara bent down and kissed her daughter's forehead.

"How are you feeling?" she asked. "We found blood but no wounds. Were you hurt?"

"No, I wasn't hurt. I was afraid, but I wasn't hurt," she replied. "I just felt tired."

"Baxter, we need to speak with our daughter," Lara said, as she sat down on the edge of the cot eager to learn what happened in the clearing.

Baxter stood and started to move toward the door.

"Mother, I want Baxter to stay. I need him to stay," she insisted, as she reached for Baxter's hand. "Mother, I care for him, and I need for him to stay with me."

Lara looked up at Thomas and then at Baxter's surprised expression.

"All right, he can stay," she smiled. "Now, what can you tell us about what happened in the clearing? We know how

Woodward was wounded and that your father attacked Franco. When did Magna arrive and who killed her?"

Laralynn looked at Baxter, and she took a deep breath.

"Take your time," coaxed Baxter. "You're safe. No one can hurt you."

"I saw father slam into the man you called Franco. He was a vampire, mother. He was scraping his fangs against my neck when father knocked him away from me," she said, as she lifted her hand to her neck searching for marks.

Remembering his cold breath, her body began to shiver uncontrollably. Baxter sat down on the cot, pulled Laralynn into his lap, and wrapped his arms around her. He noticed the uneasy look that Lord Thomas gave him but continued to offer her the comfort she needed. Laralynn sighed and leaned back against his chest causing heat to race through his body. He saw that Lord Thomas continued to frown at him, but he wasn't about to release her unless he was forced to let her go.

Once the shivering stopped, she took another deep breath and continued, "They fought each other, father and Franco, and then they just stopped moving. They were so quiet; I feared father was dead. When I pulled father back away from Franco's body, I saw the dagger in father's chest. I pulled it free and blood poured from the wound. I was holding the bloody dagger when Magna suddenly appeared. She screamed at me and blamed me for killing Franco."

Laralynn closed her eyes not wanting to relive what she had seen.

"I'm with you, Laralynn. Just get it all out," Baxter whispered into her mind.

She could feel relief almost instantly upon hearing Baxter's voice.

"As she made her way to Franco's body, I slowly moved toward Woodward. I was kneeling by him when she came toward me with a dagger in her hand and ordered me to stand. Strange red smoke was all around me and it burned my skin. She told me she was going to . . . kill me . . . and deliver my body to you, mother."

She felt her mother stroke her arm and knew she would cry if she looked at her mother's eyes. Keeping her eyes focused on the bed linens, she forced herself to continue.

"When she started to grab my arm, I saw a look of intense pain on her face and watched her fall to the ground before me. Behind her was an old woman, but I never noticed her until Magna collapsed. She was holding Magna's bloody heart in her outstretched hand. When she dropped it to the ground, she smashed it with her boot, and turned to walk away. She told me I was free, and that Magna would no longer hurt me. I asked her name and told her I wanted to thank her. She kept walking and said there was no need, that a promise made is a promise kept. She acted so strange. It was as if she knew me."

Looking over at Woodward and up at her father, she smiled when she thought of how grateful she was that they had survived.

"I was able to heal father and Woodward using my gift of healing. When I stood up and looked at all of the bodies, I couldn't breathe. I only remember backing away and calling for Baxter before everything went dark."

"You are safe, Laralynn. It is all over," her mother whispered and kissed her cheek. "You were very brave, and we are very proud of you."

"Mother, who was the old woman?" she asked.

"I believe she was the witch, Velsa," her mother replied.

"The witch that cursed Astra?" she asked.

Her mother nodded and stood looking down at her daughter in Baxter's arms. It was clear that Baxter loved their daughter, and she loved him.

"Yes, I believe it was," she said. "Now, you need to rest. I will visit you later. Thomas, we need to tell the council of what we have learned. We have nothing to fear."

Her father stepped forward and kissed his daughter's forehead.

"I owe you my life, daughter," he said, as he wiped a tear

from his eye.

"We saved each other, father," she smiled. "I love you, father. I love you, mother."

"We love you too, Laralynn. We love you too," he replied, with pride. "We always will."

Thomas took Lara's arm and led her through the doorway. Looking over his shoulder, he saw his daughter lean her face into Baxter's kiss. She was no longer his little girl. He knew that she would soon belong to Baxter. He was sad that she had been his precious girl for such a short time, but he was happy she had found someone to love her.

Chapter 28

The balcony doors were both open, and Kayleigh stood leaning against the stone ledge when Gautier entered their chamber. He had received a message from Evergreen and was eager to give her the good news. Hearing him enter, she turned and reached out offering him her hand.

"Come see the night's sky. It is extremely beautiful tonight," she begged.

"Could this fondness for the night sky be due to the full moon?" he asked, as he took her hand.

"The moon does enhance its beauty," she smiled.

Gautier moved her hair back away from her shoulder and trailed kisses from her bare shoulder to just behind her ear.

"Your skin smells of lavender," he whispered. "You know that lavender is used in love charms."

"Do I need a love charm to make you want me?" she sighed.

"Never, from the day I met you my heart has belonged to you," he replied. "Through those dark days that you were lost to me, I thought of nothing but you. My love, you are everything to me."

"And you are everything to me, Gautier," she whispered her reply. "For us, our love is always and forever."

They stood holding each other until the moon was high in

the sky. Removing her robe, she stepped away from him and let her wolf come forward. An excited howl could be heard coming from far below their balcony.

"I hear Alicia's wolf," he laughed. "My two favorite little wolves are anxious for their run tonight. Best we leave this chamber or she will come looking for you."

Kayleigh's wolf followed closely behind Gautier until they reached sight of the gate that led to the forest. Alicia's grey wolf sat waiting by Gustavo's side until she saw them coming toward her. Leaping up to greet Gautier, she was thrilled when he bent down and allowed her to lick the side of his face.

"I almost forgot. I received a message from Evergreen that you will find very interesting. Magna has received her final death," he said, with a broad grin upon his face. "There is no need to doubt it. It has been verified by Meadow. You are free to run without the worry of Magna's interference. Now go! Enjoy your full moon."

Gustavo pulled opened the gate and the two wolves ran for the forest.

"Be careful," Gautier shouted. "There are dangers in the forest."

He stood and watched until they were out of sight.

"I'm sorry Gustavo. I know you were fond of Magna," he said. "She threatened Laralynn, and they believe that Velsa only took Magna's heart to save her."

"Maybe now, she will find peace," he replied. "Maybe now, everyone will find peace."

* * *

Velsa scurried about getting her cottage ready for the spell that would change her life forever. The table had been freshly scrubbed and her book of spells had been placed prominently in the center of the table. The black candles and herb bundle were waiting to be brought to flame. The black stones from Black Thistle Castle had been crushed and mixed with her blood. Two small boxes sat side by side unopened. The first contained Lara's heartbeat and the other a few strands of Gautier's hair. The leg bones from several rodents were neatly arranged in a pyramid. A wooden cup was filled with rose quartz, amethyst, moonstone, and amber. A torn strip of linen was tied around a few leaves from the poisonous weed, caper spurge. An empty teacup rested upon its saucer. A pitcher of water from Whistlers River, Gautier's favorite place, sat ready to be poured. All of the items she needed for her spell where neatly arranged, all except one. She still needed the tail from Kayleigh's wolf.

"Tonight is the night," Velsa sang and watched the book of spells ruffle its pages as she danced around the table. "Tonight is the night I'm going to take that pretty little wolf's tail. Do you like my new gown? I conjured it just for the occasion. Gautier has always had a fondness for the color lavender."

The book of spells lifted from the table and banged itself back down.

"I know, I did away with all things lavender," she grumbled. "I hated it because Gautier gave Kayleigh a ring that had a lavender stone. That is why I cursed the Wispet Canyon and the thistles that surrounded Black Thistle Castle. It will all change. Soon, I will be the love of Gautier's life. He will forget all about the little wolf. Maybe I'll send him hunting, and he can end her completely."

Laughing at the thought of Gautier hunting Kayleigh, she picked up the small dagger and stroked the silver blade before slipping it into its emerald encrusted sheath. Tying it securely around her waist and picking up the heavy hunter's trap, she took one last look around her cottage and vanished.

* * *

The night air was cool and the moon's light filtered between the tree's branches offering Velsa just enough light to set the hunter's trap. She knew the exact spot to place the deadly weapon. She had seen the white wolf enter the small clearing by the stream numerous times. With the wave of her arm, it was completely covered by pine needles and waiting for its victim. Taking her place on the branch of a nearby tree, she settled in to wait for Kayleigh's wolf.

"All I have to do is wait," she laughed.

It wasn't long before she heard the sound of what she knew were two wolves running toward her, and she could feel her heart racing with excitement. Trying to calm her breathing, she silently started counting to ten. Before she could finish, Kayleigh's wolf burst into the clearing and made her way toward the stream. With her nose in the air scenting for danger, Alicia's grey wolf stepped around her and bent down to drink from the cool water. After her fill, she padded over to her favorite spot at the base of a hollowed out tree to rest. Kayleigh seemed nervous. She stalked around sniffing the air until she was satisfied there was no danger and bent to take a drink.

Ready for a short nap, Kayleigh headed toward the mound of pine needles. As Velsa watched, she placed one paw and then another near the trap. Stopping to look at a possum that had invaded her privacy, she changed directions and stepped to push off with her back paws. The trap slammed shut around her back leg, crushing the bone. A painful howl reverberated through the forest.

The grey wolf was jolted from her nap by the sound of Kayleigh's howl, and her own wolf began to mimic her howling. She paced around as she watched Kayleigh's wolf trying to free herself from the trap. Fearing there could be another trap, she stopped moving and realized there was nothing she could do for Kayleigh in her wolf form. Her own wolf was afraid, but she needed to change into her human form and try to pry the trap open. Lying down she tried to bring her human form forward. Her wolf resisted her request and refused to listen. She only wanted to stand guard and protect Kayleigh.

"It's the only way we can help her," Alicia screamed at her wolf. "Let me out!"

Finally, the grey wolf relented and allowed Alicia to come

forward.

"My Lady, lie down and don't move. I'm going to try and open the trap," she ordered. Alicia could see that the trap had completely crushed the bone and anymore movement would cause the trap to sever her leg. "You can't move. Do you understand? You can't move. The trap has crushed the bone. Your leg is only held on by the skin and muscle."

As Alicia put her hands on the trap, the blood that covered it caused her hands to slip. Kayleigh whimpered with every attempt to grasp the trap. Once she could finally grip the thick sides of the trap, she pulled as hard as she could, but she couldn't open it.

"Kayleigh, I'm not strong enough. Have you called for Gautier?" she asked. Not hearing a response, she knew she was unable to communicate with him mentally. "I'm going to change back into my wolf and run for help. Please, don't move. I'll bring Gautier as soon as I can."

Alicia gave herself over to her wolf and raced for help.

Velsa watched and waited until she knew it was safe to leave her perch. Dropping to the ground she arrogantly stepped toward Kayleigh and stood quietly until Kayleigh opened her eyes. She was greeted by snarling and bared teeth, and she returned her fierce response with laughter.

"You, little wolf, have taken the only man I have ever loved away from me," she stated, with hatred in her voice. "Now, you will feel the pain and suffering I have felt for so long."

She pulled the dagger from its sheath and laid it across the palm of her hand.

"With this dagger, I will be able to cut Gautier from your life," she smirked. "Every time you change into your wolf, you will be reminded of your loss, and the pain will never go away. You will have pain from the moment you open your eyes until you close them."

She blew on the dagger and it leapt from her hand slicing Kayleigh's tail from her body. With Kayleigh howling in pain, Velsa retrieved the tail but left the dagger on the ground next to the trap. Waving her hand over the dagger, she changed the silver blade into an ordinary hunter's dagger. Looking down and smiling at Kayleigh's bleeding body, she began to chant.

Hide my essence from all that search for me and
  wipe clean the memory of my presence.
A hunter's trap and dagger have caused this pain,
  which will linger for all eternity.

Taking one last look at the bleeding wolf, Velsa laughed as she vanished from the forest.

Kayleigh flinched as she heard someone running toward her. Caught in a hunter's trap, she could feel her life slipping away and didn't have the strength to look an enemy in the eye. If death was coming, she welcomed it to free her from the pain. It wasn't until Gautier had released her from the trap, and she could feel his body next to her own, that she felt the need to survive.

"I've got you," he whispered. "Don't you leave me. Our love is always and forever, remember, always and forever."

She opened her eyes and tried to focus on his face. A blurry image looked back at her, and she could feel his breath against her skin as he spoke. Unknowingly, she had shifted back into her human form. Confused and unable to make out his words, she took solace in the sound of his voice. The pain roared to life as he tried to wrap her naked body in his tunic. Finding it too much to bear, she closed her eyes and retreated back into unconsciousness.

* * *

Strange music and laughter drifted through the cracks in her cottage door and up through the smoke stack. Velsa was thoroughly enjoying celebrating her success. The bones and herbs that hung from her ceiling were swaying to the music, and her book of spells merrily bounced to the notes of her magical flute. A jug of sweet tonic sat between her legs as she rocked back and forth in her favorite chair. Lifting the jug to her mouth, she swigged the tonic with unladylike abandon and wiped her mouth with her sleeve. It had been a moment she would never forget, and unfortunately, one that Kayleigh would never remember. She sat with glazed eyes reliving the moment the trap snapped shut and hearing Kayleigh's howl as her tail was sliced from her body. Her one regret was not staying to see Gautier retrieve his beloved wolf.

"Let him enjoy his wounded wolf," Velsa yawned. "Once he has tasted my potion, he will belong to me, forever. Things will be as they once were."

Feeling a bit overheated, she sat the jug down on the floor and stood to search for her hand-painted fan. It had been a gift from Balgair. An unexpected gift that he had brought her from a faraway land many years ago.

"Now where did I put it?" she mumbled, as she tried to keep her balance. "I know; my tan is in my frunk. I mean my frunk is in my tan. Oh, for toad's sake, where is the little breeze maker."

Stumbling toward her trunk and finding the leather handle, she struggled to open it. After several more attempts, she successfully lifted its lid. There before her was her beloved fan.

"Isn't it pretty," she muttered, as she admired the lovely painted flowers and stars.

"Bending to pick it up, she caught the heel of her boot in the lace of her underslip and started to fall. Trying to regain her balance, she reached for the wall. Missing it by a good foot, she twisted and turned until she landed with her rear in the middle of the open trunk. Finding her knees just under her chin, she reached beneath her and extracted what remained of her fan. Without the energy to move or to stop the room from spinning, Velsa tossed her fan aside, closed her eyes, and decided to take a nap.

Chapter 29

After arriving back at the castle with Kayleigh's limp and broken body, he had ordered Gustavo to summon Lady Lara's healer. Even though Gautier or Desirae could offer a healing spell, it would only last until the spell was broken. Once broken, the pain would begin again. She needed to be healed.

While he waited for their arrival, Alicia and her mother had helped him clean the blood and dirt from Kayleigh's body. He had dressed her in a clean sleeping gown, and they had washed and braided her hair. Even though they were all as gentle as they could be, she screamed every time they touched her broken leg or her lower back.

Comforted now that Kayleigh was finally sleeping, he thought back to the bloody scene in the forest. He could not blame the hunter for the trap. It was a common tool to gain food for the table or to keep animals from killing their livestock. What he didn't understand was the brutality of leaving an animal to die after removing its tail. It made no sense. The person that owned that dagger and committed this cruel act needed to be punished.

Gautier looked up as the door opened and Alicia entered.

"My Lord, the Lady Lara is here," she announced. "She has brought her daughter, Laralynn, and Flora with her."

Alicia stood quietly by the door ready to offer any assistance that was needed.

He stood and made his way to the door as Lara entered. Taking her hand in his, he bent and kissed the back of her hand.

"I'm sorry our meeting could not be a happier one," he sighed.

"There are happier times ahead; I am sure of it," Lara replied.

"And Laralynn, I have heard of your recent . . . shall I say . . . adventure?" he smiled. "I will tell you what I always tell my sweet Kayleigh. There are dangers in the forest."

"I will remember that and keep my dagger ready at my hip," she replied.

"Come Flora," he said, as he reached for her hand. "Come let me show you what has been done to my Kayleigh."

They walked hand-in-hand to her bedside. Releasing her hand, he carefully drew back the linen covers to reveal the bone that protruded just above her ankle. It was surrounded by jagged and swollen marks left from the pointed teeth of the hunter's trap.

Laralynn couldn't help but gasp, and she quickly covered her mouth to try and silence it.

"I agree; it is a horrible sight," he said, as he patted Laralynn's shoulder. "Forgive me, I should have warned you. What you cannot see is the harm that has been done to her wolf. She nearly lost her back paw from trying to escape from the trap. If Alicia had not warned her to be still, she would have continued to struggle to free herself. I'm sure she would have chewed herself free of the trap before I was able to find her."

"It looks almost like Woodward's broken ribs," she whispered to her mother.

"Gautier, I have brought my daughter here because she has been gifted with the power of healing. Our Forest Warden received several broken ribs when a buck charged him during their hunt. She was able to heal him using water," Lara explained.

"Child, you shall have all the water you need if it will heal my Kayleigh," he said. "I will see that it is brought to you without delay. Alicia, will you see that it is brought to this chamber?"

A single nod and Alicia left the chamber to follow his order.

"Is this her only injury?" asked Flora.

"No, there is more," he groaned, as he looked back at Kayleigh. "Had she still not been in her wolf form when I arrived, I would not have seen the worst of it. Her tail has been cut from her body."

"Oh my stars," gasped Lara. "Who could do such a thing?"

"I have been asking myself the same question," he sighed. "Had the hunter's blade not been left behind for me to find, I would have had no chance to track the hunter. Unfortunately, it left no essence behind. It was wiped clean and no footprints were left behind."

"Gautier, let's leave and let Flora and Laralynn do what they can to heal her," she said, as she took his arm. "I'm sure it would be better for them and for you, if you were not at her bedside while they worked."

Reluctantly, he nodded, and they left the bedchamber and closed the door.

"Don't you find it strange that there were no footprints?" she asked, as they walked toward the stone steps. "Even a small animal would leave footprints behind."

"At the time, I did not think to examine the ground around her," he replied, as they began to descend the stone steps. "I simply noticed there were no footprints of any kind, not even from Kayleigh's wolf."

"That eliminates an animal, for they would surely leave footprints behind and have no way of disguising them," she concluded. "A human's footprints would be deeper and harder to hide. They would simply cover them with leaves to hide them, but if you removed the leaves, they would still exist. An immortal is the only being clever enough to leave no footprints behind."

At the foot of the steps, he stopped and began shaking his

head.

"I have only one enemy, and Kayleigh has only one enemy," he choked out the words. "Could it be? Could she be that cruel?"

"I'm afraid to ask the name of this enemy, for I fear that I already know it," she gasped.

"There is no need. Hearing her name would bring bile to my throat," he said through clenched teeth. "Can you take me to the spot where I found Kayleigh? I need to feel the ground and the trees around it. If I find her essence there, it will be all the proof I need to end her life."

"You will need to show me, for I have never been to this place. Think of the place where you found Kayleigh so that I may see it," she said.

Gautier focused on the small clearing by the stream where Alicia had brought him. Opening his mind to Lara, he allowed her to see exactly where she needed to take him.

"Take my hand," she said, as they vanished from the castle.

* * *

With Alicia at his side, a tall man carried two wooden buckets full of water and sat them by the corner of the bed.

"Anything else, My Lady," he asked.

"No, that will be fine," replied Laralynn.

Flora held the corner of the bed linens and waited until the man had left the chamber and closed the door. With Alicia's help, Flora folded the linens back away from Kayleigh's leg. Alicia crawled up onto the bed and prepared to hold Kayleigh down if she tried to move. Flora stood by her knee and waited for Laralynn to begin.

"I hope I can do this," she said, taking a deep breath trying to calm her nerves.

She dipped the wooden cup that hung on the side of the bucket into the water, filling it halfway. Holding her hand palm up over Kayleigh's ankle, she poured a small amount of water into her hand. Nervously, she let it trickle onto her ravaged ankle. Instantly, Kayleigh bucked forward with her eyes wide open. She clutched the bed linens in tight fists and screamed through the pain. Alicia wrapped her arms around her shoulders trying to ease the pain. Once her screaming stopped, she gently pushed her back onto her pillow while Flora struggled to hold her knee.

"I'm sorry, My Lady. We are trying to help you. Please lie still," Alicia begged. "Scream all you want if it lessens the pain."

Kayleigh's body began to shake and perspiration ran from her forehead. With each drop of water upon her leg, her screams and moans grew louder.

"Has the healing begun?" asked Flora. "Please tell me it's healing."

"I can't be sure. The wound is so severe. I'm going to pour more water on the bone. Hold her leg tightly and try to keep her from moving," begged Laralynn.

Thinking she had not been generous enough with the water, she filed the cup again. This time, she poured the water onto her hand and let it fall directly onto the bone that protruded from her leg as Kayleigh continued to scream. Laralynn was sure that Kayleigh's screams would send Gautier charging into the bedchamber at any moment, and she feared for her life.

As Kayleigh's outbursts calmed, she noticed the bone had moved back under the skin. The swelling and redness had started to disappear.

"It's healing. It's healing," she cried. "I'm going to pour one more cup of water on the wound, and hopefully, it will be the last. Hold her down, Alicia."

"One more time, My Lady," she whispered. "It's almost over."

Laralynn repeated the same process, and this time, Kayleigh barely moved or made a sound.

"It's almost completely healed," Flora said, as she dipped a cloth into the water and began wiping the remaining blood from Kayleigh's leg.

"What do we do now?" asked Alicia.

"We need to turn her over onto her stomach. This way my hands will be close to her spine, and my healing can travel through her bones. Hopefully, this will heal the wolf that lives within her spirit," explained Flora.

Laralynn and Alicia carefully turned her over and lifted her gown so that Flora's hands could rest against her skin. With her fingers spread, Flora gently placed her hands upon Kayleigh's lower back. She closed her eyes and focused on sending her healing power toward the spirit that lived within her. Laralynn could feel a gentle warmth coming from Kayleigh's skin, and then it slowly cooled. Without saying a word, Flora lifted her hands from Kayleigh's back and smiled.

"I could feel her wolf," she whispered. "Her wounds are healed, but she is still without her tail."

"It happened so fast. You should have been the one to heal her leg," Laralynn shrugged. "I gave her so much pain."

"I would have used all my energy. There would not have been enough to heal the wolf," she replied. "We did all that we were able."

"Let's put fresh linens on the bed, bathe Kayleigh, and dress her in a clean sleeping gown. Gautier will be glad to see she is healed, and the pain is gone."

* * *

Lara stood back and watched Gautier as he circled the area searching for a hunter's footprints or any sign that would lead him to the one that harmed Kayleigh. It was clear from where she stood that there were no visible prints other than Gautier's. The only impressions in the earth were from Kayleigh's body and the dagger.

"Alicia's wolf stood over by the tree and never came near Kayleigh's body when we arrived. I see the prints from my own boots and no one else's," he offered, as he looked about for anything that may have been left behind."

She watched as Gautier pulled his dagger from the sheath at his hip.

"I believe that I know who harmed Kayleigh. If I am correct, the essence of the attacker will be hidden by a spell to shield her from any blame. Instead of searching for Velsa's essence, I will search for anyone that left their essence behind. This should be the loophole that breaks the attacker's spell. By using my Fog of Essence, I may be able to pull the essence from the earth that was covered by Kayleigh's wolf and the dagger left behind," he said. "If I can find a small amount, it will have to reveal the remaining essence to me."

Using his blade, he cut into the palm of his hand. The blood began to pool, and he made a fist. Returning his dagger to its sheath, he stood holding his fist out over the hunter's trap. When he opened his hand, a faint fog spewed from his palm. It quickly spread over the ground and up the trunks of the trees that surrounded the area. As quickly as it spread, it was absorbed by everything it touched. Lara watched and waited, but nothing happened.

"Where has it gone?" asked Lara.

"Wait, it will reveal any essence left behind," he replied.

Slowly a thick green fog began to lift from a sturdy branch up high in a nearby tree. It swirled around the trunk many times before making its way to the ground. One by one, small footprints from the base of the tree to the hunter's trap lifted from the ground. Finally, the green fog outlined the hunter's trap, Kayleigh's wolf, and a small dagger next to the trap.

Gautier ran his hand through the fog and flinched as it burned his skin. He watched the fog pulse and mix with the blood on his open palm. Taking a deep breath, he closed his hand to make a tight fist and then threw what remained of the bloody fog to the ground. The fog began to grow until an outline of a hazy figure stood before him. Slowly the thick fog cleared leaving a translucent image of a woman, the image of Velsa.

"She will pay for this," he growled, as he touched the outline of the dagger. "The witch will burn for what she has done to Kayleigh and her wolf."

Chapter 30

After Gautier returned and repeatedly thanked everyone for healing Kayleigh, Alicia said her good-byes and left the bedchamber. She was exhausted and needed a distraction. Her head was spinning from everything she had seen. Wandering aimlessly through the dim hallways, she suddenly found herself outside next to Killian's stone wolf. Standing on her tiptoes, she ran her hand over his leg and paw.

"I have missed you, Killian," she whispered.

"I have missed you, too," he replied. "You sound tired and worried."

"Something horrible has happened. Lady Kayleigh and I released our wolves for a run during the full moon. A hunter had set a trap by the stream where we go to drink. We didn't see it, and it snapped closed around her back leg," she said, as she wiped tears from her eyes. "I couldn't get the trap open; I wasn't strong enough, Killian. I had to run for help. I had to leave her all alone."

"Was she hurt badly?" he asked.

"Her leg was broken so badly that she could have lost her paw, but that wasn't the worst of it," she replied. "Someone cut the tail from her wolf while I had gone for Gautier. Lady Laralynn and Flora, Evergreen's healers, were able to heal her wounds and her wolf's, but they couldn't restore her tail. She was finally sleeping when I left their bedchamber. Who would do such a thing to a helpless wolf?"

"Someone with hatred in their heart, Alicia," he growled. "Someone full of hatred."

Alicia's thoughts immediately went to Jario and his thwarted attempt to attack Lady Kayleigh, and she was grateful he was spelled to his dagger. Thinking of the wrong done to Desirae's sister, she wondered where Desirae had been all this time.

"Killian, I must go find Desirae. She doesn't know what has happened to Lady Kayleigh," she gasped. "Forgive me for leaving so abruptly."

"You are forgiven, Alicia," he replied. "Don't stay away too long."

"I won't," she said, rubbing his paw one last time.

Turning to leave, she heard someone calling her name. Looking toward the gate, she saw Desirae and a young woman walking toward her.

"Well, now I know why I haven't seen you," shouted Alicia.

"You were looking for me?" asked Desirae.

"I was about to look for you," she replied, as she looked at the young woman beside her. "Is this Astra?"

"Alicia, this is Astra, Velsa's sister," she said. "Astra, this is Alicia."

"Welcome to Black Thistle Castle," she smiled and reached for Astra's hand. "I have many things to tell you, and I fear you will not be happy to hear them. Come, let's go to the library."

After hearing Alicia's warning, Astra reluctantly followed behind Alicia and Desirae. The stone lined hallways of the castle were too dim for her liking, and they reminded her too much of the darkness of her cave upon the mountain. She much preferred her bright cottage in Primrose Pond. It sat in the full sun, and she only had to light a candle once the sun had finally set. Seeing Desirae disappear through an open doorway, she caught a glimpse of sunlight just before she entered the library. The warm light calmed her nerves as she looked at the books stacked on the table.

"You said you had something to tell us. Tell us now, before we start reading" requested Desirae.

"Lady Kayleigh and I released our wolves for a run during the full moon. A hunter had set a trap by the stream where we go to drink. We didn't see it, and it snapped closed around her back leg. I changed from my wolf into my human form, but I wasn't strong enough to open the trap," she explained, this time without crying. "Changing back into my wolf, I ran to get Gautier. When we returned, we discovered someone had cut her tail from her body."

Desirae and Astra both gasped.

"Has a healer been called?" asked Desirae.

"Yes, Lady Laralynn and Flora, Evergreen's healers, were able to heal her wounds and her wolf's, but they couldn't restore her tail," she replied.

"Do they know who committed the cruel act?" she asked, wanting to know more.

"I do not know for certain, but I believe Lord Gautier and Lady Lara may have returned to the place where he found her wolf. His boots were clean when I arrived to help with the healing. When he returned with Lady Lara, his boots were covered in damp soil, and the hem of Lady Lara's dress was damp. He looked like he was trying to hide his anger. Once he saw that Lady Kayleigh had been healed and she was sleeping, his eyes brightened, and he happily thanked us for our service. I said my good-byes and left the bedchamber shortly before you arrived," she sighed.

"There is only one person that would be that cruel to Lady Kayleigh, and that person is my sister, Velsa," Astra groaned, as she covered her face with her hands.

"Astra is right," declared Gautier, as he stepped into the library. "I returned to the place where I found Kayleigh. I used the Fog of Essence, and it showed me her image. Lady Lara was my witness and viewed her image, as well."

"Gautier, it has been a very long time," Astra smiled, as she took his hands. "I had hoped to thank Kayleigh for the gift of her blood. Instead, I am saddened to hear that my sister has betrayed you, once again."

He pulled her in for an embrace knowing she had also endured her sister's cruelty and survived. She had warned him of the coming war, and he had taken her vision as unlikely. For her betrayal, her sister had cursed her to a life on the mountain.

"What I am about to ask you might be difficult for you," he said, as he released her so that he could look into her eyes. "I ask you to stand with me against Velsa. It is time to put an end to her hatred, by death if need be."

Astra gasped at his chilling words. She had feared this day would come, but she didn't think it would be this soon. Closing her eyes, she wrapped her arms around herself and turned her back on everyone. If he failed, she knew Velsa would return her to the mountain or worse.

A strange warmth began to fill her body before she saw three women standing within a field of wildflowers.

"Astra, you have stayed true to your path of purity," Derora whispered. *"Look to the light in your heart for guidance. Your sister has fallen too far to be saved."*

"See the future, my child. You have the power within you," reminded Ida.

"We will stand with you, every one of us. Our power now belongs to you," Ingrid declared, as she leaned forward and kissed Astra's forehead.

"I don't know what to do? How will I know what to do?" asked Astra.

"Read the books. It will all be clear," Ida assured her.

The women slowly faded and the warmth left her body.

As her body began to shiver, she felt Gautier wrap his arms around her. Feeling her body calm, she turned to look at him. Taking a deep breath, she raised her chin.

"I will stand with you," she declared. "I will stand with you against my sister."

Chapter 31

The night sky was clear, and the stars shone brightly in the sky. The air was still, and the only sound she could hear was the echo of the crickets as they played their rhythmic melody. She had decided that this was a good night for conjuring a spell. Without the wind, there was no way for her secrets to be discovered.

Velsa stood with her spine rigid, facing her table. Running her hand over the deep wrinkles on her face, she was saddened by her own ugliness. Closing her eyes, she thought back to the way she looked the day Gautier found her gazing at the sea. Feeling her beauty return, she opened her eyes to see she was dressed in a lavender velvet gown, and her flaxen hair hung loosely over her shoulders and down her back. She smiled knowing her image would surely please Gautier when she ran into his open arms.

Determined to take back what belonged to her, she held the marker and opened her book of spells. Before her was a spell written in blood. The spell that would change everything.

"This is for you, my love," she whispered.

A flick of her wrist instantly ignited the black candles and the tightly bound herb bundle. She began taking deep breaths as the smoking herbs filled the cottage with the pungent aroma of sage and lavender. Lifting a wooden bowl from a linen sack, she placed it on the table in front of her. Rubbing her hand over the smooth inner surface, she thought back to the day it had been given to her. It was a cherished gift from Balgair that had been lovingly hand carved from the lowest branch of an old oak tree. Finding it a suitable vessel, she began the process of filling it.

She picked up a small wooden cup with both hands. As she carefully tipped it, she watched one stone of rose quartz to inspire love, one moonstone to inspire passion, one amethyst to inspire happiness, and one stone of amber to relieve stress fall to the bottom of the vessel. Next, she unlatched and lifted the lids of two small boxes, retrieving the strands of Gautier's hair and Lady Lara's delicate heartbeat. She placed them gently on top of the stones. Opening a vial that contained crushed black stones from Black Thistle Castle and her blood, she poured it over all of the items.

Change his heart now dark and cold,
   to beat forever more.
With true love passion and desire,
   my vision to adore.

Feeling heat and seeing steam rise from the vessel, Velsa knew it was time for the next part of the spell. She took a moment to double check the words. If she got it wrong, she would never be able to unlock the bond between Gautier and Kayleigh.

She picked up the pyramid of rodent bones and dropped them into the vessel, one by one. Pointing her finger at the bundle of caper spurge leaves, she beckoned it toward the vessel. It willingly obeyed and fell on top of the small bones. With a wooden mallet she began to break the bones and leaves against the stones until they were nothing but powder. Taking the pitcher by its handle, she poured the water over the hissing concoction. Finally, she lifted the wolf's tail and submerged it into the liquid.

Unlock and break this bond for me.
Detach and isolate the pieces.
Forget all that you once shared.
While awake, your pain never ceases.

Dipping a wooden ladle into the steaming liquid, Velsa poured a few drops into her teacup. With the rim of the cup at her mouth, she inhaled the scent of her future. Tipping the cup up, she let the potion run over her tongue and down her throat. It didn't burn or have an unpleasant taste. It was perfect.

"It is finished," she signed. "All I have to do now is put some in a vial, take it to Black Thistle Castle, and pour it into a goblet for Gautier and Kayleigh to drink."

She let a nervous laugh escape, and plopped down into her rocking chair.

* * *

As Gautier walked into the library, he was greeted by Astra's smile.

"Lord Gautier, good morning," she called. "How is Lady Kayleigh?"

"Her body has healed, but she still has terrible pain," he replied. "She cries out in her sleep and screams when she wakes. I believe that Velsa is the cause of it. I couldn't bear to have her in pain and have put her in a sleeping spell until we can end this trouble with Velsa."

"I am truly sorry. Had I known, I might have been able to warn you or stop my sister," she replied. "I had been trying to live a simple life, and I wasn't listening to the wind."

"You are not to blame, Astra. Velsa is to blame for all of it, the war, the curses, and the attack. No one blames you," he reassured her. "We are grateful for your return."

"Lord Gautier," whispered Desirae.

He turned around finding that he had been blocking the doorway.

"You've brought Meadow with you," he exclaimed.

"Lord Gautier, I am sorry to hear of the attack on Lady Kayleigh," she said. "If I can be of any help, you need only ask."

"Has Desirae told you of our needs?" he looked at Meadow and then at Desirae.

"Yes," she replied. "I have come to read the books and help you communicate with the witches in the otherworld. I will do all that I can to help you."

"Please sit. I will let Desirae and Astra show you what they have found while I return to Kayleigh's bedside. It breaks my heart to leave her alone," he replied with a sigh.

"Come join me, Meadow," Astra smiled. "There is much to read."

Meadow took her seat at the table. Before she could get comfortable, several books lifted from the table and floated toward her.

"Only one," she fussed. "I can only read one at a time. The rest of you go back and wait your turn."

Astra pressed her lips together trying not to laugh. She had never seen such a thing.

"Books are drawn to me," she muttered. "Be sure to close the door when I leave, or they will follow me through the hallways."

* * *

Gautier nervously paced their bedchamber. The sight of Kayleigh sleeping soundly gave him some peace, but he feared what would happen when he woke her. It was as though the nightmare of being bound apart had claimed them again. Stepping out onto the balcony, he looked at the scene before him. He missed the small cottage in Woods Village where he used to sit and watch the sunrise with Kayleigh. He missed the smell of the salty air too. When this was all over, he would take her back to visit the charming village and watch her run through the forest.

The sudden smell of smoke had him searching for fire. Seeing the thatched roof of a cottage engulfed in flames, he ran for the door. Opening the door, he startled Alicia who was holding a pitcher and two goblets on a tray.

"I have brought you something cool to drink," she choked, as he moved her back out of his way. "My Lord, is there trouble?"

"Fire!" he cautioned. "I saw fire!"

"Go, I will set these on the table by the bed," she loudly replied, as he ran down the hallway toward the steps.

Gautier made his way outside and around toward the small cottages within the stone wall of the castle. The fire had spread and had consumed one cottage and the roofs of two more. Whispering a few words under his breath, he pointed his fist at the thatching and water sprayed over the fire. It wasn't long before the fire was out.

Gustavo had gotten everyone out in time and was questioning two women about the start of the fire.

"Do they know what started it?" he asked Gustavo.

"My Lord, a cooking pot in the hearth," he replied. "The fire doesn't make sense to them. They haven't had a fire in the hearth for over a week, and there weren't any ashes in the hearth. They swept them out, leaving it clean."

"You mean the fire was purposely set?" he growled.

"It appears that it was," Gustavo replied. "Could it have been a distraction?"

"Kayleigh!" shouted Gautier.

Both Gautier and Gustavo raced to the bedchamber and burst through the door. Kayleigh lay sleeping quietly. Nothing appeared to have been disturbed.

"What has happened? We smelled smoke?" Desirae asked, as she and Alicia looked beyond Gustavo to see Kayleigh was sleeping.

"I already told Alicia there was a fire," he muttered, as he lifted Kayleigh's hand and kissed her palm.

"My Lord, I was in the library. I haven't seen you this morning," she countered, as she followed Desirae into the chamber.

"You were standing right there when I opened the door. You were holding this tray in your hands," he barked, as he lifted the pitcher to pour the cool liquid into the goblet.

"My Lord, she was with me," Desirae defended her statement.

"Then someone that looked like you brought me this goblet," he laughed, as he lifted it to his mouth.

Desirae knocked the goblet from his hand, as she gasped. "Don't drink it."

Shocked by her reaction, he looked down at the berry wine that had splattered across the floor. A fine mist of steam rose from the liquid and vanished.

"It's cursed," Desirae muttered. "My Lord, it's cursed."

Velsa stood invisible outside the bedchamber door and watched the goblet knocked from Gautier's hand.

I will have to figure out another way to get him to drink the potion, she thought. You can't hide from me, my love. Soon, we will be together.

Knowing her attempt had failed, she vanished back to her cottage.

Chapter 32

With another attempt to harm Gautier and Kayleigh prevented, they all felt the urgency of ending Velsa's powers. Huddled in the library, Astra, Desirae, and Meadow discussed how to handle the vengeful witch. They had determined the only way to counter her strength was to absorb the power of the witches that had gone on to the otherworld. Since Derora, Ida, and Ingrid had willingly visited Astra's mind, she was the obvious choice. They would need to go to the Hill of Entrance in the mountains behind Evergreen Castle within sight of Witches Weep. There they would perform the ceremony to acquire their power.

The journey to the Hill of Entrance was unsettling to Astra, even though it had taken only a few moments. Desirae had taken hold of her hand, and the next thing she knew, she was standing before a stone pillar. She had never seen the stone pillar. She had read how it had been erected by the people to honor the kindness of the White Witches, but it had all happened after she had been cursed to the mountain. Feeling herself being drawn to the grey stone, she stepped forward and knelt at its base with her eyes closed.

"Place your hands upon the stone," whispered Derora, into her mind. *"Feel our strength."*

Astra obeyed and placed the palms of her hands flat against the stone pillar. She could hear singing, but she couldn't make out the words.

"All of the witches that have crossed to the otherworld are here to help you. Calm your heart and listen to the music, there is nothing to fear," she heard Ida softly sing into her mind.

A gentle warmth replaced the cold stone beneath her hands, and she could feel it move up her arms and throughout her body. An overpowering feeling of joy filled her heart, and she thought she recognized the feeling.

"Yes, Astra," a woman's voice sang. *"It is me. It is your mother."*

"Mother?" she choked back the tears.

"I have come to tell you that I understand how hard this is for you. There is still love for your sister in your heart. I can feel it. Do not let that feeling prevent you from doing what needs to be done. She has betrayed us all," she sang. *"Her heart has turned black like the magic she wields. It is time to take it from her."*

"I am afraid, mother," she confessed. *"I am afraid that I will fail."*

"My child, you are a Seer Witch. Look beyond your worries to the future. Astra, trust in yourself," she said, as her voice slowly faded away.

The singing grew louder, but every note sounded sweeter than the one before it. Their voices merged perfectly into one beautiful voice, and at that moment, Astra felt her body collapse.

Astra woke to the feel of someone's hand stroking her forehead. Her head was in Desirae's lap, and she could feel the soft grass beneath her arms.

"It sounded so beautiful. My mother . . . sang to me," she cried, as she sat up and looked back at the pillar.

"I could hear the music, and it was very beautiful," Desirae replied. "Are you well enough to return to Black Thistle?"

"Yes, we have work to do, and it must be done quickly. Let's hurry," Astra urged.

* * *

Alicia could hear the women talking as she approached the library. She wanted to be of use to them, but knew she would just get in their way. Quietly standing in the doorway, she noticed Astra's hair and shrieked, startling everyone.

"What has happened to your hair?" she asked, as she hurried through the doorway. "The ends of your hair are red. They are red like the berries that we pick in the forest."

"The witches did it," laughed Astra. "I think it is pretty. Don't you like it?"

"Why? Why would they do that?" she gasped, as she lifted the red stained curls.

"We think it was caused when the witches gave her their power," Desirae laughed along with Astra.

"Who has power in their hair?" she asked and then regretted her words when she looked at Meadow's apricot curls floating above her head. "I'm sorry Meadow. I wasn't thinking."

"You are forgiven," she laughed. "We are all a bit confused over it. I have accepted it."

Looking down at the table, Alicia saw the spent candles and herbs.

"Have you finished reading the books, and are you ready to take Velsa's powers?" Alicia asked.

"We are," replied Desirae. "We are waiting for Lord Gautier. He is hesitant to leave Lady Kayleigh alone while we all head for Velsa's cottage."

"My mother and I will be glad to stay by her side," she offered.

"That is kind of you, but we think it is better that you return to your chamber. He is going to spell the chambers to prevent intruders," she explained. "We may be starting the next war. Once we leave, do your best to protect yourself."

Alicia froze for a moment and then quickly hugged each of the women at the table.

"Be safe," she said, hearing her voice crack. "There are many here at Black Thistle that care for you."

As she turned to leave, she saw Lord Gautier standing in the doorway with an eager but stern look on his face. Alicia threw her arms around his waist and hugged him with all her might. Before he could speak, she released him and ran for her bedchamber.

"Are you ready?" he growled. "Let's go take the magic from the wicked witch."

* * *

Laralynn was just closing Starlight's stall when she heard Tolin open the stable door, and she saw Oliver, Elda and Will enter. She knew they had been sent to inform Lord Seth of Magna's final death, and she had wanted to go with them. Curiosity about the vampire's two huge tattoo's and the rumors of a love affair with a mermaid had driven her to ask her mother's permission, but her mother had immediately denied her request. She didn't know enough about the vampire and what she had heard about him wasn't good.

As Oliver and Will dismounted, Tolin took the reins of Will's horse and led him to his stall. Will slapped Oliver on the shoulder and quickly left the stable. Seeing Elda lead Arrow into his stall, she stepped up on the gate as Elda pulled it closed.

"How was Lord Seth?" she asked. "Did he cause you any trouble?"

"He was angry at first, but his temper calmed once we explained what happened in the clearing," she replied.

"What was he like? Did you see his tattoos?" she laughed and covered her mouth with her hand.

"He's the biggest vampire I have ever seen," she blurted. "He was taller than Oliver by this much." After pointing from her elbow to her wrist, she started to laugh. "I couldn't see his arms; he was wearing his tunic. I did see what looked like bones tattooed on his neck. He is a vicious looking vampire."

"What are you two laughing about?" teased Oliver, as he closed Mona's stall gate.

"Lord Seth and his tattoos," laughed Laralynn.

"I think Elda has found herself a mate? I saw the way she was looking at him," Oliver taunted her."

"Just because you have found your mate doesn't mean I have to look for one," she snarled. "If I was, it wouldn't be that big ugly vampire."

Laralynn jumped from the gate and couldn't stop laughing.

"What is so funny," he asked.

"You two are always fighting with each other," she coughed trying to catch her breath. "It's a good thing you two aren't mates. I fear that you would kill each other."

"Enough of this talk of mates. I need to report to Preston. Elda, are you coming?" he asked.

"Can she stay? Please, I wanted her to help me with my truth gift," Laralynn begged.

Oliver looked at Laralynn and then at Elda. He saw Elda nod her head, and he gave Laralynn a big grin. "As long as you promise not to use it on me," he hissed.

"Oh Oliver, I know you would never lie to me," she replied, as she reached for Elda's hand. "Does Elda know any of your secrets?"

"No," Elda blurted. "Not a single secret."

As she waited for a sign, she was surprised when her hand began to tingle. She looked at the back of her hand to see the outline of a red flame.

"Elda look," she gasped. "What does this mean?"

"I believe that it is your gift telling you that I lied. I know several of Oliver's secrets," she confessed.

"I trust that you will not repeat them," Oliver said, as he glared at Elda.

Seeing her grin, he threw up his hands in frustration and turned to make his way to the Command Center.

"Oliver, I vowed to keep them secret. I will keep that vow," Elda shouted. "I expect the same from you."

Oliver turned and raised his fist over his chest.

"Lady Laralynn and my friend, Elda, I leave you to your game of truth and lies," he said, as he continued with a word of warning. "The truth may not always make you happy, but it will always be honorable." He turned and left without looking back.

"Oliver has been different since he learned about Astra," Laralynn suggested.

"I think he was surprised by the marking. He admitted that he misses her. He may be quick with a sword but not of the heart. Oliver will act when he feels he should and not before," she replied. "Now, let's see what happens when I answer truthfully."

"I'll ask an easy question that I know to be true," she declared. "Are you a vampire?"

Elda rolled her eyes and laughed. "Yes, I am a vampire," she replied.

They both watched the back of Laralynn's hand to see what would happen. The same outline of a flame appeared, but this time, it was blue. After several more questions, the truthful answer was always confirmed by the blue flame, and the lie was always confirmed with a red flame. Laralynn experimented with both hands and with her hand upon Elda's covered arm. She was satisfied that as long as her hand was touching the one that answered the questions, the flame would appear on the back of her hand.

"This is a wonderful gift," whispered Laralynn, as she ran her fingers over the back of her hand.

"Always remember it is a gift. Do not abuse it," she reminded Laralynn. "Keep with Honor - Forfeit with Shame."

"I will," Laralynn replied. "Now, hurry on after Oliver. I'm sure he is worried that you have told me some wicked tale about him."

"There are many to tell, but none that I can repeat," she laughed, as she headed for the stable door. "I am glad I did not receive that gift. It would have gotten me into trouble. I am sure of it."

Seeing the door close, Laralynn returned to Starlight's stall.

"Did you think that I had forgotten about you?" she laughed.

Reaching to unlatch the gate, she felt something unsettling. It was a faint thought of fear from someone she knew. It felt familiar, but the image was hidden in the forest. Not knowing where, she opened the gate and readied Starlight for a journey. Leading her to the gate, she stepped up on the rail and mounted her back. Taking the reins, she hurried through the door Tolin had left open before anyone could stop her.

"Hold tight my sweet Starlight. We are going to flash together," she whispered in her ear and then they were gone.

Chapter 33

Velsa could hear the wind howling, but she knew it was an unnatural wind. The swirling wind was carrying anger and danger directly to her door, and she immediately knew its source. As the howling grew louder, she made her way to the door and drew it open. There before her stood Gautier and his pathetic group of magic hurlers. Entertained by their appearance, she boldly stepped from her cottage to confront them. Making eye contact with every one that dared to stand before her, one side of her mouth began to smirk before she emitted a horrendous laugh that caused them all to grimace from the pain. Noticing that they had all taken a step back except Gautier, she directed her focus on him.

"Gautier, you honor me with your visit," she sarcastically snarled. "Have you missed me? Have you come to pledge your undying love to me?"

Seeing his look of disgust, Velsa pursed her lips and reached out her arm to make a sweeping circle over her head. Purple sparks flitted about her head and body. The air around her sizzled as her image began to change from the old hag into the lovely image of Aslev. Her hair fell loose from its braid and fluttered in the wind.

"Is this more to your liking, my love? Is this not the image that you worshiped for so many years? Did you not hold this body against your own in the moonlight and whisper words of affection to me? Is this not the golden hair that bewitched you when we first met in Cobb Cove?" she asked, waiting for his reply and hearing none. "What is wrong my love? Oh, how could I forget? This is the image that you betrayed with that frisky fur covered bitch. I remember every kiss you hid from me, every embrace, the ring you gave her that held a stone the color of the thistles, and the day you wed. I remember all of the painful betrayal."

Gautier took a step forward and glared at Velsa. He remembered the day he first met her, the overwhelming desire to know her, the times he held her, and the secrets they shared. None of those moments compared to the pure hatred she had shown him by binding him away from his beloved Kayleigh. Those moments were filled with an unending feeling of complete agony that tortured him even now to think of them.

"Yes, Velsa," he shouted. "I remember all of it. I remember the good and the bad. Most of all, I remember all the horrible things that you have done to me and my Kayleigh."

"Must we have a conversation that includes her name?" she snapped. "All of this hostility has been because of her. She has been the problem, all along."

"It is you, Velsa. You are the problem. You let your jealousy and hatred fill your soul. You let it take the goodness that you once possessed, leaving you with nothing but ugliness for all to see. Changing your appearance does nothing to hide your evil nature. You have harmed the one that I love, and I intend to make you pay for your cruelty," Gautier bellowed, as the air around him began to heat. "This interference in other's lives must end. We have come to offer you a peaceful existence to your life here on Alltree Island. If you reject this offer, you will feel the ramification of our resolve to end your life."

Standing with her back rigid after hearing Gautier's threatening words, Velsa caught a slight movement within the trees out of the corner of her eye, and she saw Gautier look in that direction. Everyone stilled as Lady Laralynn slowly emerged from the edge of the forest. Dismounting her mare, Laralynn slowly walked toward Aslev's outstretched hand.

"Come here child," she softly coaxed.

Confusion covered Laralynn's face as she took Aslev's hand. Looking at everyone standing around Lord Gautier, she looked back at her for an explanation.

"What has happened?" she asked. "Why are they all here?"

"They have come to hurt me," Aslev whimpered, looking for sympathy. "Lord Gautier has blamed me for the harm that has come to Lady Kayleigh."

Shocked by Aslev's words, Laralynn turned to face Lord Gautier.

"You must be wrong, Lord Gautier," Laralynn loudly stated. "Aslev could never hurt anyone. She has loved me since I was a child. You have made a terrible mistake."

Feeling Laralynn wrap her arms around her waist, Aslev smiled at Gautier.

"Laralynn," Gautier softly said, as he took a step toward her. "She has hidden her true self from you all these years. Who stands within your arms is Velsa, the witch that made a bargain with Jario to take Kayleigh's tail, and the witch that bound Kayleigh and myself to wander in darkness, alone."

"Jario is bound within your castle," Laralynn yelled, as she released Aslev and stepped toward Gautier. "He could not have had anything to do with the harm that fell upon Lady Kayleigh's wolf. Do not blame Aslev for the hunter's trap. You must blame the unwise and cruel hunter."

"It is true that she was caught within the hunter's trap," Gautier agreed. "However, the trap was closed upon her leg, not her tail. I have the dagger that was used to remove her tail. It seems that Velsa left it behind. I have it with me, and a trace of the wielder's essence was left behind upon the leather bindings. I can prove to you that it belongs to Velsa."

"I can settle this here and now," Laralynn replied. "I have been given the ability to see the truth in spoken words. I will ask her if she has done this dreadful deed, and she will give her answer to me. I will know the truth."

Turning to Aslev, Laralynn held out her hand and waited for her to place her hand upon her palm. As she waited, Laralynn could see the fear in Aslev's eyes.

"Please, Aslev?" Laralynn begged. "Place your hand upon mine. Show them that they are wrong. Show them that you could have never done such a horrible thing."

Afraid, Aslev took a step backward. She took in the eyes of everyone that waited for her to prove her innocence. Looking back at Laralynn, she took a step forward and moved her hand toward her palm. Hearing a sigh of relief from Laralynn, she hesitated for only a moment before she grabbed Laralynn and placed her body in front of her own. With her arm around her neck, she backed toward her cottage.

"Let her go," yelled Gautier, as he raised his hand and built a glowing ball of yellow light. You have affirmed our claim of your attack upon Kayleigh and your death."

"You cannot harm me," she shouted, as blue sparks gathered around her body. "If you do, you will harm Laralynn. We are connected. What happens to me will happen to her."

"More lies," Gautier bellowed. "Is there no truth left within you?"

Feeling a gentle hand take his arm, he looked back to see Meadow nodding her head.

"Laralynn is marked. Within that mark is the connection between them. It has been there since her birth," declared Meadow. "If you kill Velsa, you will kill Laralynn."

Gautier lowered his arm and the light slowly faded. Seeing her smile made him furious. He raised his arm again, but this time, the light grew from yellow to bright orange and then to red. He began to chant and pace back and forth. Knowing what he was doing, they all began chanting along with him. The sound of the chanting grew louder and stronger. They could see Velsa begin to stagger, but she wouldn't release Laralynn. The wind began to swirl around the two women.

Holding her hands over her ears, Laralynn begged, "Release me, Aslev. I know the truth. I feel it. I know that you harmed Lady Kayleigh."

Hearing Laralynn's words made Velsa flinch from a sharp pain deep inside her chest.

"It is true, my child. I cut the tail from the white wolf," she whispered. Closing her eyes, she placed her mouth next to Laralynn's ear. "Laralynn, forgive me. Please know one truth. I have always loved you, and because of that love, I release you."

With tears in her eyes, she pushed Laralynn as hard as she could away from her body. As she watched her fall to the ground, she saw the tiny red mark that bound them disappear. Standing with her arms spread wide, Velsa knew it was over. Looking directly at Gautier, she shouted as loud as she could, "I loved you then, and I love you still. Do as you please with me!"

They were the last words she uttered before the spell flew from their hands and blasted her in the chest knocking her to the ground. As it made impact with her body, the earth beneath their feet began to violently shake, and they all watched as Velsa's cottage crumbled before their eyes. The trees around them began to sway and a few were not strong enough to stay upright toppling others in their path.

As the shaking slowly ended, Laralynn rushed toward Aslev. Taking her lifeless hand within her own, she looked back at Gautier.

"You killed her," cried Laralynn, as she brought her limp hand to her lips and kissed her palm. "She told me that she loved me. It was the truth. She confessed her evil deed to me. Gautier, you have the truth." As the tears ran down her cheeks, she felt Meadow's gentle hands take her shoulders.

"Child, she is not dead," Meadow softly said. "We have removed her powers. She is no longer a witch. When she wakes, she will not remember her past."

"She won't remember me?" asked Laralynn.

"No, my child," she replied. "She will start her life over. We will find a safe place for her to live."

"She can live in our old cottage in Primrose Pond. She will be safe there," Laralynn offered. "People are friendly there."

"Let's go home. Your mother will be worried," Meadow said. "She will be eager to hold you within her arms."

"First, I must see after Aslev," she declared. "I am her only friend. It is up to me to see that she is safe."

* * *

Gautier's spell shook not only the ground around Velsa's cottage but all of Alltree Island. It was so strong that stones fell from the walls that surrounded Black Thistle Castle. The flames in the hearth leapt high and sparks flew about as the burning logs jerked against each other. The banners that hung around the Great Hall waved violently as if a strong wind had blown through an open door. One by one they toppled to the stone floor along with several of the burning torches.

A loud crash echoed through the halls, as the elaborate shield that hung above the hearth fell from the wall and smashed against the floor. Jario's quivering arms pushed his chest up off the floor. He could feel the floor still vibrating from the strange blast he had heard earlier. An eerie sound of cracking glass caused him to cover his head as pieces of stained glass fell to the floor. He couldn't imagine what had caused it, and he didn't care. Whatever it was, he was finally free of his imprisonment inside the dagger and free to leave Black Thistle Castle.

He had to escape before anyone realized he had been released from Gautier's spell. Maneuvering his body up on one knee, he felt a strange sensation as everything before him began to spin. Trying to stand, he lost his balance and collapsed to the floor. He could feel the madness wrapping its evil hold around his mind, and he desperately needed blood to stop it. He needed blood to clear his mind and his vision. His best chance for blood was in the castle, but that was a risk he wasn't willing to take. The safest place to find blood was in the forest. Looking up at what was left of the stained glass windows, he saw their colored panes were dull and lifeless. Without the bright sunlight, it would be safe to leave. Even if the dim light was only temporary, he would be willing to risk the burns to elude capture and his final death.

Struggling to stand, he crawled to a chair that had fallen on its side. Clutching its leather covered arm, he pulled himself up onto his knees and tried to focus. Slowly his blurry vision began to clear. Not wanting to delay his departure, he forced himself to stand as he held tightly to the chair for support. Swaying, he made his way to the closed doors that led into the main entry of the castle. There he stood listening for any sound of the army or Gautier's little wolf. Off in the distance, he could hear the army starting to search the castle and women sobbing from fear. He pulled open the doors and stumbled into the entry. One entry door hung precariously from a large metal hinge and offered him the first glimpse of the outside.

Desperate to leave, he climbed up onto the front of the damaged door that leaned inward and leapt onto the stone steps below. Trying to keep himself from falling, he leaned against the base of the stone pedestal. His vision blurred once more as he tried to move. Stepping away from the pedestal, he lost his balance and grabbed it again with both hands. Feeling the rough stone beneath his hands, he looked up to see a stone wolf with a medal hung around its neck. A memory of a fight with a black wolf flashed in his mind. Looking down at his hands, he quickly pulled his right hand away from its rough back paw.

The sudden sound of Gustavo shouting and his boots running through the hallways made Jario freeze. If he didn't run now, he would be captured and sent to the dungeon.

Do I still have my gifts?

He closed his eyes and focused on his haze. Little by little he disappeared. Not taking time to look back, he ran from the castle steps and over the drawbridge. The sight before him made him gasp. The thistles that surrounded the entrance to the castle lay withered upon the ground. In all his years, he had never seen the slightest weakness in the crop of deadly thistles.

Something dreadful had happened, and he didn't want to meet the danger face to face.

Hearing the army shouting his name, he knew they had discovered he had escaped. Even with his haze, Jario knew he would no longer be safe upon Alltree Island. There would be a price on his head, and everyone would be looking for him. His only chance for survival would be to leave on the next ship that left the harbor.

I need to find blood first, he thought, as he turned toward the forest. I will board a ship and start fresh on some distant island. I will find a distant island where no one has heard of me.

Without looking back, Jario carefully made his way through the lifeless thistles running for the safety of the forest and his escape from Alltree Island.

Chapter 34

After helping Laralynn and Astra settle Aslev comfortably in her new cottage, Gautier was eager to return to Kayleigh's bedside. Finding Desirae at the gate waiting for him, he took her hand, and they both vanished back to Black Thistle to find the entrance blocked by armed guards.

"Is the Lady Kayleigh in danger?" he shouted.

"My Lord, she is safe," the guard replied. "A guard stands at her door."

Desirae bent down and picked up the medal that once hung around the stone wolf's neck and looked up to find the pedestal empty.

"My Lord, it appears Killian has been freed," she said, as she handed the medal over to Gautier.

"I don't understand. What has caused this?" he looked at the guard for an answer.

"There was a strange blast, and the earth shook violently. I am surprised you did not feel it. It shook me from my cot in the barracks," he replied. "As we searched the castle to be sure that no one was hurt, we found the shield that once hung above the hearth in the Great Hall smashed on the floor. The blast must have caused it to fall."

"And the dagger?" he asked. "What of the dagger? Is it still secure?"

"The dagger came loose from the shield, and it still lies on the floor. We were afraid to touch it," he said, as he gulped in a large breath of air. "It troubles me to tell you that a page saw Jario stumble from the Great Hall. He ran for help, but when he returned with Gustavo, Jario was gone. My Lord, Jario has escaped. The army is searching the forest for him."

"That monster will simply disappear into his haze. If he is smart, he will leave this island for good. He is no longer safe here on Alltree. Send word for the men to return to the castle. Their presence is better served here," he ordered. "Desirae, can you shield the castle from the traitor for me? I need to go to Kayleigh."

"Yes, My Lord," she replied.

"I see the stone wolf no longer stands upon the pedestal. Where is Killian?" he asked. "Where is the Guardian?"

"He stands guard at Lady Kayleigh's door," he replied. "His wolf has not left her door since he was released from the stone."

"Go," coaxed Desirae, as she began to wave her hand over her head. "Your place is by Lady Kayleigh's side. Nothing will penetrate the walls of this castle until you give the order."

Gautier leapt over the broken door and ran through the hallway toward the stone steps that led to their bedchamber. Taking them two at a time, he reached the landing and could see the black wolf sitting in front of their chamber door.

"Killian, my good friend, it is good to see you again," he said, as he ran his fingers through the wolf's thick black fur. "You honor me with your presence at this door. Now, go find Alicia. Hurry, she has missed you."

Killian's wolf backed away from the door allowing Gautier access. He lowered his head and then raced toward the stone steps that would lead him to Alicia's arms.

Gautier slowly opened the door and made his way into their chamber closing the door behind him. He could see Kayleigh lying beneath the soft bed linens sleeping soundly. He wanted to wake her, but he feared the pain she would endure by doing so. Seeing the fire had gone out in the hearth, he filled the grate with more wood and brought them to flame. A beam of amber sunlight upon the floor caught his attention, and he walked out onto the balcony to see the grey clouds part allowing sunlight to fill the sky. With both his hands resting on the stone ledge he looked out over the stone wall that encircled Black Thistle Castle. Not sure of what he was seeing, he focused on a dark strip of earth that lined the stone wall.

"What has happened to the thistles?" he muttered.

He studied their strange appearance and tried to determine what could have caused the wicked weeds to die. He clearly remembered the day they changed. Velsa stood at the castle gate screaming his name and threatening Kayleigh. Ignoring her threats, he had stood on the balcony holding Kayleigh in his arms. Furious over the sight of them together, she raised her arms, and the air began to swirl around her head. One by one the purple thistles turned black. Their shrieks of agony filled the air, along with Velsa's laughter. She had cursed the purple thistles to an eternal existence of darkness and bloodlust. They had been cursed out of hatred. Now after all this time, they were finally dead. Giving them one last glance, he noticed a hint of green among the black stalks. It seemed to spread from one stalk to another. Slowly, the once deadly stalks stood full of life displaying their green stalks and purple flowers.

Leaving the balcony, he paced back and forth at the foot of their bed as he thought of all the strange things that had happened since they had thrown the spell at Velsa.

Her curse upon the thistles has been broken, he thought. Would the curse put upon Kayleigh be broken as well? Do I dare wake her to find out?

Taking a chance, Gautier began to undo the sleeping spell. He raised his arms with open palms. Small red flames danced in his right hand and then jumped to his left as he chanted silently in his mind. With the last word of the spell, he closed his hand and extinguished the flames.

Gautier moved to the side of their bed as he waited in silence for her to awaken. He began counting her breaths until he saw Kayleigh's eyelashes flutter against her cheeks. Fearful of what would happen next, he waited for the shivering and painful sobs, but he heard none. Slowly, Kayleigh opened her eyes and then closed them again. Opening them once more, she looked about the room and then tried to focus her eyes on the person that stood by her bed.

"Gautier, is that you?" she murmured and raised her hand to reach for him.

"Yes, my love. Has the pain left you?" he asked.

Sitting down on the edge of the bed, he took hold of her hand and brushed his lips against her fingers. He saw her close her eyes and feared she could feel more pain. Instead she opened her eyes and gave him a beautiful smile.

"The pain is gone, Gautier. There is no more pain," she laughed. "It is gone."

"And your wolf . . . is she," he hesitated and searched her eyes.

Kayleigh, pushed back the bed linens and quickly pulled her sleeping gown over her head before Gautier could stop her. Within moments, the white wolf stood in the middle of their bed. She jumped about the bed linens chasing her tail. He reached for her face and felt her wet nose against his cheek before she pushed him back against the bed.

"My little wolf has returned to me," he whispered, as her tongue licked the side of his face.

* * *

Alicia had listened to the army running through the hallway ever since the sudden jolt had shaken the castle. She wasn't surprised when she heard the sound again of someone running outside her chamber door; however, the knock on her door startled her. Cautiously, she approached the door. Placing her ear to the wooden surface, she listened for any sound of danger.

The silence stilled her heart, and she took several steps back away from the door. Her wolf could feel her fear and was desperate to come forward to protect her.

"Who is there?" she called out.

"It's me, Killian," he anxiously replied. "Open the door, Alicia. It's me."

She ran to the door and opened it wide to see Killian standing before her.

"It's . . . You're . . . Killian, you're really here," she gasped, and reached out to touch his arm. "I can't believe you're really here."

Killian pulled her against his chest and wrapped his arms around her. Feeling her body tremble, he gently pushed her back so that he could see her face.

"I'm here, Alicia," he whispered. "Please don't cry. I'll not leave you again. I never want to live another day without you."

"These tears are tears of happiness," she smiled, as tears fell from her lashes. "I have carried you in my heart for so long, and now, I can finally hold you in my arms."

Lifting her chin, he watched her eyes close and the slightest offering of her lips to him. Without hesitation, he claimed her mouth and felt his wolf howl with delight. Pulling away, he heard her sigh before he saw her beautiful smile. Dropping to his knees, he covered both of her hands with his own.

"Will you have me, Alicia?" he asked, as he looked up to see the look of surprise on her face. "I promise to love and protect you with my life. Will you have me as your one and only?"

"Yes, Killian," she replied. "My heart is full of love for you. I will have you, forever."

The sound of someone running toward the open door startled Alicia, and Killian stood moving her behind him to shield her.

"Stay behind me," he ordered. "Jario may have returned. I fear he will be full of blood lust."

"But, he is bound in the Great Hall," she gasped.

"No longer, I saw him run toward the drawbridge," he

whispered, as he moved her further from the doorway. "He is the reason I am free."

"Why would he free you?" she whispered, bending down to look under his outstretched arm for the danger.

"Hush," he said into her mind. "Be still."

"Alicia, are you here?" shouted Gustavo.

With a sigh of relief, Killian took Alicia's hand and walked toward Gustavo as he entered the chamber.

"We believe the danger has passed . . . Killian? My friend, it is good to see you," he bellowed, as he gripped his arm and slapped him on the shoulder. "We have all missed you."

"It was lucky for me that Jario was shaken free during the blast. Had he still been secure, I would still be trapped within my stone prison," he laughed. "I never thought I would give thanks to that evil vampire."

"But, how did he free you?" she asked, confused by his explanation.

"He lost his balance and touched the paw of the statue before he ran from the castle. That had to be the loophole that set me free," he laughed. "He had the power to turn me to stone, but he didn't realize that by touching the stone it would release me."

"I am thankful he released you. I am thankful that he is gone, but I will not think of him again," she muttered. "EVER!"

Chapter 35

An excited crowd had gathered in Black Thistle's Great Hall. They had all been asked to join Lord Gautier and Lady Kayleigh for a festive evening of food, drink, music, and dancing. The festivities were his way of celebrating Kayleigh's safe return.

Thomas stood near the hearth holding Lara's hand, as he remembered the last time he had stood in Black Thistle's Great Hall.

"What are you thinking about?" asked Lara.

"The last time I was here," he replied. "You were missing, and I was still searching for you. I had come here for Gautier's help." He glanced around the room and saw his daughter smile back at him. "Little did I know that searching for you would lead me to our beautiful daughter."

"I know it was a sad time for you. It was for me too," she confessed. "I promise I will never leave you again. I couldn't bear a day without you."

Lifting her hand, he brushed his lips against her fingers.

"Would you honor me with a dance, my love," he smiled and waited for her reply.

"I would love nothing more," she blushed, as she followed him to the cluster of couples that moved about to the sound of the soft music.

Laralynn smiled as she saw her parents walking hand in hand and returned her attention back to Baxter. He had been her protector, her confidant, and her friend.

One day, I hope Baxter will be much more to me.

Baxter leaned toward her and whispered, "One day I will, if you'll have me?"

"You were listening," she gasped.

"If you don't want me to hear your thoughts, you need to learn to shield them," he laughed. "If you like, I can teach you."

"I would rather practice listening to your thoughts," she replied. "Will you teach me?"

"I will, but if you want to know what I'm thinking, you need only ask," he replied.

"I always want to know what you are thinking," she said, as she took hold of his hand. "What are you thinking now?"

"How nervous I am to tell you that I love you," he replied.

She had longed for him to say those words and found herself dreaming about the day he would say them to her. Looking down at the back of her hand, she saw the outline of a blue flame.

"They are the truth, Laralynn," he said, as he covered the back of her hand. "I will always tell you the truth. You will never need to look for the flame upon the back of your hand to prove it."

"I wondered if you would let yourself love me. I hoped you would, and that you would tell me one day. I had hoped it would be soon," she replied, as she pulled her hand from his. "But, it wasn't your truth that I was seeking. It was mine. I wanted to show you that my love for you is real. I love you, Baxter, with all my heart, and the blue flame upon my hand proves it." She lifted her hand to show him the blue flame. "This is my gift to you."

Baxter reached for her hand and kissed the blue flame that she had proudly displayed to him.

"I hate to interrupt the two of you," Oliver blurted. "Lord

Gautier is going to make an announcement and he wants you to bring Lady Laralynn to stand beside him."

Laralynn blushed as she saw Oliver wiggle his eyebrows behind Baxter's back.

Lord Gautier and Lady Kayleigh stood before the crowd. To his left stood Laralynn, Flora, and Alicia. To Kayleigh's right stood Desirae, Astra, and Meadow. Clearing his throat, he looked at a quiet crowd.

"We have much to celebrate today," he began. "My lovely Kayleigh is well, and we have these wonderful women to thank for it. Lady Laralynn, Flora, and Alicia graciously cared for Kayleigh and healed her wounded body. For that, I will be eternally grateful." Taking hold of Kayleigh's hand, he brushed a kiss against her fingers. Looking back at the people that stood before him, he continued, "As you know, we have endured an evil curse for a very long time. Desirae, Astra, and Meadow have helped me end that curse. It no longer surrounds Black Thistle Castle or Alltree Island. I could have never done it without them. I am truly grateful for their help and their courage. Now, please . . . everyone . . . take a moment from the festivities to give these women your thanks."

The crowd cheered as they watched Lady Kayleigh stand before each of the women to offer her thanks and a warm embrace before she returned to Lord Gautier's side.

Gautier lifted his hands to quiet the crowd one more time.

"It has come to my attention that we have a very special announcement to make," he smiled, as he looked over at Alicia. "Our Guardian, Killian, has proposed to Alicia, and she has accepted."

The crowd began to cheer, and two men lifted Killian up on their shoulders for all to see. Gautier took hold of Alicia's hand and waited for the men to bring Killian toward him. After carrying him through the crowd, he was finally lowered to stand next to Lord Gautier. He took hold of Killian's hand and looked at the happy crowd.

"It is a good day when love can be proclaimed to all," he

shouted, as he looked over at Kayleigh and then at Alicia and Killian. "Make this the beginning of your forever and always."

While listening to Gautier and the cheering, Oliver had managed to work his way through the crowd to stand beside Astra. He casually hooked his little finger with hers. Hearing her gasp, he waited to see if she would pull her hand away. Comforted by her continued touch, he bent down to whisper in her ear, "One day you will be my forever and always. One day, when you are ready."

* * *

It had been several days since they had all returned to Evergreen. A sense of peace had filled the castle with the knowledge that Magna and Franco were no longer a threat to anyone. Thomas and Tate were comforted that the death of their family had been avenged, and Magna would never seek to harm anyone again. Even though Velsa had not directly harmed anyone at Evergreen, it was a great relief to know that her powers had been removed. Only Laralynn struggled with what had happened, and she had stayed in her bedchamber trying to understand the change in Aslev.

Thomas and Lara sat in their courtyard enjoying a goblet of sweet berry wine trying to decide what they could do to help their daughter. They had seen the change in her and knew something had to be done. Hearing the door open, they looked up to see their daughter walking toward them.

"Mother, Father, may I speak with you," she asked.

"Of course," her father replied. "Come sit with us."

Laralynn sat down and folded her hands in her lap. Now seeing her parent's faces, she wasn't sure where to start.

"There is obviously something on your mind," her mother smiled. "Tell us what is bothering you."

Laralynn took a deep breath and tried to remember everything she wanted to say.

"I have decided that I don't want to travel down the path

that you have taken, mother," she confessed. "I want something more. I like being outside in the forest and feeling the bow in my hands. It is clear to me that I was never meant to be dressed in satin and fine slippers. I find comfort in the breeches and tunics that Elda has given me."

"What are you trying to say, Laralynn," her father asked. "Do you want to leave us?"

"Never," she gasped. "I want to do something meaningful with my life. Being human, I know I won't be here forever. I don't want to be remembered as Lady Lara's daughter. I want to make a difference. I want to defend Evergreen and its people. I am asking that you allow me to join the Evergreen Army."

"What?" her father gasped.

"It is all I want, father," she replied. "Can you please try and understand?"

Lara looked at Thomas and rested her hand upon his arm to keep him from saying something he shouldn't. Looking back at Laralynn, she could see the yearning in her eyes.

"If this is what you truly desire, I will allow it," she replied.

"Father?" she asked. "Will you agree?"

"If it pleases you and your mother, I can hardly refuse you," he said.

"Thank you," she cried, as she stood and threw her arms around her father's neck. "You have made me so very happy."

"Now that you have our approval, I will demand one thing," Lara sternly said. "You must wear a gown to Killian's and Alicia's wedding. On this, I will not bend."

Chapter 36

When Baxter and Laralynn entered Gautier's private courtyard, she was taken with its beauty. Candles circled the rim of the stone fountain and were magically suspended among the branches of the trees. A glorious full moon hovered among the twinkling stars in the night's sky, and the scent of lavender filled the air. It was a perfect night for an Eternity Ceremony.

The talking and laughter hushed as Killian entered the courtyard followed by Gustavo. Taking his place before Omar, he waited anxiously for Alicia. He stole a glance down at his black breeches and black knee high boots. They had been a gift from Lord Gautier, as well as, his linen tunic that held a fierce wolf's head surrounded by thistles, the new symbol to honor his role as "The Guardian". It was all a little overwhelming. He anticipated a simple ceremony in the forest or in the meadow, but Lady Kayleigh had insisted on something special they would remember forever.

Hearing the door open, he looked up to see Alicia coming toward him followed by Astra. Her beauty took his breath away. She wore a silver-grey dress of luscious shimmering velvet with sheer trumpet sleeves that fluttered from her wrists with each step she took. Her hair hung in soft curls down her back, and a delicate ring of moonstones and black pearls rested against her forehead. Around her neck, she wore his gift of an oval moonstone that hung from a strand of perfectly matched black pearls.

Taking her place beside Killian, she turned to face him.

"You are so beautiful," he whispered.

Before she could reply, Omar asked for quiet.

Holding a small leather book, he pulled on a silver ribbon that had marked his place.

"This night we come to witness the joining of Alicia and Killian for all eternity", he began. "Their love for one another is strong and true. It has been tested and proven to be worthy. Much has been endured to prove their love."

Looking at Killian, Omar asked, "Killian, do you pledge your trust, honor, love, and protection to Alicia forever more?"

Killian took a deep breath and proudly replied, "I will, forever more."

Looking at Alicia, Omar continued, "Alicia, do you pledge your trust, honor, love, and protection to Killian forever more?"

She smiled up at Killian and replied, "I will, forever more."

Omar looked around the courtyard at the faces that had come to celebrate this union and asked, "Do you pledge your trust, honor, love, and protection to Alicia and Killian?"

In unison their voices responded, "We will, forever more."

"For a symbol of their unity, they have chosen something unusual. Once it was explained to me, I understood its meaning. I'm sure you will find it fitting, as did I, he offered. "The breaking of the branch symbolizes the end of their separate lives. The binding of the branches symbolizes the binding of their souls and their wolves for all eternity."

Gustavo stepped forward and handed Killian a small branch. He in turn held it out for Alicia to grasp. Together, they bent the branch until it broke in the middle.

Then, Astra stepped forward and handed Alicia two ribbons, one grey and one black. Killian held the broken branches together while Alicia wrapped the ribbons around the broken branches and tied them securely together. Killian then handed it to Omar.

"This union is bound together forever by their love," he bellowed, as he held up the small bundle. "It is with honor, that I declare Alicia and Killian united for all eternity. Killian, you may kiss your mate."

Killian swept Alicia up off her feet and kissed her lips as flower petals were thrown up in the air above their heads. He could feel his wolf begging to be released and warned him to be patient. Setting her securely back down, they were immediately offered congratulations from Lord Gautier, Lady Kayleigh, and Alicia's parents, as well as, being kissed and hugged by everyone in attendance.

Music and laughter filled the courtyard. Killian had never been this happy, and he had Alicia to thank for it. After taking the time to visit with each and every one of their guests, he declared it was time for he and Alicia to depart the festivities. Alicia kissed and hugged her parents, and Killian received a firm handshake from Lord Gautier. Bidding everyone good night, they hurried from the courtyard to start their new life together.

As Laralynn watched them leave, she felt someone take her arm. Turning, she was greeted by Astra.

"I wanted to thank you for loving my sister. She was not always what she became," she sighed.

"Astra, she loved me before I learned to love her. I don't remember a day that she didn't love me," Laralynn replied. "I only wish it had been that way for you."

"Maybe one day it can be that way again," she tried to smile.

Laralynn wrapped her arms around Astra and hugged her tightly as she whispered, "Then, we shall hope that day comes soon."

Epilogue

Baxter and Laralynn stood hand in hand at the edge of Wispet Canyon looking down at the spectacular view. The curse of the Canyon of Obscurity causing the darkness, dead foliage, and crumbling stone cottages was gone forever. It had all magically been replaced with the vivid fields of lavender, fragrant scents, streams of crystal clear water, and neat rows of stone cottages with freshly thatched roofs.

"I can't believe she destroyed all this beauty because Gautier loved Kayleigh," sighed Laralynn.

"Velsa let the darkness replace the love she once carried in her heart. She hurt so badly that she wanted to make everyone else hurt too," he replied.

Feeling her sadness, he wrapped his arm around her waist and felt her head rest against his shoulder.

"Baxter, did you know she made a promise to my mother to keep me safe," she asked.

"I knew of the bargain that was made when your mother left Evergreen. She was to hide you and your mother until your sixteenth year," he replied.

"No, a promise was made after I returned to Evergreen. She willingly made a blood promise to keep me safe. That is why Velsa gave Magna her final death. She did it to protect me,"

Laralynn paused and shook her head. "That name is so strange to me. Velsa is someone I never knew. She will always be Aslev to me."

"In the end, I think she realized that she didn't need Gautier's love. She already had the love of someone very special," he replied, as he kissed the top of her head.

"Who?" she asked, as she looked up at Baxter's broad smile.

"It was you, Laralynn. Your love for her shattered the darkness she held within her heart for so long," he said. "You were the loophole. It was your love that shattered the curse and brought everything back to life."

Wrapping her arms around his waist, she placed her face against his chest and felt the warmth race through her body.

"I love you, Baxter," she cried. "I'm so glad you found me."

"I am too, Laralynn," he whispered, as he inhaled the scent of fresh apples. "I love you, and I always will."

The End

A NOTE FROM THE AUTHOR

Thank you for reading Shattering Obscurity. As a new author, I am honored that you have completed this journey with me. Even though the Evergreen Series has come to an end, there are several stories still to be told about the characters that wander Alltree Island. I am excited about what I have planned and hope you will be too.
If you enjoyed this book, please take a moment to leave a review at Amazon, Goodreads, or your favorite eBook provider.

I would love to hear from my readers. Let me know what you think of the characters in the Evergreen Series and who you would like to hear more about. You can reach me at any of the sites below. I will do my best to respond as quickly as I can. I look forward to hearing from you.

Website: www.authorjoannherley.com

Facebook: www.facebook.com/authorjhbooks

Email: info@authorjoannherley.com

OTHER BOOKS BY THE AUTHOR

EVERGREEN SERIES

Book I   Seized by Obscurity

Book II   Escaping Obscurity

Book III Protected from Obscurity

Book IV   Shattering Obscurity

Coming Soon

Trapped Alone - Prequel to the Evergreen Series - Early Summer 2016

www.ingramcontent.com/pod-product-compliance
Lightning Source LLC
Chambersburg PA
CBHW071144170626
46809CB00002B/766